Typhon Inc.

Tina Shelton

First Print Edition
Cover design by Amy Wham
ISBN: 1-943522-08-1
ISBN-13: 978-1-943522-08-8

To MR, because I promised.

CONTENTS

WORST KEPT SECRET

In a tiny, shabby hole-in-the-wall cafe, Orochi found himself thinking more and more about his freedom. He'd had it all; unlimited access to the Web, billions of rightfully stolen dollars, revenge on the man who ordered his mother killed. Unfortunately, the United States Government, or what was left of it, didn't see it in that same light. Despite the dissolution of the states into nation-states, this secret branch still operated as though nothing had ever happened. They still upheld the original Constitution, and the charters surrounding it.

These goons threatened to throw Orochi in jail for stealing, when all he'd done is appropriate stolen funds. Then they told him they'd incarcerate him over some mild property damage. They gave him two choices - a cell or a leash. He thought he could tolerate the leash but as the months had gone by, Orochi chafed against his limits.

The little cafe seemed content to ignore the seven foot two behemoth crouched in the back of the place. The table was barely big enough for his drink and the visor he'd smuggled with him. He couldn't use his 'ware. Everything was bagged and tagged and they would know the second that Orochi crawled into the Web. It pained him not to use his state-of-the-art equipment, but better a stolen glimpse into his old life than sitting here returning awkward glances at passerby. He picked up the visor. It was heavy, definitely an older model, but that was hardly something to get picky about. He put the visor up to his eyes and clicked it on.

He had barely signed in and started surfing when he felt a hand on his shoulder. His stomach bottomed out despite himself. Pulling the visor off, he saw Pixru's wry smile, and his stomach lurched again until he remembered who was in control of her body.

She sat down in the chair across from him, uninvited. "Tsk, tsk, Orochi. I thought you swore to lay off the digital sauce for a while."

Even as she chided him, he fought down a silly urge to beam. Carnelia still called him Orochi, even though everyone else in the facility called him Jack. He didn't let it bother him. They weren't Savvy. He had to summon up a scowl for her instead. "Is your parole officer around?"

"No, if they can't find you on their own, they aren't getting any help from me." She winked. "I'm here because you've been moody lately, and I wanted to find out what was going on."

"What do you mean, what's been going on?" He blurted, grabbing the visor and turning it in his hands. "Nothing has been going on."

Her dark eyes narrowed for a moment. "I get it. You're bored."

"Aren't you?" Orochi asked, frustration lacing his tone. "How do you put up with this, every day?"

"You're the only person I know who would find bored going through training to catch ops who the general public doesn't know exists." Carnelia scolded.

Orochi shrugged. "Well if they'd present a challenge..."

There weren't many people in the room, and they all seemed to want the same thing - public privacy. Carnelia continued in a hushed tone, moving closer.

"They want to give me the 'ware again." She said, excitement pouring from her.

"No." Orochi looked confused. "Parris's ware?"

She nodded confirmation. "I'll jump again!"

"No." Orochi said again. "You can't! That 'ware is a disaster, it's so experimental it hasn't made it to rats, and it has a death rate of yes. How could you even allow this to happen?"

"I'm bored." She said, her eyes twinkling with barely repressed joy.

He opened his mouth to protest but he understood her point. They had been locked up for months, being trained as operatives. The training was difficult, and it was rewarding, but it was just about concluded. It was barely better than being imprisoned, although with more access to entertainment media. It wasn't enough. Who cared about the plight of sitcom families when there were ancient buildings to infiltrate?

"I was expecting more bluster." Carnelia commented. She reached out for the sugar holder, fiddling with it apprehensively.

"You can't." He said.

"I can, and I will." Setting down the sugar, she leaned forward, her jaw set.

"Well if you're going to do this, why did you come and ask for my opinion?" Orochi asked, tone surly.

Carnelia shrugged. "I didn't."

"So, you just came down here for a cup of coffee?" Orochi raised an eyebrow. "Your excuse is lousy, partner."

Carnelia winced. "I've got to live my own life, Orochi. I can make decisions without you, but it's nice to have a friend's input, too."

"How do they know how to implant the thing, huh? How do they know they'll do it right?" Orochi demanded, hoping his anger masked his hurt at her comment. *She can make her own decisions, she doesn't need me. You're childish, but don't be that childish.*

"They hired the doctor that does all the surgeries. She survived the night Parris went down in flames." Carnelia said coolly.

The door opened, and both of them swung their heads around to see who the interloper was. Orochi saw it was Nathan, which is who he'd been waiting for. Couldn't have picked a better time.

"So you're going to let an evil doctor do who-knows-what with your head under the sanction of a branch of government not authorized to operate outside of a hundred square miles of the state of D.C., and you think that's all normal and fine?" Orochi's voice was pitched low, despite his desire to yell at her from the top of his lungs.

"It is what it is." Carnelia said, standing up. "I can't stand living like this anymore."

It was one argument Orochi couldn't fight against. His eyes flicked to Nathan, who stood in line getting his drink, pretending he wasn't watching Carnelia and him fight.

"I'll let you get back to coping. Rascati says you get one hour away from the Bureau and then you either find your way back onto the compound or you'll be escorted back." With that, she turned and left.

He hadn't had a chance to tell her about the dreams, he realized belatedly.

When she left, Nathan appeared to take her spot. "That seemed intense."

"She was proving to me how much like me she really is." He looked out the door. He couldn't make out her long, black hair from the front windows of the cafe.

"That would be intense." Nathan allowed. "How stupid is the plan?"

"It's pretty stupid, but I'm not sure that I could possibly talk her out of it." Orochi frowned. "What do you have for me?"

"A new visor, complete with a new persona. It's meant for light diving, but I figure anything is better than being caught. I also rigged up a little something extra. It's in experimental stage but I think I have a dream recorder rigged up."

"Thanks." Orochi handed him the older visor and accepted the newer, sleeker model.

His short friend smiled warmly. "Well, it's not like I've got a lot of business now. When are you going to break out of your cage and fly free?"

Orochi looked out the window again. "I can't leave her. She hasn't decided that the Bureau is garbage quite yet. When we go, I want it to be a party of two."

Nathan's mouth quirked. "I'm sure you do."

"It'll be easier to escape if there's more inside help." Orochi backpedaled.

"Where will you go, though? I mean, if this organization is as big and as spread out as it claims, it's going to be hard finding a place to hide." Nathan took a sip from his latte.

Orochi nodded. "That's part of the slow down. I mean, you know what travel is like, outside of a greendome. The weather constantly hammering, the high winds, constant storms, it's terrible. You can't live out there, for long at any rate, and anywhere we'd need to go would involve crossing a sea. And we'd have to pick somewhere that didn't know me from the Web."

Nathan chuckled. "Yeah, no Tokyo greendome for you."

"Or the NAN, of course. The Native American Nations are not welcoming of outsiders." Orochi shrugged and grabbed his own coffee. "Not like you could blame them."

"So that leaves a lot of places that are very far away, in very difficult to traverse conditions. I can see where that would slow you down." Nathan grinned. "Except I found the very place you're looking for."

"Where?" Asked Orochi skeptically.

"Australia." Nathan said. "You wouldn't have to learn a new language, you don't have to put up with this relentless rain, and you'd be considered an average height!"

Orochi was surprised to discover he was considering it. "Who would fly that far? That's a lot of time in the can."

"I know a guy who provides dome to dome service. Of course, he does the Tokyo route more regularly but I bet for the right price we could get him." Nathan leaned back in his seat.

"There's a lot of difference between flying to Nippon and flying to Australia." Orochi said.

"There's almost no difference. It's about seventeen hours commercial speed to Nippon, and it's about twenty hours to Sydney. One's in the northern hemisphere and one is in the southern, but geographically they are almost in a straight line on a map." Nathan looked smug.

"Well well, someone's been doing their homework." Orochi said with approval. "I'm just not sure how to get out of the box I'm currently in."

"I'm working on that too." Nathan said. "You've never put yourself in trouble I couldn't get you out of."

"Except this time." Orochi said.

"Well, so far." Nathan said. "It takes time, these are sticky threads and a lot of spyware keeping people out. It's not a one-night stand."

"It's not a one night stand?" Orochi choked on his laughter. "At this point she's moving in and you're shopping for rings."

"Fine, I'm stumped as hell, but I haven't exhausted my resources yet. There's a way to do this." Nathan took a sip of his coffee.

"Thanks for the update, Mr. Positive Thoughts, I'll keep them in mind." Orochi said with a dismissive eye-roll.

"So, what's with the dream recorder?" Nathan said. "The one you asked me for out of the blue."

Orochi, coffee to his lips, almost poured the black liquid out of the mug and into his lap. "You're kidding, right?"

"Of course I'm not kidding. I'm not even sure it works, but you sounded really intent on it, so I cobbled something together based on the Preston-Mellan brainwave principles. It's not my usual forte in science, I had to do a lot of reading. I want to know what I did it for." Nathan looked around. True to form, the little cafe was nearly empty, with only a handful of characters in the place. "Do you think this place is a front?"

"Why don't you ask that louder, or when our waitress is pouring our coffee." Orochi snapped. "Look, I've been having really intense dreams. Dreams about my mom."

"How weird." Nathan didn't need an explanation; Orochi had already filled him in about the unusual subconscious passenger that he'd been hosting for years. "She's gone though, right?"

"I thought she was." Orochi said. "Things have been different. There's files that I can see, but I can't guess the password."

Nathan snorted.

"Shut up. It's one thing when you have a random password generator to do the work, it's another when it's meat vs. machine. They don't trust me with tinker toys in lockup, let alone something I can connect with." Orochi was pained to admit it, but without tech to assist he wasn't much of a Savvy.

"Anyway, you were saying?" Nathan looked up from his latte.

"I never could access any of this stuff before, and I want to see if maybe those dreams are some kind of password that my brain's filtering wrong. That technology is such vaporware to begin with. Who knows what you could do with tech that can let you jump into other people? Especially the way this stuff works, according to the end user. I mean, think about it. You don't have to be hooked in to anything specific, you just have to be patched in. How can you think that any receiver would be compatible? Some people run old 'ware because it's all they can afford. Some people have cutting edge stuff with high end security 'ware to filter out anything that is deemed an intrusive software, and that's a pretty intrusive software. Sure, I could see exploiting a weakness to a particular set of 'ware, like say, if HaikenSoft was vulnerable, but that's still less than a fifty-fifty chance that the person she'd jump into had the right stuff. Unless you did serious homework on your target, you'd have no way of knowing what 'ware they had, and if you could even successfully jump in." Orochi shook his head. "There's something else going on, and I think my mom left me a way to figure it out. I think those dreams are the key to how the jumpware works. I just have to be able to capture it, to go over it a few times. That's why the strange request."

Nathan nodded. "I hope you're right. It would be a shame if..." He trailed off, looking pale.

Orochi looked over his shoulder, unsurprised to see two large men wearing state-of-the-art body armor, flanking a silver-haired man in a gray suit. Rascati's expression remained unreadable as the two bruisers cruised like sharks over to their table.

"Recess is over." Rascati said, his tone controlled. "Time to come home."

"I'm coming, I'm coming." Orochi stood slowly, keeping his hands visible. "Sorry you had to see this, kid."

Nathan smirked. "Nothing I haven't seen before."

"I'm glad you got your playdate, but there's responsibilities waiting at home." Rascati said as his twin bruisers each took possession of an arm and aimed Orochi out the door.

Rascati's words were pitched for Nathan's ears but Orochi overheard him as they escorted him out. "You could always try out for the team. It's pretty small but I know the guy who runs the place, I'm sure I could get you in."

"You don't want me on your team. If you did that, what would keep Orochi in town?" Nathan said.

Orochi smiled.

"Don't get caught, little thief, or I will requisition you." Rascati warned. "And then you two can have your little coffee klatches in my house."

As they loaded him in the van, Orochi vowed to find the tracer they'd stashed on him before the next time he left the compound.

INSTALLATION

The surgical theater was small, bright, and cool. It was early. Carnelia's scalp tingled. Losing the weight of her hair had been strange. From her body's response she'd guessed that Pixru had worn it long her entire life.

Dr. Galia Aaren gave her a cursory glance as the gurney wheeled into the room. The two orderlies arranged her under three large LED arrays. They didn't give off a lot of heat but her naked skull detected the temperature change. Carnelia's skin crawled as she recognized Dr. Aaren as the woman who implanted the jumpware the first time. She wished Dr. Aaren had died that night. But then, she wouldn't be here to do it all over again.

She wanted to sit up but she'd been strapped to the table. A fugue state descended over her thoughts as the sedative kicked in. She wasn't sure she wanted to do this. There was no backing out now.

Then again, didn't she want this? She wasn't putting up much of a struggle. Despite the fact that she knew she didn't have a choice, she didn't have to agree to this and walk into it willingly. She could have made demands.

I want this. Carnelia thought. The truth was, this was the only job she'd ever been good at, and if that made her a bad person, so be it. Being trapped in Pixru was bad enough, being trapped permanently...

"...I wasn't told, could be a risk..." The doctor's voice drifted into her hearing.

"Nobody knew, but it answers a few questions." It was Rascati. "It's too late now, complete the procedure and we'll inform her on revival."

The words, tell me what, rested on Carnelia's lips like rose petals drifting down. She knew there were none and yet her mind assured her that the LEDs shed them instead of light, and she was warm and thoughts were slippery as the fish in the canal by Ganada's house. Hadn't seen Ganada in two months or more, missed her pigeon and tomato sandwiches...

Her consciousness twitched, an unexpected jerk before falling asleep. Suddenly she was seventeen, skinny as a post, with long kinky hair and clothes that barely clung to her bones. Tears slid down her cheeks in fat, wet streaks. Her big, brown eyes were searching her brother's face for any trace of compassion. They were outside, where Michael was guarding the door of Parris's brothel, The Wild Night. She'd been looking for him, and when she found him she almost wished she hadn't. The club was high end, with a generous helping of underclad young women. Many of them were underage. The police were all paid to look the other way and Parris made sure that no gang violence broke out in his territory.

White light made her jerk to her senses. The familiar enclosure of an M-pod reassured her of where she was.

"Carnelia?" Dr. Aaren's voice interrupted. "Tell me if you feel this in your right index finger."

Carnelia felt a disconcerting sensation of scratching from the inside of her finger. "Right middle."

"Ah. This?" The doctor asked again.

Again a scratching sensation, although this time it was in her right index finger. "Yes."

The doctor lapsed into silence, focusing on her work. The quiet left nothing for Carnelia to hold on to, and she felt herself sinking back to her memories.

"They hurt me, Michael!" She gasped breathlessly as her brother looked on, trying to remain detached. "They held me down and took turns! I can't work in a brothel! I can't be a whore! Give me a gun, put me in the line of fire, I will do it, but I'm not a thing! I'm not a doll you throw away when you're done!" Her lip quivered and she barely kept from crying again.

Michael took a step forward and wrapped one careful arm around her, sheltering her in his embrace even as he watched for danger. "If I had my way, I would have you show me each one of those bastards and I would shoot them." He kissed her forehead and looked into her eyes. "I would kill them all for you. But you know I can't. You know that if I do, then I have signed the two of us up for being hunted for the rest of our lives. We don't have any friends, or any powerful allies, or even a place to live. We signed on with Parris because that's the choice we had, this or living hand to mouth, on the streets, starving to death. I'm sorry you can't live under those conditions, but they're the only conditions we can live with. You need to do as you're told, and maybe you can work your way out of your punishment and into a better position."

"That's your solution?" Carnelia hauled back and struck her brother in the chest. "Hiding from your sister behind your 'brothers'? You're going to let Parris get away with this because you're afraid of living on the streets? Well, we lived on those streets just fine for years, before we were kidnapped and carted off..."

"Listen to yourself. Kidnapped. Carted off. Yeah, we were, and we were because we didn't have anywhere to turn, or anyone to turn to. No one is going to dig us out of this mess, and we're going to have to spend time figuring out a way to get away. And I don't just mean away, I mean like, out of the fucking greendome, risking life and limb to try to immigrate to another greendome where we're out of Parris's reach. That's what it's going to take, Carn. Risking those damn storms, risking death, to get out of this mess." Michael hugged her close, then let her go. "Go back inside. You're in a bad spot but we've been in bad spots before. We'll survive and we'll come out stronger."

Carnelia pushed past her brother, her cheeks burning from the shame and the fury. "Easy for you to say."

The scalding anger forced her back into the M-pod.

"Carnelia?" Dr. Aaren's voice floated back into her thoughts. "Are you with us?"

"Is it done?" Carnelia raised her head. Emotions rolled through her, but she pushed them away. It was old business; this was new.

A hand pressed on her forehead to stop her. "Now, let's not get too enthusiastic. Everything has been installed, but we won't be able to test the 'ware for another day or two. Right now we're just making sure you came through with everything intact. It's a complex matrix."

Thinking through soup, Carnelia's memory clung to a conversation she wasn't supposed to overhear. "So, what were you supposed to tell me?"

"Let me take a couple more readings and I'll get to that." The doctor's discomfort was distinct.

Carnelia sighed. She remembered the long wait for the anesthesia to wear off. She probably wouldn't be able to walk for another hour or two. She tried to move her hand and was rewarded with a slight twitch in her left pinkie. She had to be awake for the surgery, in order to respond to the doctor's questions. She remembered doing that, although those memories were detached, much less distinct than her conversation with her brother. The blocks were precautionary, but necessary.

"Okay, doc, I know you're not excited about whatever it is, but just get it over with. Was it a tumor? Did you have to remove a chunk of my brain while I was under?" Carnelia's tongue felt thick. She concentrated on making her words understandable.

"No." The doctor paused. "This is going to come as a shock, but I know you aren't the original owner of this body. And it seems that the body that you jumped into has an additional passenger."

Horror soaked through her bones and she tried to sit up straight. Her abdominal muscles betrayed her and left her limp. "What?"

The click-click-click of flat soled shoes filled the silence surrounding the doctor.

"Ah, I missed the big news." Rascati said.

"You knew?" Carnelia tried to turn her head to face him. It happened, far more slowly and painfully than she would have imagined it could.

"Not until Dr. Aaren brought it to my attention." Rascati said. "It was too late, you'd already had the anesthesia administered."

"Which would have provided a convenient refurbishment." Carnelia growled.

"Do you know who the father is?" Rascati leaned over her, looking grim.

She struggled through the clouds of thought to reach the conclusion he sought. Revulsion shot through her fog as she realized exactly whose baby she was carrying. "Michael."

"I'm reasonably certain that's true." Rascati said. He ran his hand over the counter top, then clapped his hands together. "One would understand why you may not want to carry that particular baby to term."

There had been signs. Morning nausea, no period after six weeks, feeling inexplicably tired. She thought that Pixru had some kind of nutrition disorder. She'd tried various diets, and had found one that worked. From that point on she didn't think about it much, just assumed that Pixru's health problems were something she'd kept secret. After all, Pixru was a secretive person.

"It's all I have left of him." She heard herself blurt. "It's not like I had sex with him."

"You don't have time to be a mother. You have a contract." Rascati pointed out.

"Nowhere in my contract are there stipulations for pregnancy. This isn't a deal breaker, it just requires some creative problem solving. I don't know what I'm going to do. I only just found out fifteen minutes ago, I need some time to think." Carnelia's mind raced, stumbling over the anesthetic and vaulting beyond it. With it came the first hints of pain.

"You're on the table right now. It would be a ten minute procedure to resolve this problem." Rascati said.

"Easy for you to say." Carnelia snapped.

"Damn right it's easy for me to say! The world is overpopulated. Worse, we have less living space available on the planet than ever in human history. It's not responsible for you to have a baby, especially if it's not yours."

Carnelia drew back. "You just sounded like every don't get pregnant slogan I've ever heard."

"Just because it's political rhetoric doesn't mean that it doesn't apply." Rascati smoothed the front of his suit, a habitual gesture.

"You don't own me, you just have my services. Don't forget that." Carnelia bristled, feeling the fog clear further. "I need time to think before I come to a decision."

"Oh, yes, you'll definitely want to talk things through with Orochi on this one. He's going to be so understanding of the situation, you being pregnant with your dead brother's kid and all. That Orochi, he's a rock." Rascati frowned. "I'll just swing by his room and let him know you're out of surgery."

The pain wasn't as bad as she'd expected, but the anesthetic hadn't worn off entirely, either. She could feel nerves tingling, raw from being connected to the jumpware. "That won't be necessary. I've recovered from this before. I'm going to spent the next six hours in a lot of pain, which will taper off to only distracting, exhausting levels of pain, and then maybe by dinner tonight I'll be able to eat and then go directly to bed. I don't have the energy to listen to anyone else's 'too many humans' speech. I just want to be alone."

Rascati cocked a silver eyebrow at her in surprise, but then nodded and turned to go. "Understood. I'll let him know you pulled through, but it took it out of you."

"Thank you." Carnelia laid back on the table. "Doctor, are you still in the room?"

"Yes, of course." Dr. Aaren appeared at her side as if by magic.

"I'm in a lot of pain, do you think you could..." Carnelia let the words taper off as the spasms began to hit.

"Of course, let's get you comfortable." Dr. Aaren busied herself with controls to adjust the pain managers.

Idly, Carnelia wondered if she'd ever be comfortable again.

BACK IN THE SADDLE

"Wake up, Carnelia." Rascati's voice cut through the filter of pain medication. "Wake up, Carnelia, we need you in the C-pod."

"You're kidding." Carnelia's mouth framed the words but they didn't sound intelligible. "I haven't been out of surgery for twenty four hours."

"It's almost three in the afternoon. You've been out for nearly thirty-six hours. Our mark logs in at eight o'clock her time, we can't miss this opportunity." Rascati grabbed her arms and pulled, heaving her out of the bed and almost into a sitting position. Her head didn't want to sit atop her neck, and her spine felt like it was a broken circuit board.

"I can't do this yet. You'll kill me." Carnelia flopped back onto her bed. "She'll go to work tomorrow."

"Carnelia, you do realize that I'm not a heartless beast. If I'm telling you it needs to get done today, then there's a reason it can't wait for tomorrow. I wish we'd done this procedure a week ago, but decisions hadn't come down from the top, and that's what we were waiting on. Please, Carnelia, I know you don't feel well, but we have reason to believe that she's part of a body-jumping ring, and we need to catch her. We already have good evidence on her, but she also has access to information that we would kill for." Rascati's features were tight, a rictus of a smile that disturbed her. She couldn't believe she found him attractive at one time. When he was a cop he was a tough but fair kind of guy. This new Rascati was something she couldn't fathom, and she didn't like the change.

"Tell me what we know. I don't go into this blind, you know." Carnelia realized that sounded like acquiescence.

"She's a sora no me, Nipponese for eye in the sky. She's one half of a cop duo, where one is in a C-pod, gathering intelligence for a specific location, and the other is in an exo-skeleton, making the arrests." Rascati supplied.

"Ah, so she's already got her hands in the cookie jar at work, and she started taking some of them." Carnelia sat up. The broken circuit board feeling had lessened. Maybe she could do this.

"Something like that." Rascati agreed. "Her partner's name is Daizo Hayanari. He appears to be untarred by his partner's brush."

"A clean cop? No such thing." She watched his mouth flatten into a thin line and hid her own smirk. "You're not a cop anymore."

"Glad to hear you think so highly of me." Rascati grumbled. "She's got suspected connections to a bodyjumping ring."

Carnelia snorted. "Impossible. How'd they get the 'ware?"

"That's what you're going to find out. They have files on crimes where the perpetrator swears to being asleep or out of town or the like, and yet they are caught on security feeds as being a perfect match. Sounds like what Parris was pulling off." Rascati pointed out.

She nodded. "Is she one of the bodyjumpers?"

"No, we think she's being bribed by the bodyjumpers to alter the TPD files. We have intel that she's going to do it today. And that's why you have to go now." Rascati urged.

"Love those last minute escapes," Carnelia said, grabbing her clothes.

In a few minutes they had her dressed and walking, Carnelia leaning on Rascati more than she'd like. Despite the aches of fresh connections, Carnelia felt anticipation rise as she thought about using her jumping skills again. She thought it would be nice to get away from Pixru's influence, and start seeing the world through fresh eyes.

Orochi leaned against the door jamb of the C-pod room, fiddling with a toothpick. "Well, well, well, what do we have here? What a touching scene, Rascati, helping a lady out. Only, if she needs this much help, don't you think the right answer is leaving her in her room to heal up?"

"I don't have time for your vitriol right now, Orochi. Take it up with our employers. I'm just the messenger." Rascati tried to push past him but Orochi moved into the door frame, taking most of it up.

"She had the surgery yesterday. She's been sleeping all of today. Don't you think that's... I don't know, maybe a fucking sign that she's healing? Give it another day. Or are you trying to kill your strongest asset?" Orochi looked down and glared at Rascati. Carnelia's heart swelled a little. Orochi didn't have any right to interfere, any sway with anyone that mattered here, and he was risking his ass standing up for her. Not wanting to say anything stupid, she bit her bottom lip and stayed quiet. She wanted to hear more chivalry before she stepped in.

"I'm not at liberty to share the parameters of the situation with you. We don't have a lot of information on this target, what little we have tells us where she'll be at eight a.m. this morning." Rascati took a step forward.

Orochi refused to yield. "She hasn't tested it on anyone yet and you want her to use it for an international case? You're just chucking her in the deep end while she's hungry and tired, aren't you? What the fuck did Carn ever do to you? I mean, between the two of us, you should be doing shit like this to me, not to her."

"Orochi, I'm going to give you a chance to move voluntarily. Then I'm going to call in assistance. I understand you're concerned for Carnelia, but again you choose to go about it the wrong way. You're going to be a great asset to her in the field, but she's got to get out in the field first." Rascati met Orochi's glare with his own hypnotic brand of level calm.

Carnelia sighed. "Orochi, it's okay. I'm doing this under my own power."

Orochi snorted. "You can't even stand up under your own power."

"Then carry me." She said, brooking no argument. "But stop making me stand out here, it's uncomfortable."

"I don't think that..." Rascati began.

Orochi reached past him and gently plucked Carnelia from where she stood. Carnelia tried not to yelp in surprise. She hadn't thought he'd take her seriously. What was worse was her inclination to snuggle in and tell Rascati to get bent.

"I'm staying." Orochi informed Rascati. "If anything looks even a tiny bit wrong, you pull her out, intel or no."

Rascati heaved an enormous sigh. Carnelia buried her face in Orochi's chest and laughed quietly, hoping that he didn't hear her. Orochi's scent was very masculine, sandalwood and tobacco and leather. She forgot how much she liked it. She pulled her face away from his chest and looked out towards the C-pod they had prepared.

Orochi put her down, and she managed to walk towards the C-pod without help. She pulled herself inside, used to the motions. She lay down, letting the servos connect the contact patches. "Ready."

Inside the C-pod, she felt the needle puncture the delicate skin on the inside of her left arm. She started breathing deeply, calming her mind and focusing on her jump. She hadn't done an international jump before. Parris was too afraid to let his jumpers that far out of his sight. She would be in unfamiliar surroundings, reading unfamiliar symbols, navigating unfamiliar systems with no security protocols beyond the ones she had on entry. She didn't know much about the Nipponese police. At some point she'd seen a movie poster of an exoskeleton-clad police officer walking the streets of Tokyo. Before Rascati mentioned it, she didn't know they had partners feeding them information about any encounter in progress.

"Are you ready?" Rascati's voice sounded in her ear, bringing her back from her reverie. "Your target is Kasumi Yamamoto, and her partner is Daizo Hayanari."

"It's not like you're going to stop if I say no, so why ask?" Carnelia asked, not caring how snotty she sounded. They were asking a whole lot out of her, and not giving her much in return. Orochi had the right of it, she shouldn't have done this.

"Initiate," Rascati said in response.

Carnelia felt a long, slow slide and she was suddenly free from her moorings; the body she'd been inhabiting slipped free and she felt the rush of a new body drawing her down. She decanted herself from Pixru to the career police officer and eye-in-the-sky. She felt herself settle into new dimensions, stretched in her creche, and looked into the complex world of readouts that was Kasumi's job to interpret.

The readouts were insane. Temperature, barometric pressure, school attendance, the parole roster of the nearest three prisons to her precinct, and a host of other information scrolled in. Carnelia realized with a start that she was reading Nipponese. She knew Pixru could, but she could only read the language when she was in her body. Apparently one of the perks of her ability was borrowing some of the host's inherent ability.

"Kasumi, how are things looking today?" The question rolled in with the quiet confidence of a man who asked the same question every day. She didn't recognize the voice, but a name popped up in the corner of her vision. Daizo Hayanari. A green light blinked, verifying the identity of the speaker.

"Quiet." Carnelia said after a moment's hesitation, relieved to discover that she spoke in Nipponese.

"Good!" Officer Hayanari didn't seem to notice anything wrong with his partner. "Contact me if necessary."

Carnelia could feel several things that were different about Kasumi than Pixru. Kasumi was definitely taller, by at least three inches. Her skin had a darker tone, although not as dark as Carn's had been. She had short hair, dolled up into some kind of style. Her cheekbones weren't as sharp as Pixru's, but her lips were more inclined to smile.

She looked into the systems that Rascati asked her to look through. All of the necessary data was open to her, as Kasumi had logged into them before Carnelia jumped. She saw a list of earmarked cases with the same last name. Hitochigai. She imagined she'd find lots of other cases with the same last name, seeing that Nippon was an island, and the Nipponese were particularly proud of their heritage. However, this file was the last thing that her host saw, so she scanned it to see what was so interesting.

Carnelia read with a fluency that pleased her. The Hitochigai file was littered with mistaken identity cases. People who were caught stealing, caught on camera if not in person, who had a second identity as someone with a well-established life. Mortgages, credit scores, car loans, jobs... the works. What would make them want to moonlight as a thief? And when they were picked up for questioning, they swore they never were at the place, like any good thief would.

Carnelia's mouth quirked in a half-smile. She remembered those days.

"Kasumi?" A voice sounded as though it were right at her shoulder, but she was all alone in her C-pod. It was Daizo again.

Carnelia responded, hoping that it was in the right language. "Yes?"

"Any chance you can find me a perpetrator? I'm bored." His tone was light and playful.

"Uh..." Carnelia tried a couple of hand controls before one swept the Hitochigai files out of view. She looked at multiple screens, each scrolling with different information. She had what she needed, it was time to run.

Focusing on a point within her mind, she reached back across the ribbon she rode in on, that tenuous connection she could feel to Pixru's unconscious body. She could feel Pixru across the expanse, her heartbeat regular, her breathing deep and slow. Knowing it was time to go, Carnelia jumped.

Angry red claws clamped down inside her head, breaking the connection to Pixru and wracking her with pain. Carnelia reached out for the receding connection, clasped it, and felt it dissolve in her mental grasp.

Oh no what if I can't jump back because it's not my real body? The thought made her feel sick.

She tried again, furiously trying to latch onto her exit strategy. What was happening? She'd been stuck before. This wasn't the same feeling she'd had when Orochi had trapped her. This was something entirely different, and much more painful. Was it something to do with Kasumi? Or was it something to do with her being a transient spirit housed in another body?

The information better be worth my life, Carnelia thought. *Because I'm trapped and anyone who can help me is in another greendome!*

She reached out for the C-pod's communication arrays. Pain rose in her mind, making it hard to concentrate. What would she say that wouldn't be intercepted by the Tokyo police?

"Kasumi?" Daizo's voice queried. "Any luck?"

Carnelia knew Orochi's private comm channel by heart; it was the only thing she could force her mind to concentrate on. There wasn't any time for a long message. She tapped out an SOS and prayed that Orochi had been paying attention in class on Morse code day.

SOS

Waiting for Carnelia to check in was exhausting. Orochi had been practicing creating a program in his mind. Rascati saw to it that he had almost zero access to anything that would allow him time on the Web. If it weren't for Carnelia he'd have already escaped by now. As it was, he was beginning to give up on her leaving with him. If she didn't give up on this little idea soon, he may have to start making plans with Nathan.

He heard something in his audio. He flipped to look. It was on Carnelia's old channel.

· · · − − − · · ·

It was short, and then long and then short. Something about the pattern tickled his memory.

Behind him, a technician began flicking switches and twisting dials.

Orochi closed his eyes, listening to the internal chatter.

"We've lost contact." The technician was a young man, younger than Orochi. His eyes told Orochi the story though. All theory, no practice.

"What was she doing? What was she looking at? I want everything she transferred." Rascati said sharply.

The smartboards flared to life. Images littered the boards. Names sprouted across faces. Orochi noticed that all the last names were the same. Hitochigai. There didn't appear to be a familial connection. He saw faces that were Caucasian, Yorban, and Latino mixed in among the Panasian.

It was a code, but what did it mean? It seemed to be just a name, nothing that translated into something specific. Whose code was it? The TPD? That was terrifying to think. The SPD hadn't known, or had been paid off by Parris when he'd last had dealings with them. Was something like that happening again?

Blue hexagons outlined each separate file and tiled neatly over the next one. He'd seen that interface before, once. Some bithead showing off their Savvy skills by taking pictures of the insides of Nippon's Sora No Me technology. If he recalled correctly, that particular login was a shell account now, whose last login date was the day after he posted the pictures. The pictures had been removed from the board.

Orochi bore down on the gray man in his gray suit. "You did not send her to Nippon."

Rascati remained calm. "You see those cases up on the board?"

Orochi didn't trust himself to speak, so he nodded.

"They're bodyjumping cases." Rascati continued. "These are from the TPD, but all across Nippon they're seeing cases of impostor theft. Each of the victims believed they were at home asleep when the theft occurred, even after they were shown the damning evidence. We've offered our support in assisting these cases, but thus far we've had our hand slapped away. So, we've decided to step in and help, whether they want the assist or not."

"Hardly governmental." Orochi said.

"Extremely governmental," Rascati replied. "Not that you care about laws."

"I care about large bodies of people coming together respecting the little guy." Orochi clarified. "You sent her into one of the most well-funded police agencies on Earth. They have tech toys that would make this room look a century out of date. Even after everything went to hell in the Great Crisis, they managed to keep their shit mostly together. There was no way they were going to miss their sora no me getting nosy about files she shouldn't have been in."

"She was supposed to ripcord." Rascati said, running a hand through his steel gray hair in frustration.

"She's fresh out of surgery, and you didn't test it. What the fuck did you think was going to happen?" Orochi felt his anger push up through his layers of calm.

"She's used the technology for over a year, done dozens of jumps that we know about. She's successfully left multiple bodies before." Rascati snarled. "You're the only one that gave her problems, and you're safely out of the way."

"Your answer is up on that screen." Orochi pointed at the Hitochigai cases. "They're not like Seattle police. They are aware there's a fucking problem."

"Being aware and being able to do something about it are two different things." Rascati's tone had lost its heat.

"She's in another greendome. Do you know what it's going to take to mount a rescue?" Orochi asked.

Rascati looked up. "You're not going to be on that team."

"The hell I'm not." Orochi said. "She sent me a distress signal just as you lost contact. SOS. She's in trouble. That's my partner in there and I'm not going to leave her to a bunch of assholes who sent her there in the first place."

"It's not your call to make." Rascati said.

"Yeah, like not telling me about Carnelia's surgery because you knew I'd object. Like not telling me her destination because you knew I wouldn't let her go. Yeah, not telling me things has been serving you well these past couple of months." Orochi folded his arm across his chest and turned to the smartboards.

"Well, you're such a team player, Orochi, if we included you we'd be guaranteed to never get anything accomplished, just sit around being safe." Rascati fixed Orochi with a stare. "Pardon me if I get this wrong, but weren't you out breaking the law, getting shot at by bad guys and good guys alike, and getting jumped by Parris's crack team of bodyjumpers before you joined our rig?"

"This is different. Carnelia isn't as strong as I am." Orochi said, fists clenching.

"Is that why you risked her life in a bank heist, as well as dragging her halfway across Seattle? Didn't you get her shot? In your body and in hers?" Rascati stood patiently, waiting.

"This is way beyond the trouble we were in in Seattle, and you know it. I'd shoot her myself if it meant bringing her home safely." Orochi said firmly.

"All the more argument to leave your ass out of play. We have people. As far as our outfit is concerned, you only just graduated. There are people here who have been tasked with dangerous missions for much longer than you. I am sorry that I can't send you out to rescue your partner in an appropriately manly fashion. You're going to have to sit this one out, and once we rescue her, you can go back to doing insanely dangerous things." Rascati looked as though he wanted to pat Orochi on the shoulder, but decided against the action. "We'll keep you informed on the progress."

"Yeah, sure, boss." Orochi said, anger lacing his tone. "You do that."

He headed out of the room, where Rascati had already turned back to the smartboards to glean more information.

Orochi wanted to punch something. Preferably Rascati but any stuffed-shirt bureaucrat with delusions of grandeur would do.

Did they forget who I am? Just because I'm working for them doesn't mean that I suddenly became a tame animal. I can't leave her out there with no backup.

He knew he had to leave the facility, which was locked down tighter than a frog's cloaca. He thought he had an idea of how he'd do it, though. It was a mind exercise he'd begun when he first walked the halls. He didn't have anything in his room that he couldn't replace... except the Zerorez. Well, he could replace that too, he'd just have to get Nathan working on it.

Nathan. To call or not to call. Eventually he'd have to, but on the highly probable chance that they monitored the frequencies, he'd probably need to wait until he got out the doors.

Now all he had to do was get outside.

Rascati probably put an alert on all the exits, but some exits were better covered than others. Or, he could be clever and make his own.

He walked to his room. That alone wasn't suspicious behavior, he spent a lot of time in there, and that'd be where they wanted him. Next, he did a quick savvy of the video camera he wasn't supposed to know about, and took 24 hours of recorded time with him in his room, eating, reading, coding, all the things they would expect from him. He slid the file into the spy camera and got to work. He grabbed his Zerorez, glad that he wouldn't have to leave his favorite gun behind. He guessed they wouldn't come looking for him for a while, not wanting to put up with him in a mood. That allowed him time to step into his closet and climb up into the getaway tunnel he'd made to the roof. He hadn't used this one yet, wanting to save it for an important situation. He took the time to weld a patch over the hole using the mask and torch he'd squirreled away. He had to remember to thank Nathan for having the forethought to set this up.

Once through the hallway and upwards, Orochi was greeted by the cool, moist kiss of Seattle's air. Most days he didn't consider that this biome was monitored and adjusted for by complex machinery. Everyone knew that there were greendomes, and that it was the vigilance of these weather controlling systems that allowed people to survive the elements. Outside the greendome was a world gone mad, a world where weather systems were out of control. Hurricanes, tornadoes, tsunamis, volcanic eruption - nature seemed to attack itself with vicious ferocity. There were ways through the greendomes, but most of them were land based.

And there was a large ocean between him and Carnelia.

He pulled himself up and out, and decided to maintain radio silence until he was free from the building. He could be seen by the outside cameras, but he didn't have anything to loop. He had to rely on the fact that they were poorly staffed, and needed to focus on Carnelia. Hope was a bad plan component but it was one that had worked out in his favor in the past. He raced to the edge with cameras that had blind spots. He climbed down off the rusty, rickety ladder quickly, making sure his boots were solidly on each step before dropping to the next one. This was the most dangerous part of his plan; if he were caught before he reached the bottom, he'd have nowhere to go.

Having faith in the low numbers of the Bureau's office, Orochi hit the pavement and broke towards the next building. He tried to keep as much metal between himself and obvious camera angles as he could manage. Once he'd figured he'd gotten far enough, he started running. He didn't like running, because it drew attention. However, he'd learned long ago that whatever a seven-foot-two monster like himself decided to do was likely to attract notice.

Glancing around to orient himself, he realized he'd made it to the docks. He was now far enough away from the building to transmit, he thought. He got on comms.

"Did you quit yet?" It was Nathan's standard greeting ever since Orochi signed on with Bureau.

"Yes." Orochi said. "But what matters is that Carn's in trouble."

"Fuckers!" Nathan's voice was filtered to normal volume. "What did they do?"

"She's trapped in Nippon." Orochi said tersely.

Nathan gave a low whistle. "How'd she get there?"

"It's a long story, which I will gladly catch you up on when I get there. In the meantime, we're going to Nippon to save her." Traffic was sluggish where Orochi was. He noticed the pointing and staring, but he chose to ignore it. "I'm on my way to the tarmac."

"Ugh." Nathan's distaste flooded over the line. "Couldn't we get a boat?"

Orochi's laugh was mirthless. "Oh, yes, I suppose that getting capsized and drowning a thousand klicks from land does sound like a better plan. Maybe we'll get lucky and mermaids will rescue us from a watery grave."

"Nobody flies, Orochi." It was a statement of fact.

"Your friend does." Orochi remembered Nathan's earlier comment. "And you said he does the Tokyo route regularly." He wished there was a visual component to the comm, just so he could see Nathan's face.

"You're serious." Nathan sounded haggard.

"Dead serious." Orochi said, climbing down towards the ground.

There was a long sigh across the comms. "Why do I listen to you?"

"I put zest in your life." Orochi grinned.

"Zest." Nathan echoed. "Fine. Meet me at the airport in 2 hours. And buy us a plane."

After cutting connection with his friend, Orochi ran across the street. He was certain that no car would want to wrap its plastic bumper around him, and he was right. People honked and glared, but no one pressed the accelerator. He left the cool air of the city and stepped into the underground, looking for an entrance to the Hyperloop.

He was far enough outside town that the Hyperloop was fairly empty. It left him with time on his hands and a wireless connection. He couldn't risk his own 'ware so close to the Bureau, but he remembered he still had Nathan's visor. He booted up and started searching chartered, outbound flights. He found one being stowed at the airport. It was owned by a large, local corporation. Before his incarceration, this would be as easy as pie. Orochi looked through his files. Nathan left him a copy of all of his favorite toys in the visor. Smiling, Orochi accessed his shell company and began fleshing out an aviation division, complete with CEO, bank accounts, and credit scores. As he waited for his stop, he made an offer to the CEO of the local corporation that was too good to be true. He waited impatiently for the CEO to make a counter offer, but when he did Orochi grinned, knowing that he'd found the right leverage.

By the time the Hyperloop had reached SeaTac's airport, Orochi was the proud owner of a sleek plane, complete with weather screen.

Nathan caught up with him, a backpack bulging full of equipment that would never make it through customs. He looked at the airport, and sucked air in between his teeth. "Man, this place has seen better days."

"It's seen better decades." Orochi eyed the concrete-and-glass building. "C'mon, it's not like we'll be here long."

"Yeah, soon we'll be plummeting to our death in a windstorm so violent they don't have the ability to record it." Nathan grinned. "Go team us."

FLY LIKE AN EAGLE

The airport was slowly dying of neglect. The escalators didn't run, and neither did the baggage claim. There were illuminated signs advertising for products that had been out of circulation for decades, but most of them had been spray painted over with various tags. Holes had been chipped into the concrete. The floor was a hazardous mess of rubble. At one point there had been brass fish embedded into the walkways as an artistic embellishment, but long ago someone had dug the fish up for their metal.

This was not to say that the airport was deserted. There were many people loitering at the niches that used to be restaurants or retail spaces. Families huddled together, as though waiting for their departure. Their clothes were torn, their hair in disarray. Gangs patrolled various areas, declaring territory and watching closely over it. The airport was little more than a tenement building at this point, with people holing up in the hopes that they could find a way out.

"Why are we here?" Nathan asked, looking at the outcasts and then down to the ground. "This place is terrible."

"I bought us a plane, and to make it convenient I bought it here at the airport." Orochi said.

Nathan gave him a dry look. "You're not complaining nearly as much as you should be. What aren't you telling me?"

"Please, don't act like I don't TMI you twice a day." Orochi said defensively. He lifted his chin towards the milling people lining the walls of the airport. "Look at those people. They have it the way we used to."

"Yeah they do." Nathan sighed. "They don't even have walls to call their own. This isn't a way for people to live."

"I know." Orochi said quietly. "But it's better than living on the street. And they're in a greendome. No matter how bad someone has it, someone else has it worse."

"If The Ark hadn't left..." Bitterness filled Nathan's voice.

"We didn't know then. We thought the world was going to end." Orochi said soothingly. "I mean, look at us. It almost did."

"Who says it didn't?" Nathan looked up at his friend, then back to the people along the walls.

"Oh, yes, I can see how an extinction-level event would put those people in a much better position." Orochi rolled his eyes. "I'm tired of listening to the Ark's Lament. It's Savvy 101 and you know better. It was a fucking shame the world plunged into chaos with isolated islands of survivability. It would have been livable by itself, if the corporations hadn't called in all of the Ark's debt at once. Crashing the economy for their own benefit was a stupid maneuver. They were short-sighted and that's what collapsed the world, not the Ark itself. We're lucky we have rebuilt some infrastructure since then. As much as I hate cops, having them is better than not. Let's just let that go for now and focus on international air travel, shall we?"

"Sure." Nathan sighed and settled into silence.

Orochi looked for the S concourse. It involved a ride on a mini-Hyperloop. It was a mystery how it retained enough power to move, but the little cars trundled along their designated routes, stopping at each set of doors. People got on the tube with them. They didn't meet with any curiosity. It reminded Orochi a little of a zombie thriller. He thought of the billions that he spent on a plane to rescue Carnelia. He decided once he was back, he would sell the plane and distribute the funds where they'd do some good.

They were the only two to get off at the S gate, and they made their way up the dormant escalator and onto the gate. A ginger man, quite trim, dressed in dress slacks and a white button down shirt squinted as he saw Nathan and Orochi approach.

"Nathan!" The pilot smiled as he saw them. "Packing light, I see."

"I didn't have time to pick up my dry cleaning." Orochi said, sticking out a hand for a handshake.

The pilot took his hand without reservation and pumped enthusiastically. "I'm honored to meet you, Mr. Orochi."

"Just Orochi is fine." Orochi corrected, taking his hand back. "Like, Madonna, or Calliope."

"Understood. Shall we talk business?" The pilot asked, looking to both Nathan and Orochi.

"Ah, a businessman, I approve. What's your name, sir?" Orochi asked, realizing Nathan hadn't mentioned.

"McCune, sir."

"Well, McCune, you know how banks are. I transferred the payment from my account to yours and it got held up by transaction bots, checking legitimacy, that sort of thing."

McCune nodded sharply. "I see."

"Damned inconvenient, but I'd be willing to give you a million in cash up front if you're willing to accept a slightly delayed final payment."

"Sir..." McCune's eyes lit up. "The plane is gassed and ready to go."

"Good." Orochi nodded, and shouldered his bags. "So, if you know Nathan, then you know he's a nervous flyer. Any thoughts?"

"Nerves are normal." The pilot said, his laugh shot with a thin shake. "Especially over the ocean. This plane has a state-of-the-art PTS-1722 windscreen installed. This plane will navigate the storms like we were walking in the park."

"The windscreen is state of the art but the plane isn't?" The whites shone around Nathan's eyes.

"Planes have been built with the most efficient body in mind for centuries." McCune said, leading them down the gangplank. "There are more efficient styles than the one we're taking, but it is no slouch. I regularly fly to Tokyo and back, I'm familiar with the machine... there shouldn't be any worries."

"Oh, there's worries all right." Nathan said, holding his equipment bag close.

Orochi put his hand on Nathan's shoulder. "Hey, it got me out of the box and out doing adventures with you. That's what you wanted, wasn't it?"

Nathan eyed Orochi's earnest expression. "Oh yes, it's so much better now, thank you."

"Nothing ever makes you happy, does it?" Orochi asked, and ducked his head low to enter the plane.

"Pie is good. I could go for pie." Nathan stepped through the plane's door, eyed the surroundings of the plane, and picked a seat from the twenty in the cabin. "Are we really doing this?"

"Be sure to thank Carn when we rescue her." Orochi said, stretching out and leaning back his seat.

"Oh, I will." Nathan said.

Pre-flight checks cost them half an hour, a half an hour where the plane on the tarmac earned the scrutiny of those who milled outside the airport. Most kept a respectful distance.

"I've never parked here." McCune said, concerned. "Those people know to stay back, right?"

"I'm pretty sure they're planning on stealing the plane." Orochi said conversationally. "They just haven't figured out how to do it yet."

"Does the plane have a defense system?" Nathan asked.

"Yes. The PTS-1722. We're worried about chaotic storm fronts, not ambitious predators." The pilot went back to his smartboard, keying in information.

"Can you take off with the hatch open?" Orochi asked thoughtfully.

The pilot turned to look at him as though he was insane. "Nothing would prevent it."

"Okay, then I can take care of them." Orochi offered.

"How?" McCune stared.

Orochi made a twirling gesture with his finger, encouraging the pilot to get back to work. "There are two words in the English language that remain very important to this day. Plausible deniability. I want you to contemplate this concept and bask in its glory, and hurry the hell up getting this plane off of the ground. It will make my job easier."

McCune saw that several people were moving with purpose towards the landing struts. "Right. I'm on it."

Orochi turned to Nathan. "You don't happen to have a tether in that bag, do you?"

Nathan withdrew a line and a carabiner. "Sure do."

Finding a place to anchor the line, Orochi tied it around his waist and cracked open the door on the side of the plane. "Any time now, McCune."

The engines fired to life. McCune dealt with dials and switches. "I'm going to start rolling forward, towards the runway."

"Roll forward, get clear. I'll do the rest." Orochi drew his Zerorez.

The door swung open, and Orochi leaned out as far as he could. He took aim at the feet of the closest would-be boarder, and squeezed off a round.

The engines roared, pushing the plane away from the people stalking it. Many of the would-be boarders dropped to one knee and drew weapons. They started shooting back, aiming for the tires or Orochi. Others covered their heads and ran the other way. Chaos reigned as they milled, trying to decide how best to regain their advantage.

Meanwhile the plane rolled forward, faster and faster.

Orochi noticed one person who had grabbed onto the leg above the wheel. They climbed the landing gear towards the interior of the plane. Orochi stretched his arm as far as he could go, and pulled the trigger.

The climber fell onto the tarmac and rolled into a heap.

Satisfied that there were no other boarders, Orochi climbed inside and wrestled with the door to secure it.

"Those poor people!" Nathan accused him when he was done. "What was that about?"

"If they'd made it, they'd be going to Nippon. They don't speak the language, don't look Panasian, and have no allies there. Better a shot hand and a short fall among friends than being dragged to another country." Orochi shrugged and kicked the clip out of the Zerorez to refill it.

"You're such a fucking humanitarian." Nathan said.

"We're up in the air. The PTS-1722 is kicking on in five minutes. Would either of you like a Scotch?" The pilot asked.

"You brought Scotch?" Orochi asked.

"It eases nerves for first time flyers." McCune eyed Nathan. He held the bottle out for Orochi.

"You want some?" Orochi asked as he stood up to fetch the drink.

"Love some, but probably not until we land, if that's all the same." The pilot turned back and smiled.

"I admire your restraint." Orochi said. "How about you, Mr. Sunshine? Would you care for a little refreshment?"

An electronic hum filled the air as the wind screen turned on.

"That must mean we're close to the edge of the greendome." Nathan said. "Yeah, Scotch would be great."

The plane dropped thirty feet as a wind pocket sucked it down towards the ground.

"Whoo, looks like we've got a SIP - storm in progress." The pilot clapped his hands together and rubbed them briskly back and forth. "Hold on, you two, the flight's ten hours long."

"We should have brought our own Scotch." Orochi said, pouring himself a drink.

The plane shook as the real world tried to break in.

WIDESCREEN

The signal went out, she was certain that it had, but at best Orochi was still hours away from her. At worst, it could take days. She had to deal with the situation as it was dealt.

"Kasumi?" Daizo asked again. "Are you all right?"

Carnelia looked at the screens in front of her. "I may have found a perpetrator near the Shinjuku Oak Tower. A teenage kid with a concealed something. Could be paint, could be a weapon. I can't see from here."

"I'm on it. What are they wearing?" Daizo sounded eager.

"Black pants, red top, blue sneakers." She hoped this call wasn't being monitored real time, or they'd see she was sending Mr. Insistent on a goose chase to quiet him down. Meanwhile, she had to get out of her gear. She could stay in this C-pod all day trying to hop home, but she felt certain that if she did, whoever set this up would pluck her out and haul her off.

She also couldn't just leave. From what she knew of the Tokyo police force, the officers were teamed up with an eye in the sky and feet on the ground. It was her job to read information and feed it to her partner, who would act on it from inside an exoskeleton that hosted the most top-of-the-line robotics in existence.

She couldn't leave, she couldn't stay, she had no idea what she should do. She knew her SOS was a long shot. She was trapped outside of her greendome with little chance of getting home.

Was the fact the jump was international part of the problem? Parris deliberately kept her jumps local, but she wasn't sure if that was why. She assumed that it had more to do with keeping his jumpers from leaving forever. There was no way of finding out what was going on while she was here. She'd be as poorly prepared to pretend to be Kasumi as she was to play Baxley. Better on the run than made by the cops. She would just slip away, out the back, and find some coin-op C-pod joint that didn't question their clientele. She could try to jump out again, or maybe just make a long distance phone call the old fashioned way, and beg for help.

C'mon, Carn, it's not like you haven't lived rough in the past. This body lets you read and speak the language, you're not even that poorly off. She flicked a switch to end her C-pod session, glad that the old tech worked the same way across the globe. C-pods had been invented at the time of the Great Crisis. People thought the world was going to end. C-pods were made for cryo-sleep originally, although the ones used now didn't support that feature. When the Great Crisis had passed, someone had found C-pods to be perfect for babysitting bodies while the mind was out on the Web. C-pods had changed since the Ark, but they still owed their ancestry to those days.

Stepping out of the C-pod, she figured she had twenty minutes lead time before her "partner" came looking for her.

Few people looked up to see who was passing. They were involved in their cases. All she had to do was not be suspicious.

She managed to get outside without incident. She almost leaned against the door in relief before recognizing she would be seen. Instead, she picked a direction and started walking, knowing that even if Kasumi's car was parked in the parking lot, she would have no way of picking it out. She picked a point and started walking towards the street beyond the lot.

"Going somewhere?" Asked a familiar voice from behind her, with an echoing boom that brought her shoulders up.

For a moment, Carnelia closed her eyes. She took a long, slow breath and opened her eyes again, hoping beyond hope that the face wouldn't match the little ident icon she'd just seen a few minutes ago in her berth.

He brought the exoskeleton to a stop. It was tall, probably ten feet tall, and it was very wide. The arms were too long for the torso. The whole thing looked like a scaffold, painted white, with a small platform that allowed Daizo to sit or stand. The controls were obscured behind smoked glass. He poked his head out from the platform and waved.

"Daizo." She said. He was supposed to be off on her goose chase! "How are you?"

"Confused." He bit the word off. "You sent me on a false mission and then slipped away from your desk. That is not the actions of the woman I know. What are you doing that you can't tell me?"

"Nothing!" She raced to assure him. She backed up into a sedan, and slid towards the hood, still trying to get away. "I needed some time away from my desk."

"You could have said that." Daizo growled. "Instead you have me looking for a ghost!"

"You're my partner. I don't want to get you into trouble." She said, folding her arms across her chest. "This is something I need to do by myself."

"We're partners." Daizo said brightly. "You can tell me anything."

She looked at him. He was handsome, clean-cut, with lively dark eyes and a well-defined jaw. He was so clean he squeaked, and Carnelia knew he wasn't the kind of person who would accept the reality of the situation without complete mental reprogramming.

"I can't, I really can't." She shook her head. "I just need to go home now."

"I'll give you a ride!" Daizo offered, his even teeth glinting in the sunlight. "In my new car."

"Thank you, but no." She said firmly. *What am I going to have to do to ditch this guy? He's more insistent than Orochi!* "I mean, what about the exo? You can't just leave that in the parking lot."

Daizo's face fell as disappointment overcame his cheerful disposition. "I don't understand, Kasumi. I have tried to do everything you've asked, and you continue to shut me out."

So that's what this is about. I should have known. Carnelia didn't have time to assuage his wounded ego. "Daizo, you're a nice man but it wouldn't work. You need to stop pursuing me or I will have to ask for reassignment."

"That won't be necessary." Said Daizo, sounding wounded.

She looked up the steps that led up to the TPD building. It was a white building, very crisp and proper, standing for justice and propriety. She heard steps behind her, but thought nothing of it. What she did note was that Daizo's eyebrows had shot straight up, reaching his hairline. Then a storm cloud of emotions rolled in, and his expression went from open and friendly to guarded in a moment.

Whatever caused it was behind her. She turned to see what had caused this transformation. An older Panasian man wearing a Stetson hat and a brown oiled canvas duster stepped up towards them. He nodded towards her and smiled. "Kasumi."

There was no way to access the memories of the person whom she had jumped, but if there was ever an upgrade she'd desired for jumping, it was that. She had tried to pretend to be the person she'd jumped into in the past, to poor effect. She smiled and nodded, trying to think of how to get as far away from him as possible. This guy's fashion choices made her skin crawl.

"Haidora." Daizo said crisply.

Haidora. It translated to Hydra. She didn't know a Hydra, but she knew a Hyde. A supposed to be dead Hyde. A bodyjumper Hyde? The realization left her stunned, breathless on the steps. Parris's go-to guy had somehow survived. Rascati had assured her that he'd shot the man down, but obviously not fast enough to prevent a jump. But how? He wasn't hooked up...

"Come on, Kasumi, let's go someplace with a few less cops around." He put his arm around her neck and shoulders, drawing her in.

Daizo looked away angrily, and missed her pleading eyes. Suddenly the man she'd been driving away was the last person she wanted to leave.

"Daizo." She said quietly.

He turned, still angry.

"Haidora" put pressure on her neck, which Carnelia assumed was a polite threat. She managed a soft, "I'm sorry." There was nothing else she could say.

He turned away and stormed back inside the police department.

"That pup better be careful. He's sniffing a little too close to what we're doing." Hyde said, pitched low for only her to hear. "You need to be a little colder to him, make sure he's disinclined to follow you. Otherwise I'm afraid we're going to have to seek a more permanent solution."

Carnelia swallowed. She had a feeling that Hyde was connected to her being stuck in Kasumi. That said, he spoke to her like she was Kasumi, which could work in her favor. She still had a chance to get away from him and follow her plan. "I understand, but it's hard. He's a puppy. I don't want to talk about him anyway. I was on my way home, I'm not feeling well."

Hyde's face took on a surprisingly empathic look. "I'm sorry to hear that, darlin'."

Oh no.

He smiled at her then, and she closed her eyes. "I'll take you home and look after you, how's that?"

The incongruous idea of this warped killer taking care of her almost made her bark a bitter laugh, but she held character. "That'd be fine."

How do I get out of this how do I get out of this how do I... Carnelia took a deep breath and thought about how she would extricate herself from her problem. Hyde was the immediate threat. She was sure that he was acting in boyfriend capacity, rather than some kind of criminal play. Or maybe she was helping him, but the fact remained that they had an intimate relationship. Hyde would notice her slip faster than anyone else. How was she going to get away from him?

They walked. Hyde seemed content to be quiet, which let Carnelia formulate ideas. The files Kasumi had open were filed under the same name, Hitochigai. It was just a name, but the people whose files had been opened weren't just Panasian. There was a small likelihood that every person in those files were related by family, but it was small. There were also pictures of items that went along with each face. Stolen goods?

Bodyjumpers.

Was Hyde a bodyjumper?

How did Hyde jump when Rascati shot him down? He wasn't plugged in. Even still, he'd never done bodyjumping before that I knew of. There were just the four of us, Gage, Lisbet, Daign and me. If Hyde was a bodyjumper, Parris wouldn't have let him run around killing people... would he?

She hadn't been plugged in when she jumped into Orochi. She had been in her own body, though, with tech in her head. It hadn't been easy, but she'd pulled it off.

"You're awful quiet." Hyde interrupted her thoughts.

"Sorry." She said reflexively. Kasumi must say it a lot.

"You and your apologizing. You don't need to apologize around me. I like a woman with some backbone." He leered at her. "As long as it's flexible."

Her hand flew up in front of her mouth, hiding a smile that Carnelia didn't feel. It had been a while since she'd felt someone else's habits. In the beginning she'd had to deal with nothing but habits with Pixru, but finally she'd managed to put her mark on that body.

Not that she wanted to think about Pixru.

Pulling her hand down. Carnelia forced herself to look into Hyde's eyes. "I was just thinking about the Hitochigai files."

"I told you to leave those alone. You're just asking to get in too deep." Hyde chastised her gently.

They had been walking for a while and Carnelia wasn't sure where they were going. The streets were thick with traffic, small families pushing strollers, kids throwing balls that returned to them, teenagers flipping tricks on hoverboards. Drones sailed through the air, ranging from the small to the bowling ball sized, while a class with matching uniforms stuck together in formation as they wandered down the sidewalks.

Now that she was observing it, she saw that Tokyo had fared better than Seattle had since the Great Crisis. The skyscrapers reached higher, and fewer seemed to show structural damage. The streets had smaller, more efficient cars on the road, and moving sidewalks that still moved. The kids she'd seen seemed to have homes. Of course, she hadn't gone out at night, and she hadn't left the center of the city. Doubtless there were areas less clean and well-mannered than this. However, downtown Seattle had a lot of shady content, and here everyone seemed less guarded and more relaxed.

"Don't you think that I'm in deep with you?" She asked, hiding another smile.

"That's different. You can be with me and not know what I do." Hyde said, trying to sound stern.

"I know what you do." She chanced. "I am trying to become more involved."

"You don't know what you're asking, darlin'." He said, frowning. "You're gonna lose your job, and then you're going to have to work with me and the other lowlifes."

"If it means I get to be with you..." She trailed off suggestively.

He chuckled. "I'm warning you, if you go down this rabbit hole you'll never look at life the same way again."

"Funny, I think I heard that one before." Another limb, but it sounded good.

She was rewarded with his laugh, and a, "I don't think you're not feeling well."

"Being around you helps me feel better." Carnelia wanted to gag, but she wanted to live. If it meant flirting with Hyde, she'd have to manage that until she could slip away from him.

"We're not far now." Hyde said.

She let that comment go, but now she felt uncertain again. Was he testing her? Was all of this a test? Had she already failed and he was not letting on?

The skyscraper he walked up to had a decorative front. Painted vines coiled up the windows, in various shades of green. Tiny flowers dotted the vines, but as she got closer she saw that the detail work was impeccable. The bower above the doorway threw shade, and she looked up to see rows upon rows of balconies.

"Home sweet home." Hyde said.

Is there anything you say that is not a homily? Carnelia held her tongue.

They rode the elevator up to the thirty-ninth floor, and Carnelia leaned in to Hyde to feel where they should be going. She let him lead, and grabbed for her keys, dreading unlocking the door.

"I've got it." He said, and heroically rescued her from fumbling. Her heart sank as she realized how deeply these two were involved.

She stepped into the dimly lit room. Inside the furniture consisted of a table, plastic chairs, an unadorned smartboard, and a couch that looked like it had been fished out of a dumpster.

Which were the least of her problems when Hyde's hand wrapped around her throat and squeezed.

"Who are you?" He demanded. "You ain't Kasumi so you best identify!"

Her eyes widened and she looked around for a weapon of opportunity. The spartan space offered her nothing to grab, throw, or even kick into his way. He lifted her off the floor, and her feet kicked despite herself. She grabbed onto his wrist, trying to force the tendons to release their grip.

Recognizing that she couldn't speak, Hyde lowered her to the ground. He grabbed a pistol from his duster and pointed it at her belly. "I can make your new place of residence a living hell with one twitch of my finger. You had best be telling me who's in my girlfriend before I have to apologize to her for shooting her."

He'd loosened his grip but hadn't released her. She called up her best false bravado, shoving the fear way down. "I'm offended that you don't recognize me, Hyde."

His eyes narrowed. "You were flirting like Lizbet but she's well and truly gone. Daign would rather get gut shot than flirt with a man, and Gage was too terrified of people to flirt with 'em. I'm guessing that it's you, Carnelia."

She sighed, and he knew he had her, so he let her go. "So, tell me what you're doing in my girlfriend."

"Honestly I was just trying to get an eye in the sky, I had no idea she was associated with you." She wasn't sure what she could tell and what she couldn't, but the Bureau could just tough it out if she turned over a few of their secrets.

"Why didn't you jump out while you were in her C-pod?" His mouth turned down, a bad sign. "You could have just gone back.. say, who are you staying in these days? I heard you were dead."

"Funny, I heard the same thing about you." She searched the room, but it was too high up for any heroic escapes. It would be shot in the elevator or shot in the stairwell, but neither instance looked good. Except for the part that this was his girlfriend's body... but she wasn't willing to put a lot of trust in his behavior. "Had I known who she was, and that you were here, I never would have made that jump."

"Who are you working for?" Hyde asked. "The Bureau?"

Carnelia blinked. She didn't know that Hyde knew about them. "I'd rather not say."

Hyde laughed. "You'd rather not say. You're stuck in my girlfriend with no one to rescue you, and you think you can just opt out?"

"I'm just embarrassed. Working for yourself and screwing it up this bad is going to make me less hirable later." Carnelia prevaricated.

"Well, it just so happens that I could use a woman with your skills." Hyde said. "And to get you the hell out of my girlfriend."

"I'm listening." She couldn't help but be interested. As fucked up as working for Parris had been, it had been the only life she'd known for a long time.

"I know a place where they got people. People who can help you out of Kasumi, and into something a little more your style. It's a better operation than Parris ran. And I know they'd be thrilled to get a hold of a talent like you." Hyde smiled, warming to the idea. His eyes widened, and he'd thought of something, but he didn't continue.

"You really know how to talk to a girl." She smiled, while on the inside a knot of terror slipped inside her heart. Anything that Hyde thought was a great idea probably wasn't. "Where are we going?"

"That's the bad news." Hyde stepped in to close the gap. "I can't tell you."

She tried to duck but his fist caught her under the chin, snapping her head back and tossing her into unconsciousness.

MANY HEADS

Her footsteps echoed loudly in the wide, empty corridors. Her heart raced, and she glanced over her shoulder every second step. Blue strands of her hair fell into her eyes, and she anxiously swept them out of her view. Everything about this place was a lie, and she had to find a way out.

"C'mon, Diane," she muttered under her breath. Diane, not Chimera, not even K1zm3t, not any more. She never wanted to touch a computer again. She was still Diane Lourdes, and she would escape.

She found the hallway that she sought. As far as she could tell, the space was an old, abandoned army base. She couldn't tell how old. The symbols had been painted over with a thick black paint, and any mention of this place or its location, on the Web or inside, had been expunged before her arrival. This place was a hollowed out shell of its former self. The people who brought her here had plans. They set up shop prior to bringing in the Savvy, the fifteen or so test subjects that they'd selected. The Orochi Group, it was called. Each of the Savvy were given a code name. They were all mythical creatures. The creatures she was familiar with all had more than one head. She was sure that mattered, but she'd been too embroiled in plans for escape. She didn't care about their mysterious mission.

Savvy. Diane had been so proud to be one of the elite. Someone who understood computer languages and could make them dance to her tune. She thought she was invulnerable. She covered every trace, every scrap of her Web identity so that no one could follow the breadcrumbs back to her. Her illusions of safety had been slapped away from her like a treat out of a child's hand. Diane couldn't bring herself to think about what happened to her since her abduction. She just had to escape.

She couldn't sit here and take it, be a guinea pig to her captors and be used for her greatest skills. If they'd offered to pay her for her services, she may have had a different answer for them. She hurried down the empty hallway, looking for the marker. She may have had a different answer for them, but now all they would get from her now was a vanishing act.

The dull green paint faded to gray as she left the lit hallways. Her shadow led her down the hall as she looked for the spot. There. This one marker, someone had let the paint run down the wall, and it served as a milepost for her. She could be chasing dreams but after what she'd seen, she'd rather chase dreams than be next.

Her thoughts played without her permission as she searched for a hidden door. Hydra... his name was Carl, but it was hard to think of her fellow prisoners as anything but their call signs now... Hydra had been one of the outspoken ones. He was brash, he was charismatic, and Diane would admit to herself, even if she admitted it to no one else, that she'd had a bit of a crush on him. He was up for a test, and went to the test chamber with his usual cocky swagger. When he came out again, something was wrong. He called everyone by name, but his eyes were flat and heartless. He had a drawl, which Diane never heard before. He called her darlin', when he used to call her Kizzy. She didn't know what the point of the experiments were, and she didn't care. She wanted out of this monkey cage before someone changed her brain patterns.

She felt along the walls. It was too dim to see any patterns or catches even if she wanted to. She followed the seams of the walls, hoping to find anything that might give away a hidden door. The staff had a way of getting in and out, and it was hidden from the prisoner's eyes. The idea that she thought of them as 'staff' made her angry. It was giving in to their conditioning. They were her guards, her jailers. They were the enemy.

Diane would find an exit. She had to. Anything less could mean death, or worse.

In the hush of the metal walls and stained concrete floor, Diane searched each section of the walls, running her fingers up and down. The wall with the drizzle hadn't paid off, but she would try every section of this facility until her fingers wore off.

A noise caught her attention at the end of the hallway. She froze, and she didn't have to feign the fear she felt as the guards rounded the corner and saw her crouched on the concrete.

"Little rabbit got lost in the maze?" The guard who spoke was a big, beefy Cauc. His comrade was a wiry Ethiopian with a shaved head and a trim goatee. The fear she felt being alone with these two in these hallways spiked as she realized the position she found herself in.

"We can't hurt her." The Ethiopian said with a rich, accented voice. "She's worth too much to them."

"Oh, I'll be very gentle." The Cauc promised, flexing his hands.

She gripped the wall reflexively. She felt something with her right index finger. She inched it upward along the wall, and she found a plastic depression in the metal.

"You're right!" Diane sprang to her feet, thinking as quickly as she could. "You're right, I shouldn't be... hey, I thought I was going to the latrine. You two wouldn't mind escorting me back, would you? I should be getting back. I think it's my turn for testing soon, I'm sure the Big Guy would be mad if I missed my appointment..."

The Cauc looked disgruntled but the Ethiopian looked relieved that she wasn't going to fight them. He took a step forward. "C'mon, girl, there's nothing to see this way anyway. You should stay closer to the group."

"You're right." Her enthusiastic nod succeeded in avoiding the creepy Caucasian man's gaze. "You're so right. I don't know what I was thinking. I definitely need to get back to my space."

It took every ounce of willpower not to look back over her shoulder. She'd have to be extra careful. Chances were good that the staff were aware of that spot, and they wouldn't let her just waltz back to it. Escape from this place was going to be a long con. She would have to recruit some help.

Who on Earth would she be able to trust?

TOKYO

Something crashed into the side of the plane.

By Orochi's estimation, it had been a boulder the size of a car, but the wind screen pulverized it down to a manageable size - say, as large as Korden, his dog - so the thunk was endurable, and the plane flew on, dent and all.

Nathan sat looking miserable in his chair, his knuckles white from gripping the seat. He looked as though he wanted to throw up, but wasn't sure where he could. He had some audio equipment out on his lap, but he wasn't paying it any attention. He was simply too frightened. "How much longer do we have? I feel like we've been in this plane forever."

Orochi thought that was fair. He wasn't thrilled with how the flight had gone thus far. Looking out the window to see endless swirls of hurricanes below, having occasional rocks hurled at them, and seeing the sky red with debris wasn't his preferred method of travel, either.

The plane shuddered, and he grabbed onto his armrests for balance.

"How are you holding up back there?" The pilot asked, voice steady.

"How do you do this regularly?" Orochi yelled back. "What on Earth makes this worth it?"

The pilot grinned. "I've got a family on either side of the water."

Orochi laughed. "How'd you father children when your cajones are pure brass?"

Nathan retched somewhere behind him. Orochi didn't look over to check.

"He okay?" The pilot yelled.

"Nothing that we can't handle." Orochi said. "You just keep focusing on getting us there."

Coming up from the side of the chair, Nathan frowned and reached out for the Scotch. He'd already had a couple of glasses, but Orochi let him be. He figured he'd need to replace at least some of what he'd lost.

"You alright?" Orochi asked after Nathan cleared his throat.

Nathan nodded miserably. "There isn't a sense of level in this entire plane."

"Well, we're more than halfway through the trip by now..." Orochi said encouragingly. He'd lost track of time since takeoff.

The plane tipped up on its side. Orochi looked out the window to see streaks of black cutting through the red hued sky. Arcs of lightning streaked out towards the plane.

Nathan scrambled to hold on to the equipment on his lap. He spared a glance to his friend to hear what was happening.

Orochi slid the screen down over the window. "You don't want to know."

"How does he make this trip so many times?" Nathan asked, his eyes bloodshot. "On purpose?"

"He's handling the plane." Orochi said. "He's got the controls. I imagine that makes it easier."

"Or worse." Nathan supplied. He set down his Scotch. "Have I told you how much I hate you today?"

"Only hourly." Orochi said dismissively. "C'mon, it's not so bad..."

Something crashed into the side of the plane. It left a bigger dent than the last one.

"This shouldn't be done. It's impossible." Nathan started shaking, his eyes going wide. "We're going to die!"

"We're not going to die." Orochi said calmly. "The windscreen is built to smooth out the air stream and to reduce impact from strikes. It also reroutes electrical discharge so that it doesn't touch the plane. Sometimes the air currents are at cross purposes and it takes a second for the tech to adjust.

"What about those boulders?" Nathan demanded.

"I'm not sure. I know the wind screen should reduce their size, so I'm guessing they were big to start. Hey, McCune! What's the story with those boulders?" Orochi yelled up to the front.

"Sorry about those. We should be past that point, now, the rest should be smoother than it's been."

The plane tilted nose-down and started to lose altitude.

"No you don't!" McCune shouted. His fingers flew over the smartboard controls of the airplane. The plane leveled, leaving Nathan looking green, Orochi looking white, and McCune flushed red.

"I'd tell you it's not normally this bad but this is about average." McCune said, not looking up from the controls. "If it helps the greendome should be around here."

"Comforting." Orochi said levelly.

The difference between the wilds and the greendome was immediate and a relief. The plane leveled out, and the landing at the airport outside of Tokyo was smooth. They filed off the plane quickly, applying boot to concrete as swiftly as possible.

"McCune, I will say this. I thought no one was crazier than we were." Nathan said, sticking out his hand. "I'm glad to see that I was wrong."

McCune shook Nathan's hand and nodded. "If you think flying is the crazy part, you're wrong."

Remembering his comment about a family on either side of the divide, Orochi chuckled. "I can't argue with that. We may be here for an extended trip, but when we need to go, we'll need to leave right away." Orochi said. "Can we keep you on a retainer?"

"I try to stay two weeks between jobs, the jet lag is awful. Think you'll need longer than that?" He asked.

"If we do, we'll be ash art." Orochi said.

McCune chuckled at the colloquialism. "Hey, they don't have room to bury their own dead these days."

"Yeah but selling remains is still a pretty cold reception." Orochi said. "I doubt ours will go for much."

"Here's my comm ID. Don't worry about the time of day, I'm used to odd hours." McCune passed him the data.

"I bet." Nathan said, looking slightly less green.

With business concluded the group split, McCune to the plane to requisition repairs, and Orochi and Nathan to find a place to sleep.

They didn't speak for a while. Orochi thought it best to give Nathan time to get a handle on his nerves. Instead, Orochi looked around at the architecture. This was a private field, not a big commercial airport like SeaTac. This surprised Orochi, as he didn't think anyone flew that much. There were houses on either end of the runway. They were small houses, but space was a priority in Nippon.

Catching a taxi to the city, Orochi watched as what little plant life remained wild slowly surrendered to orderly, maintained rows of city enhancement projects. Cherry trees grew up from the street meridian, as well-trimmed gingko grew in cones up from the manicured grass of business lawns. The skyrises weren't as tall at the outskirts of the city. If Orochi were any judge, he'd say they were only twenty or thirty stories high. As they drove towards the center of the city, the buildings got taller and taller.

What surprised Orochi the most were the proliferation of crows that sat on every tree and street sign. Black as night, larger than the ones he was used to, and when he heard them, their raucous caws sounded slightly different than his local fair. He chuckled at the idea that animals might develop accents.

"Where are we going to start?" Nathan asked, looking considerably healthier in color than he had on the plane.

"We should probably feed you." Orochi said.

"Nope." Nathan said. "I will pass."

Orochi nodded. "Okay, then next order of business is to find somewhere to chuck our gear and sleep."

"Ugh, there are so many, I don't know what's good." Nathan grumbled.

"We don't want good. We want cheap, lower end stuff." Orochi said.

Nathan groaned. "Why can't we ever do something where we're living it up for a change? The bad guys would never expect it."

"Now now, I'm not ready for that part yet. We want to stay under the radar for as long as we can. We don't know what took Carnelia, all we know is that she couldn't come back from jumping into that cop. If cops are responsible, then this is going to be really tricky. The

Nipponese police force is one of the most intimidating forces on the planet, and judging by their tactics, we're working with the dark side. Bad cops are hard to anticipate." Orochi allowed himself a moment to look worried. "Ideally we end up with a couple different locations to work from, but as we just got in and the flight was rough, I thought we could start slow."

Nathan nodded. "You had me at place to sleep."

By then they had walked to the road. Cars drove up and down the lanes, but no one looked interested in stopping for them. A taxi changed lanes and slid over, farther away from their side of the street.

Orochi growled. "You'd think they'd never seen a seven foot two monster before."

"They're used to monsters a little taller than that." Nathan quipped.

Finally a minivan pulled up to the curb and stopped for them. The driver was Cauc. "Let me get you a lift."

"Thanks." Orochi said, throwing his bag and Nathan's in the back. "We need a cheap place to sleep."

"I know a place. It's got small rooms," He warned.

"We'll manage." Orochi promised.

The driver seemed content to let the radio blare baby metal as he drove, not attempting to initiate conversation. Orochi listened to little girls screaming about wanting chocolate in Nipponese. He had to admit, it was catchy.

"Here we are." The driver said, breaking the silence. He pulled over to the curb.

They stepped out of the cramped cab, Orochi stretching as he did so. He ran his hands over his head, where the top of his mohawk should have been. He balled his hands into fists and brought them down.

Outside the hotel was a little koi pond. A young girl was splashing in the shallows, under the supervision of her mother. The mother said something in Nipponese. Orochi wasn't sure, but it sounded like it was time to go. The little girl started crying, throwing a tantrum. In seconds she was at full blast, stomping her boots and thrashing her arms. As she thrashed, she looked up to see Orochi striding towards the entry. She stopped crying mid-sob, and stared at him silently as he and Nathan walked towards the hotel doors. Orochi watched her out of the corner of his eye. She stood stock still, frozen like a prey animal. It unnerved him.

"Welcome to Tokyo," Nathan said under his breath.

Orochi didn't respond. He didn't know how. He watched the little girl as she ran to her mother and buried her head in her mother's shoulder, looking away from him. He was fairly sure he scared her. He pulled his coat around him, the smile he'd managed to scrounge up flattening.

Instead they walked up to the counter and asked for a room. Orochi paid through one of his accounts and they headed upstairs for some sleep. The room was minuscule. It was not tall enough for Orochi to stand up straight, and the bed was barely long enough to accommodate Nathan. Nathan wasted no time and belly flopped onto the bed, sighing happily.

There was a tiny water closet that Orochi had to struggle his way into. The toilet had more controls than a C-pod. He stared at it, looking at the instructional icons that meant nothing to him. He just wanted to piss.

"I can see why you wanted to go cheap." Nathan said after listening to Orochi swear profusely for fifteen minutes. "The savings really add up."

Orochi glared at Nathan. "You know, the one time I say let's not go ostentatious, and you give me shit about it."

Nathan rolled onto his back and stared at the ceiling. "Oh, so this is my fault."

"I didn't say that." Orochi said flatly. "I'm just here to get a job done and you're lying around."

"What happened to just relax?" Nathan asked, propping himself up on an elbow. "What happened to it was a long ten hour flight?"

"It was a long ten hour flight, and in that time anything could have happened to Carnelia. Let's set up our equipment so that when you pass out, I will still be able to do something useful." Orochi reached out to his bag and unzipped the main compartment.

"So, when this is all over and we've rescued her, will you finally ask her out?" Nathan asked, rolling off the bed.

"What?" Orochi spun to look at his friend.

Nathan tsked. "Orochi, you are hung up on this woman. I've been friends with you for years and I've seen you date lots of girls, but I've never seen you act like this."

"I can't date her." Orochi said brusquely.

Nathan put his hand over Orochi's duffel bag. "What? Why not?"

"I don't want to talk about it." Orochi moved Nathan's hand and continued to draw out pieces of equipment.

"Seriously? Monosyllabic pubescent answers? This is what I'm going to get?" Nathan made a rude noise. "How old are you, thirteen?"

Orochi glared at Nathan. "This isn't up for discussion. I'm saving Carnelia because I owe her. And she's your friend, too, so don't act like this is all on me."

Nathan narrowed his eyes. "I'm not sure I'd fly to another country to get you out of a jam."

"Thanks." Orochi said sarcastically. "I'll be sure to remember that when you need me."

"Oh come on." Nathan walked over to his bag and started to unpack. "You wouldn't do that for me either."

Orochi narrowed his eyes. "Says you."

"I'm flattered." Nathan grinned. "Nice to know I rank at least as high as Carn."

Bit by bit, they assembled their gear. Nathan crashed quickly after that, after having a protein bar for dinner, not wanting to wait for food to get sleep. Orochi ordered in, the favored method of Savvy everywhere. He sat down and clicked his visor on. Keeping his eyes open was preferred over keeping them closed, and this visor didn't run around screaming, "I'm Orochi! Come take me on!"

The code that washed over him was mostly Nipponese, but fortunately for him he'd had a run-in with a Savvy that had forced him to up his game and learn the language. Pixru. He tried not to think about her, tried not to think about what happened in the months leading up to Carn ending up in her body. It was too complicated. She was in an on-again-off-again relationship with Michael, and when she was off again she seduced Orochi. It was flattering, having one of the best Savvy in the industry finding him interesting for more than his mohawk. Not to mention the fact that she was beautiful as well as smart, and treated Orochi like an equal in the field. He hadn't realized he'd been used until it was too late. It was a poor choice, for her and for him, but she was a force of personality and Orochi had been pretty sure he was going to die. Now he got daily reminders of what happened whenever Carnelia entered the room.

If only she wasn't stuck in Pixru! But her body had been killed, something Orochi hadn't been able to prevent. Worse, he had a hand in getting her killed, if he was honest with himself. He wondered if he could get her a new body. Scope out the coma ward at Seattle's general hospital, find a new model. *Yeah, because that wouldn't be creepy, offering Carnelia a new body. Jeez Orochi, what has become of the freedom fighter now?*

He realized he wasn't making any headway into the code he was reading. The complexity of reading a second language, the long flight, and even the kid hiding from him added up. It was time to get some shut-eye.

Nathan snored. He'd taken the tiny bed, but there was no hope of Orochi getting any sleep on such a short bed. Instead, he grabbed a pillow and lay down on the floor. He lay there for a while. Sleep, despite its phantom promise of release, dangled right before him without settling in for the night. He sat up and rubbed his eyes, then donned his visor and sat with his back against the bed, leg over leg, and dove into the codesphere of the Web.

Rascati hadn't given him anything to work with. He wanted Orochi in the dark so he couldn't do any damage. He knew that Carnelia had jumped to Nippon, and there'd been those pictures from the TPD that Rascati showed him. It was his guess that Carn's target was a sora no me, someone who processed a lot of data and ran that data to their partner on the ground. That left him with a need to crack the highest level security police force in the entire world.

He grinned at the prospect and started looking for a way in.

Orochi spared a moment for thinking about her. If it weren't for her, he wouldn't stand a chance with the Nipponese code structures. This code looked familiar, if not nearly as exciting as what she could whip up. He spent several hours testing programs, trying to find one that would worm its way into the usual programming without setting off any alarms.

When he was ready, he launched it. He saw names on the roster, from all departments, but he focused on the sora no me. There were a lot of women doing the job; it was most likely seen as a support role. He had to keep winnowing it down, there were too many options to simply go house to house. That was when he noticed the entry and exit logs of the sora no me. Each had their patterns, but one fell out of step. She logged off early the day that Carnelia went missing, and had not logged back in. Her name was Kasumi Yasutoro.

He had his place to start.

BAD GUYS

Her jaw ached. Her eyes snapped wide open, but to no effect. There was a hood over her head.

She was in a van, she surmised, from the feel of the wall behind her back. It was cool to the touch and had both metal and plastic parts. Plus, it smelled like a vehicle. It was possible that she could play possum, try to take on her captor when he grabbed her to move her. She'd done that before. The result was a broken rib, and six weeks of painful breathing. She needed a better plan. She knew she had to try something, but the what eluded her. She felt as though playing along and getting more information was probably in her best interest. Or, at least, would save her another broken rib.

"Hyde?" She said, voice muffled. To its credit, the hood was dry and didn't stink. "What's going on?"

She felt the van go into a turn. "Good mornin', darlin'. I trust you slept well?"

"Like a brick." She replied tartly. "Where are you taking me?"

"We're almost there. Lean forward, I'll take that hood off." He said.

Leaning forward, she felt his fingers grope her hair through her hood. He jerked, and she felt the tingle of several pieces of hair being jerked from their roots, as well as her eyelids fluttering to half-mast to protect her from the light. It wasn't as bad as she'd feared; it was twilight. She thought it was early afternoon when she jumped in but that was early afternoon Seattle time. It was full daylight when she'd talked to Daizo, but she had no idea how long she'd been unconscious. The time difference was huge. She didn't know if this place was far from where they'd started or not. She would have to find out if anyone was going to rescue her.

Before them, an enormous complex crouched. It was only ten stories tall, but it went out along the ground in all directions. The middle section of the building was rounded outward, like a ball pressed down firmly from the top. The top was flat, and seemed to have some kind of structure built around it that was hard to make out in the gloom.

The building glowed from the inside, a yellow-white light that shone against the coming of night. Dark patterns of horizontal and vertical bars were visible inside the building. Carnelia's eyes were adjusting to the half-light of the setting sun and the unusual architecture. The glass appeared to be smoked. She could see the glow, but she couldn't see anything inside the central area.

The van pulled to a stop. Hyde turned off the vehicle and she heard his door open. The door she sat next to opened. Hyde grabbed her shoulder and directed her out of the van.

"What is this place?" She asked.

"You're about to find out." Hyde said. "Let's get inside."

Hyde put his hand on a print-reader and the glass doors swished open, admitting the pair of them. There were sentinels standing guard, wearing body armor and round helmets that obscured their facial expressions or any identifying marks. Carnelia wasn't certain what she was seeing, but she already didn't like it.

"Hyde." A baritone voice caught their attention. They looked up to the mezzanine level to see a Panasian man with spiked hair, a black suit, and shiny leather shoes. "What have you brought us?"

"Kaito, this is Kasumi. Do you remember Kasumi?" Hyde asked.

Carnelia said nothing.

"Ah, yes, she sings so sweetly. I don't mean to pry, but why is she tied up? I am not one to judge, but perhaps these things are best done in private?" Kaito's eyes twinkled as he teased Hyde.

"She's tied up because, we have a bodyjumper in residence." Hyde said, and the anger in his tone was a sharp contrast to how he'd been treating her.

"Ah." Kaito nodded, and walked down the stairs to meet them. "Do we now? How lovely."

Carnelia glanced at the ground floor of the building they were in. The yellow-white glow seemed to be everywhere, fit into strips along each of the window's sides. The smoked glass looked almost opaque from this angle, and she could see the sweep of an enormous desk, as well as the furniture associated in a big waiting room. However, she knew there was more behind the curtain, as where they were only took up approximately a third of the bulging bubble space. The wall behind the desk was completely opaque, black and shiny to reflect what was going on in this room. She caught sight of security cameras, and wondered what exactly Hyde had dragged her into.

Kaito got to the bottom of the stairs and gazed at Kasumi's face, to try to see the truth beyond. "Who might we have here?"

When Carnelia didn't volunteer, Hyde supplied, "Carnelia Cesnos."

"Oh my." Kaito said. "A celebrity among the Hitochigai."

"The who?" Carnelia asked.

"My bodyjumpers." Kaito said proudly. "They do things a little differently, but the effect is the same. Confusion, disorder, and very low capture rates."

"That's all well and good," Hyde interrupted. "But, she's in my girlfriend, and I'd like her back."

"I'm trapped in here." Carnelia said. "I tried to get out and something held me back."

"Interesting." Kaito stroked an imaginary beard. "I wonder how that could have happened."

His infuriating smile made Carnelia want to jump into his smug body and punch himself right where he stood.

She knew that Hyde would stop her before she could manage to get to him. "What's Hyde going to do about this? I mean, you using his girlfriend for your aims?"

"That which I turned on, I can turn off. We'll get you out of there in no time." Kaito promised. "Hyde, please escort her off of the showroom floor. Drama tends to dry up business."

Hyde shoved her forward, and it was move or fall. The mirrored wall had a door cleverly hidden in the joins to mar the mirror as little as possible. They walked through, closing off the corporate face.

"That's impossible. How would you know whether or not I was going to jump Kasumi?" Carnelia asked, looking around. They seemed to be in a holding area, with another door next to them.

"A fair question." He put his hand on her shoulder. "Hyde, why don't you let her go."

"But boss..." Hyde's eyes flicked to Carnelia.

"Hyde, I've been unfair to you. I set up Kasumi here as a delicious morsel for a particular department that specializes in bodyjumping. They've been sniffing around, and getting close. I had no idea that Miss Cesnos worked for them, whether directly or as a freelance agent. Fortunately for you, Miss Cesnos, I have been waiting for you to investigate my little palace. Despite your current ties, I believe we can work together, and with much better rapport than that idiot Parris." Kaito pointed at Carnelia's bindings, and Hyde reluctantly took them off her wrists.

She was tempted to jump at him and attack, just to surprise him, but she figured that making the nervous marksman jerk for her amusement would only be paid back in spades later. She rubbed at her wrists and glowered instead.

"Oh, come now, when you see what we're doing here, you won't feel quite so ill of us." Kaito said, taking Carnelia's hand. "In fact, it doesn't matter what brought you here, what matters now is that you're here. I have something rather special to show you, and I think when you see it you'll change your mind about me."

Jerking away, she glowered at Kaito. "Don't touch me."

"Very well." He started walking, indicating Hyde to follow. "You see, when you have a technology that is as great and terrible as bodyjumping is, putting all of your eggs in one very limited basket is not how we grow. We all knew that Parris was unstable, but he was very good at what he did. Here at Typhon, we don't run the same kind of ship. We are businessmen, first and foremost, and we run our business exactly as that - a business."

"On the backs of people who steal for you." Carnelia said, unimpressed. "I guess if this is what gets you through the night."

"Our Hitochigai are employees. They wouldn't be as proficient at what they do without someone running the ship for them. Parris was a little more... chaotic in his dealings. You have proven that you aren't just any employee, but someone capable of being more. Without us, our Hitochigai would not succeed. You on the other hand seem to be doing well, although it seems as though your work is on hiatus. Or, at least, we haven't heard much from you since Parris's death. Are you just in a lull?" Kaito's expression was one of rapt attention.

Carnelia was a little put off by his intensity. "I don't want to talk about this with you."

Kaito threw back his head and laughed. "Ah, Carnelia, you don't understand! I'm offering you such things, a better job environment, actual health benefits, an HR department when things go wrong, everything a bodyjumper needs to be the best at what they do."

She opened her mouth to tell him she didn't want to be a bodyjumper, but that wasn't true. She'd just undergone the surgery so she could do it again. Still, she didn't want to do it this way. She wasn't stealing things with Rascati's team. Orochi was with her. It was better. "I don't want the job."

Kaito spun on his heel, his eyes locking with hers. "What? You are talking nonsense. As I deduced, you're either working for the department or you're working freelance for the department. Either way, you're not being treated as you deserve."

"I'm sure you wouldn't know." She looked backwards, from where they came, and caught her reflection in the mirrors there. Kasumi looked pale, with dark circles under her eyes. Worse, Carnelia thought she should look like Pixru. The image of her face was hard to recall.

"Wait until you see what I have to show you." Kaito assured her.

Turning away from the mirrors, they walked through the second portal, which was smaller and less impressive than the first one they'd entered. The door opened up into a glowing room made up of stacks of glass and metal cubes.

Stages and scaffolding sat on a brushed concrete floor. Three levels of glass and steel sat above the floor, and the fourth level appeared to house some sort of mechanism that raised and lowered the scaffolding. The cubes weren't perfect cubes; they were rectangular in shape, six to seven feet long, and three and a half feet wide. They were evenly spaced, with thin catwalks for someone to walk between the... glass coffins, Carnelia decided to call them.

Upon her inspection of the setup, something caught her eye. She saw a hand, pressed against the glass! She looked around, her eyes darting between coffins. Inside each rectangle appeared to be water, and floating in the water was a person! Each person had apparatus on their faces which seemed to be for breathing, but the few that Carnelia could see clearly had their eyes closed, as though they were beyond the need to breathe.

"The Ark's Lament!" She shouted, her voice echoing as she got a good look at how many of these glass coffins were stretching back into the open part of the bubble. There were five stations, each with four levels, with what looked like four rectangles across and three down. There were over two hundred people here if they were all full. "What is all this?"

"Your co-workers." Kaito said confidently. "Ones that haven't been activated yet, anyway."

Carnelia shivered. *This* was better than Parris? She couldn't help but disagree. Then the penny dropped. They were going to give her one of these bodies.

Claustrophobia clamped down on her like a vise. She stopped walking, and Hyde bumped into her, pushing her gently forward. "No... you can't..."

Hyde patted her shoulder. "It's all right, Carn. I think I know where he's going."

"You're not the one that has to..." She snapped at him.

Hyde made a hand gesture; his hands flowed down his middle and up to his chest.

Carnelia glared at him but said nothing else. She didn't want to think about it.

"Ah, here we are." Kaito stopped at one of the stacks of coffins. There were four empty coffins surrounding a fifth. Kaito looked over to Carnelia. "You wanted to know which body you would be in? Well, I have chosen a very special body to house your wandering spirit. Please, take a look."

She didn't want to, but she overrode her instinct and looked at what was in store.

She gasped.

Floating before her, eyes closed with an apparatus on her face, was her body. She was perfect, her face serene in sleep, long hair floating around her in swirls. Carnelia dropped to her knees, reaching out to the glass with one hand. Her fingers trembled. Feelings rushed through her, desire meeting with terror, the horror of the idea of her body in cold storage, the raw need to have her body back. *My body. How do they have one of me in here? How is this* me?

Tears stung her eyes. "How is this possible?"

"Just be thankful that it **is** possible." Kaito smiled warmly. "After all, not many of us get this kind of a chance."

"Wish you'd had my body on ice." Hyde said with envy in his voice.

It was that envy that cut through the cocoon of Carnelia's shock and stabbed her. This was real. Hyde was a terrible actor, he was gruff and rarely showed any emotion at all. The fact that there was longing in his voice convinced her in a way that Kaito never could that the floating girl in the glass coffin, whose skin was dusky with golden undertones, peacefully asleep in suspension liquid, was her.

SEARCHING CODE

Having an entry point was the first step. Orochi yawned and yearned for a coffee, and continued his search. His inquiry involved Kasumi Yasutoro. Thirty-two, single, a police officer for seven years, promoted to sora no me within the first year of duty. Sora no me were high tech. Her partner was Daizo Hayanari, twenty-nine years old, single, a police officer for five years. His record was so clean Orochi assumed that he'd arrest people for spitting gum out on the sidewalk. Kasumi's record was similarly spotless. Which meant either she hadn't got caught yet, or she had but she had Savvy friends to take care of it.

Orochi flicked through video and pictures taken in the last few days. He found cameras on the doors to the TPD and looked for something he could use. He placed Carnelia's jump at somewhere between two and three pm, and rewound back to that day's footage.

"Jackpot," he muttered aloud. "There's only one man that goes to that much effort to play dress up. I don't care what Rascati said about him being dead." He was wearing a different skin, but that wasn't as unbelievable as it might have been a few months ago. What bothered him was that of the bodyjumpers Carn told him about, Hyde wasn't on the list. He was supposed to be just a thug. Which meant that he knew more about Parris's operation than Orochi ever realized. Memories of dreams he'd been having swum to the surface, flashed, and descended into the depths of his subconscious before he could identify them. He pushed them away, focusing on the footage.

He watched the altercation between Hyde, Kasumi and Daizo. He noticed the moment when "Kasumi" recognized Hyde, and moved towards Daizo. Hyde ignored the interplay. One thing Orochi noticed was that Daizo clearly did not like Hyde. In the video, Daizo's stance shifted when Hyde showed up, as though ready to attack. Orochi thought this was excellent. A common enemy meant that Daizo and he may be able to work together.

Following the couple's path via video took time. No single entity owned cameras that lined up with their route, which meant he had to hack multiple companies for the footage. He managed to see where they went, which was not to the address that matched Kasumi's home. Hyde's address, then. They disappeared and hours passed, but then Orochi saw Hyde dragging Kasumi out and into a short box van. As soon as the van drove out of sight of that camera, it vanished.

Orochi spent two hours proving to himself that it had vanished. The camera's footage was forged; all frames with the white short box were gone. He could prove the missing numbers on the frames, but that was all he could prove. The Savvy that did this was excellent at their job, and had remembered to remove their finger prints. Orochi styled himself as a ghost hunter, and even by his standards, this was a clean getaway. Proof then, that Hyde was protected by one or more competent Savvy. They had disappeared him completely, and his trail ran cold.

He sent out a seeker for white, short box vans. If Hyde had parked in a parking garage, there would be footage. If Hyde parked outside in an open air lot, there should still be something to see. Unless he'd gone to where the Savvy resided, but Orochi doubted that they could erase every step of his travel. Tokyo was a big city, and encroaching on too many different cameras would no doubt irritate the people keeping their eye on things. Other Savvy would get involved at some point, some profit seekers, some thrill seekers, and of course data collectors. He wasn't sure what the Savvy climate was but he was sure he'd soon find out.

Despite more hours searching, Orochi couldn't find his van. The Savvy had been thorough and Hyde had taken Kasumi to the Savvy's hideout, hence the total scrub. There were too many variables for extrapolation. He didn't know which direction or how long their route was. The only thing he had now was... a Stetson.

Orochi changed his search, looking for cowboy hats in the city. They were an uncommon variable with a very distinct form. He adjusted for color and material when he came across a couple of cowboy hats worn by children. Black Stetson hats were rare occurrences, and Orochi found that only one man in the city wore one. He caught a flicker of Hyde on a camera. It was recent, within the last few hours. Kasumi wasn't with him. It was a lead. Orochi had worked with less.

As sunlight began streaming into their room, Orochi got up and stretched. He decided to let his hunger lead him downstairs to look for food. A small bakery perfumed the air with vanilla, strawberry, and matcha, melded together into a tantalizing whole. The bakery didn't have donuts, but they had this old-school machine that caught Orochi's attention. The bottom of the machine was a griddle, and the whole thing was made of gears and metal parts and belts, encased in a glass box. The starting point was a round band of metal that sat on a circular griddle. An arm came out, and poured a measured amount of batter. Above, on a belt, a disc of bean curd dropped on top of the batter. The disc slid to the next station. Batter filled up the rest of the disc, covering the bean curd. Next, a spatula slid under the cookie, and flipped it. Orochi watched in fascination at the precision of the little gears. Each part of the contraption allowed the next piece to work. He thought about buying it, but he couldn't imagine getting it safely to Seattle. He knew Nathan would love it. Maybe he could get a facsimile made.

Orochi bought two dozen of the resulting bean curd cookies, and brought them up to his sleeping friend.

"Nathan!" He boomed as he stepped into the room. "There's this machine, you have to see it in action! I need to find out if I can buy it, Ganada would love it!"

Blearily Nathan found his way to consciousness. "Is coffee involved?"

"They had coffee. It's just diner coffee, I'm warning you." Orochi said, putting the cups down gently before plopping the bean curd cookies down on the bed.

"If it can strip the paint off of the walls, then it might be strong enough." Nathan sat up, rubbing his eyes and dry-washing his face. "Did you sleep?"

"Some." Orochi hand-waved the question. "I made headway, but I haven't found her yet."

"You should have started with something simpler, like a needle in a haystack." Nathan reached for the coffee and ignored the sugar packets. "You're looking for a Panasian woman in the largest city in Panasia. It's going to take time."

"It doesn't help that Hyde's got serious Savvy on their team. He left with Carn in his van, and the damn thing vanishes after the first camera."

Nathan let out a low whistle. "That's impressive." He did a double take. "Wait, did you say Hyde? I know you didn't say Hyde, because Hyde is dead. Our commander-in-chief killed him, remember? Dead to rights?"

"Well, I am going on information that there's an older Panasian man running around in a duster and a Stetson, but I'll show you the footage and you can decide for yourself. One thing I've found a few traces of doctored cameras, factoring an average speed in a radius around the departure point, but nothing that gives me a route, or even a direction." Orochi grabbed a cookie from the box. It was still warm from the griddle.

"How many cameras did you find?" Nathan asked, grabbing his own cookie.

"Thirty-five." Orochi said. "Do you know how many cameras are online for every square foot of this city?"

Nathan took a deep drink of the black coffee and shuddered. He coughed once. "I think this could strip paint."

Orochi gave him a patient look. "Well, do you know?"

"I think that we take your thirty-five and make them loci for another cross section." Nathan said. "You can be a great Savvy and still not catch every available camera. They slipped somewhere. I gotta take a piss, then I'll back to it."

Orochi looked up from his cookie. The last step of the machine had been to put a brand on the top of the cookie, a kanji that Orochi thought meant, 'beauty.' Or maybe, 'sheep.' Kanji were versatile, after all. He went back to his machine and pulled up the cameras. Taking half of them, he webbed out a block radius of each of the Savvied cameras and started pulling up their footage.

"We need this to go faster." Nathan said. "I'll try to write a program for the cameras. The problem is that a program is a great way to leave your signature hanging around.

"You should definitely leave our signature out there." Orochi said. "I want them knowing that they've got someone stalking them. They may come looking for us, which would save us a lot of time."

They left once to go sit down and eat, but otherwise were engrossed in their project.

Orochi looked up from his visor. "I think I got something."

Nathan stood up and walked over to his machine. "What is it?"

"I cracked the TPD's cameras, and I found the trail again. It goes out towards the outskirts of Tokyo, but the van pulls into a distinctive building. I think we can find it."

Nathan winced at the mention of cracking the police cameras. "You realize that we can't sleep here tonight."

"I think we should pretty much pack up now and move shop." Orochi said. "Just to be safe."

"You got us a starting point. Can't complain about that." Nathan said, heading to his own gear.

They got out the door, just in time to see an exoskeleton headed in their direction.

SLEEPING BEAUTY

In the palace of glass and steel, Carnelia stared at her body, floating just out of her reach. The glass was cold beneath her fingers.

Her body was shot and killed in the Glass House in Seattle, months ago. How would they have retrieved it, and how would they have sent it across the greendome to this strange place? She had no doubt Parris could coordinate something like that given his resources, but the cops swarmed the Glass House and they had taken him out by surprise. He wouldn't have had time to organize this kind of thing, and why on Earth would they have a plan like that ahead of time?

Cloning technology was completely outlawed everywhere on the planet, but it didn't look like these people cared about the legalities. This body appeared to be her in every way - including appropriate age. In reality her clone would only be about two months old, the same age as the little being tucked away inside Pixru. If she was the right age, that meant they retrieved her genetic material twenty years ago. What were the odds that was possible?

Yet, before her, floating in some kind of suspension fluid, her hair streaming in the small waves generated by the thrum of machinery, was her very own body. No, it couldn't be hers. She'd never worn her hair that long. It floated in streamers around her face, down her neck, and around her shoulders and upper arms. It had been a long time since she'd seen her untreated hair color.

She turned back to Kaito. She tried to form words but the disbelief and confusion filled her mind. She stared at him because she couldn't process the enormity of the situation.

"I imagine you have questions." Kaito prompted her.

"A few." She nodded her head, eyes drawn back to the coffin and its contents.

"Most of these questions will not be answerable until you decide to join the group." Kaito said. "There are a lot of secrets that many organizations would like to get a hold of, you understand."

"I bet." Carnelia managed.

"However, what I can promise is that you would hold a special place in our organization, above the employees that we typically hire." Kaito began.

"I've been through this speech." Hyde said dryly. "Can I go now?"

"Of course, Hyde. I won't have anything for you until tomorrow." Kaito waved him off.

Carnelia watched Hyde stride away, back towards the smoked mirrors. "How long has he been a bodyjumper?"

"Does it matter how old you are when your abilities make you functionally immortal?" Kaito asked.

Functional immortality. It wasn't something she'd considered. Of course, Parris had taught her that more than twenty-four hours out of her body would kill her. No wonder he said that. "What do you want from me?"

A smile brushed the corners of Kaito's mouth. "Well, you see, you are the very girl we were hoping to find once we got word that Parris's empire crashed down. We heard you had died, such a tragedy! It seemed for a while that your clone was going to go to waste. But then, we heard rumors that Pixru wasn't behaving like she had been before, and that she'd sold out to the Bureau. I hadn't heard of any more bodyjumps, but there were whispers. The name Carnelia was still in circulation. There was hope! What I want is for you to accept this body. Become a bodyjumper here at Typhon Inc., and enjoy the many benefits of being a high-level executive. Everything I've told you is true. I offer you your body as a symbol of goodwill between us. A second chance! How many people get to come back from the dead?"

"Yes, you've told me what you're offering me. What do you want me to do for all this glamour?" Carnelia tried to keep the tiredness out of her voice.

"Of course." Kaito took a step back from her, leaned his hand deliberately on the glass coffin containing her body. "You will be a bodyjumper. You will get assignments, and be expected to jump into people's bodies. To steal things, to learn things, to bring back intel."

"And when I'm not working?" She asked.

"Your time is yours." Kaito promised. "We will set you up with a place to live and transportation."

She paused. "I don't speak Nipponese."

"But you're speaking it fluently." Kaito tilted his head, curious.

"Kasumi speaks fluent Nipponese. I speak fluent English. I can only use the languages that come installed."

"You are such a valuable employee that we will spend some of your time training you in the language." He started drumming his fingers against the glass.

"How do you have a me?" Carnelia asked. "How could you have gotten it through the midspace between the greendomes?"

"Those are company secrets." Shaking his head, Kaito put his finger to his lips. "You get to know them once you are in the company."

Carnelia looked at her doppelganger, floating silently. "What about her? What about her life?"

"Sleeping Beauty has been waiting for her kiss to wake her from stasis. You will be what brings her to life. Worry about yourself, for a change. Trapped in Hyde's girlfriend doesn't seem like the epithet one would want on their headstone." Kaito coaxed.

Deep down, Carnelia wanted to be in this body more than she'd ever wanted a thing in her life. A second chance, to be herself and take care of the body she was in. To be suited to the body, and her own habits, as opposed to battling with a lifetime of someone else's physical mannerisms, wasn't something she could explain to anyone else. Here, she was with people who understood what she could do. The temptation would be there even if the body weren't there. The body simply took this from polite fiction to mandatory. She knew it would be a bad idea, knew that they were holding all the cards, and knew they could make her life just as rotten as Parris had.

She just didn't care.

Her decision reached her eyes and Kaito smiled, even before she said, "I'll do it."

"Excellent. There will be paperwork later but first, let's get to the important task. This body will need to acclimate, which means this will take some time. Let's get you to a C-pod."

The back of her mind ran wild with the scenarios that could make this turn ugly, but she forced them down. Her concern was getting her body back. It didn't matter what she agreed to. She could figure out how to get out of it from there.

"Allow me to escort you." Kaito put his hand on her shoulder and took her away from the glass coffin and its Sleeping Beauty.

"Wait." Carnelia said. "I'm stuck in here, how am I going to get out?"

"Don't worry. Once you get into the C-pod, I'll delete the program from Kasumi's 'ware and you'll be free to jump into your body." Kaito released her shoulder. "You have nothing to fear."

And why did that make me so afraid? Carnelia wondered, but decided not to voice her concerns. Anything now was just a delay to her getting into her body, and that just wasn't going to work for her. And yet, a voice screamed in the back of her head. *He trapped you. He knows about the Bureau, he set up a trap for you, he put his own "employee" on the line to get jumped, he didn't tell the most dangerous person you know about his plans and he just walked away. He's had my body on ice since before I was dead. This cannot go well.*

Another voice replied, *I'll have my body back.*

Kaito brought her back to his office. There was a small C-pod tucked in the back corner of the room. He waved his hands to the machine, and she walked over to it. Her nerves were warring with her needs, and she felt terrible. She crossed the room quickly, trying to get this part over with. She settled into the C-pod's couch, felt the kiss of the hypodermic needle and nearly panicked. She told herself that it was just nerves; that if they had wanted to kill her, a bullet to the head would be much more efficient than this song and dance.

She leaned back and breathed. In a few moments she heard Kaito's voice in her ear. "Program decommissioned. Here are your coordinates."

Visualizing the floating body in the glass tank, she started counting down from one hundred to calm her nerves. She felt too much; fear, anxiety, anticipation. Her own body. It was in her reach.

She stretched out her mind, diving into the strange electronic transfer of her soul leaving for another destination - her body.

A RUN IN WITH THE LAW

They were down the stairs and out the doors when they saw a chijo no ashi walking toward them. The exoskeleton was eye-blinding white, and the steel making up the joints shone in the sunlight. Little kids followed in its wake, making finger guns and 'pew pew' noises. There weren't any visible weapons on the machine, but it was well documented that the weaponry was stowed until necessary. The tempered glass that surrounded the human operator swung upwards, and a man around Orochi's age leaned forward.

"Anata wa nihongo o hanasemasu ka?" The cop asked.

Nathan looked at Orochi. "Is he here for us?"

"Probably." Orochi said, and held up his hands in the universal "I don't know" symbol.

"Ah, English then?" The cop asked.

Orochi nodded. "Yes, we speak English."

"Oh, I see. Well, I am sorry to say this but I must escort you now to the Tokyo Police Department." The cop looked sorry, which surprised Orochi.

90

"What for?" Orochi challenged.

"There were files broken into, and they lead back to this address." He said.

"That's some fast fucking service." Nathan said, shaking his head.

"It's a hotel. Surely it could be anyone inside." Orochi said.

The officer shook his head. "There are very few internationally famous Savvy registered to this building."

Nathan leaned in closer to Orochi. "Funny, I didn't book us under our internationally famous identities."

"Listen.. uh, what's your name?" Orochi asked.

"Officer Daizo Hayanari." The officer supplied.

Orochi's heart lifted just a bit. Here was the one guy they could talk to. "Look, Officer Hayanari, how are you going to bring us in? You're in an exosuit."

"I'll show you." Officer Hayanari said, smile bright.

Orochi looked at Nathan.

"The only way this is going to get better is if we get through it now." Nathan said sagely.

"Hmm." Orochi said. "Okay, show us."

In a swift motion, the exoskeleton's hands scooped Orochi up in one and Nathan in the other, curving gently so as not to crush their cargo. The floor tilted to orient as flat, and then restraining bars sprouted from between the fingers. Orochi kept his hands well back in case there were any added bonuses like stunning weapons or deterrents.

"Okay, we are going." The tempered glass lowered back over the officer, and the exoskeleton began taking long strides to get back towards home base.

Orochi commed Nathan. "You okay?"

"It's always so much fun, going on adventures with you." Nathan muttered.

"Never a dull moment." Orochi promised.

The Tokyo Police Department was a building almost as white as the exoskeleton. It had stone stairs in the front, but exoskeletons came in from the side, as they found out. Daizo put handcuffs on both Orochi and Nathan before setting them loose, and their bags were confiscated during processing. Nathan and Orochi kept silent. They had dealt with the police before, and knew what they had to do.

They were separated, and Orochi was brought into an interrogation room. It was different from Seattle's set up, with space pooled together for a single purpose. It was a room, one wall mirrored and the other three the brilliant eye-blinding white. Their color of choice, apparently. There was a table and two chairs. Orochi sat down immediately. To his surprise, Daizo followed him into the room.

"Where's Kasumi?" Daizo asked as the door clicked closed.

"Wasting no time, I see." Orochi said. "You're not supposed to be in here."

"I ask the questions." Daizo said, words abrupt. "You were looking for her."

"I'm concerned for her health." Orochi said. "I think she may have been coerced."

"How do you know her? She's never mentioned you." The officer seemed agitated. Orochi tried not to grin.

"May I call you Daizo? Look, Daizo, there's stuff going on with Kasumi that you may not be aware of. She seems to have fallen in with a dangerous crowd."

The door swung open, revealing an older Panasian man with short cropped hair and a tweed suit. "Officer Hayanari!"

Daizo stood stock still, mouth partially open. His jaw clicked shut.

"Wait for me outside." The older man dismissed him with a short wave of his hand.

"I'd rather talk to him, if it's all the same to you." Orochi said.

"It is not the same. Our station has strict policies, Orochi. Officer Hayanari is leaving now." The older man gave Daizo a significant look.

"Hai." Defeated, Officer Hayanari left the room, looking over his shoulder at Orochi.

"Forgive me." The older man said as soon as the door was shut. "I was not expecting to be interrogating anyone today, but I'm one of the few qualified that also speak English. My name is Takeshi Shin. So, please inform me, what were you doing breaking into the Tokyo Police Department's files?"

Orochi resisted the temptation to put his boots up on the table. "Inspector Shin, is it?"

He nodded gruffly.

"Well, you see, it's like this. There is a cop by the name of Kasumi Yasutoro. You may or not be familiar with her. She's a sora no me." Orochi watched Inspector Shin's reaction.

"I am familiar with Officer Yasutoro. The question is, how are you?"

"Oh, she's never met me in her life. However, she seems to be associated with someone that I have unfortunately had dealings with. I'm not sure what you call him here, but we call him Hyde." Orochi made a motion of a hat on his head. "Wears a big cowboy hat, boots, a duster, the whole accoutrement. It seems that Kasumi went to Hyde's house last night, and he and she got into a van. After that, the whole field is blank. The box van vanishes from view." Orochi knew that he was probably disclosing secrets the Bureau didn't want him to. However, they hadn't been kind enough to give him mission parameters before he took off, so they would have to live with how he handled things.

"You're admitting to savvying other people's systems, Mr. Orochi." Inspector Shin pointed out.

"No, I'm telling you how I learned that the police systems were getting Savvied. The van route is invisible to commercial and personally owned camera lines. We had to confirm that she was safe, so we used... unorthodox means to verify that the van existed." Orochi hoped that the cop was clean. This was the only way to find out.

"What our police officers do in their off time is their own affair." Inspector Shin's jaw seemed to be set on wires rather than muscles.

"Did she arrive for work today?" Orochi asked. "If she did, I'd love to have a word with her."

"That is not information we owe you, Mr. Orochi." Inspector Shin said sharply.

"I imagine not. And, just Orochi is fine." Orochi corrected him. "However this is secondary to the topic, which is that there are Savvy out there making themselves invisible, except to the police. Normally the police are the first people that Savvy want to cut out of the loop, no offense. So, this means that somewhere in your organization you have an officer or many who are working for a group capable of making one of your people disappear without a trace. That's got to be disturbing news."

Inspector Shin frowned. "This doesn't make you less culpable in your own crime."

"Charge me." Orochi said, throwing up his hands. "First offense Savvy crimes that do not lead to a subsequent criminal activity tend to have minimum sentencing, even fines. I'll be out in two weeks and the only thing you will have accomplished is that I will have to start all over again finding the bad guys. Hell, I'll skip the fine and pay a donation to the TPD to brighten up their pearly gates. My interest is finding Kasumi Yasutoro and making sure she's okay."

"You've never even met her, you've said so yourself. Your motivations are still quite murky." Inspector Shin stood between the door and Orochi.

Orochi paused, deciding. "I need to find a friend of mine and Kasumi may know where she is."

"You could file a missing person's report like everyone else." Inspector Shin said coldly.

"Does it sound to you like I have enough evidence for filing a police report?" Orochi asked.

"No." Inspector Shin looked like he'd bitten into a lemon. "Taking the law into your own hands is not how things are handled in Nippon, Orochi. It may work in Seattle - and yes, I know who you are - but here we are a law abiding citizenry and you are not following those laws."

"No, I'm following a missing person's case that hasn't been filed yet." Orochi said. "If you could produce Officer Yasutoro and let me talk to her, I would be on my way."

Inspector Shin frowned darkly, and did not respond.

"So, are you going to charge me with unlawful use and access, or data theft? I didn't steal anything, just looked at it, but that one carries the higher penalty. There is a case that Nippon has different laws but I imagine that they're pretty similar at the core." Orochi said calmly. "I've told you all I know. Doesn't that count for something?"

"I'd rather throw you in jail now and just save our city the trouble." Inspector Shin said finally. "I know who you are, I know what you can do, and I know that when you come back in this room, it's going to be after rather spectacular illegal antics. You can sit quite calmly with your degree from watching cop shows all day, but you obviously know nothing about Nippon. People will be hurt, and you will wrap your faultlessness around you like a cloak and take none of the blame for what you've done. So, I will not charge you, but understand that I'm not charging you in the hopes that you will find the plane that brought you here and climb aboard. If your friend is in trouble, file a missing persons. We will do everything we can to bring her back safely, and we will do so with resources that you do not have. Otherwise, get lost, before you injure the innocent."

Orochi listened to the Inspector's spiel, and when he was done, said, "Hey, how much do cigarettes go for here?"

"Get out." Takeshi Shin growled.

"You remind me of someone I work with." Orochi said, tipping an imaginary hat to the inspector. "And you've been just as much help."

ACT USUAL

"Concentrate, Chimera." The voice betrayed boredom and frustration simultaneously.

"How, exactly?" Diane tried to swivel her head towards the speaker, but she was strapped down on a gurney. Her wrists, ankles, and head were all bound to the table. Sweat beaded and smeared beneath the strap, making her feel claustrophobic. It didn't help that the room she was in was little more than a concrete box with a mirror that was quite obviously meant for observation of the subject without the subject observing them.

"If you don't, we'll put you in the Deep Hole." The bored voice explained. "No food, no water, just the smell of you invading your nostrils until you get sick of it and beg to be put back on the table."

Somehow, it was worse being told this in such a calm, forthright manner, as opposed to having it yelled in a threatening fashion. Threatening she could do something about. This just was.

"What am I supposed to concentrate on?" She asked, despite having been told by the tech before they left the room.

The voice became an exhaled breath, before resuming its disembodied journey. "In the next room there is a man, five eleven, black hair, dark eyes, tanned skin. He is in a similar position to you. I would like you to initiate the 'ware we've installed in your brain, and see if you can connect your consciousness to his."

This was the height of mad scientist bullshit, but unfortunately for her, this mad scientist seemed to have thought about all of the angles. They had shaved her head, installed 'ware, and after a few days of healing they expected her to test it. Everyone knew the minimum rest period for brain surgery was six weeks, but how could she refuse? They'd beat her, or worse, not protect her from the mad dogs they employed as "guards" here. Her options were limited.

"Fine." She said, and took a deep breath. She went over the activation sequence like they'd taught her, and she felt... something... kick in. Whatever it was, it didn't help her target the individual in the next room. What would it be like being a man? In some ways, she was sure it would be preferable to her current situation. Then again, men were vulnerable as well, simply to different kinds of pain. She tried to focus.

Her body convulsed. It was like a sleep-jerk magnified. The only reason she hadn't managed to sit upright was due to the straps. She frowned. What had happened? She felt something, she just couldn't describe what it was. Her eyes fluttered closed and she imagined her target. Black hair, dark eyes, tanned skin, shorter than average. She didn't know if he was overweight. She imagined a paunch, a small tummy but there. She sought out with her mind, feeling foolish, but trying for the sake of not being tortured. There had to be a better way to do this. Could they tell she was trying?

"I'm trying." She said into the quiet.

"Our machines are picking up activity. Be quiet and keep trying." The voice urged.

She closed her eyes firmly, imagining herself floating up out of her body. How would one divide the soul from the body? How could tech do such a thing? Technology was science, the soul was for the religious. If Diane didn't believe in a soul, what did she believe was being sent out across the room and into the next room? Her personality?

What would happen to her body while she was away?

What would happen to the man already in the body?

Counting to ten, slowly, she focused on transferring her energy into a new vessel. The world changed from the hard darkness of her closed eyelids to a fuzzy gray. She felt something inside her shift, although thinking about it seemed to cause her to feel more solid again. She tried to stop paying attention to the process, and let it engage itself.

When she felt the sensation this time, she let it go. Instead of weakening, it strengthened, and she could feel something at the edge of her consciousness. It felt tenuous and uncertain, but as she watched, she felt as though some kind of bridge of light unfolded before her, beckoning her forward. She felt airy and detached, as though the process were happening to someone else. She felt her awareness lose the familiar feeling of sensation. Warmth, cool, pressure, it was all lost to her in a moment of disorientation. She felt fear, and she felt the light bridge waver. Before she could assert her will, she felt as though she were slipping on a glass surface, with no purchase and no dimension. Her mind scrabbled to stop but she fell, into a bundle of sensations that were completely foreign. She felt warmth and pressure, but it was not as she had known it before. Her forehead was sore. No doubt from struggling. Her wrists were wet, and felt abraded. She opened her eyes.

The room she was in was almost exactly the same as the one she'd left, and the position she was in was also familiar.

"This is D... Chimera." They insisted they use their call signs at all times, and were punished when they didn't. It was strange, her voice was so much lower than she remembered. "Where am I?"

"Congratulations." The voice was no longer bored. It was in fact, very excited. "You've made it!"

"Ooh! Extra ration of gruel tonight." Diane couldn't disguise the bitterness in her voice. His voice. "I can't do very many tests in this body, with it being tied down."

"You can do enough. Begin by raising your right leg." The voice began.

While the voice droned on, Diane's mind whirled. She had to find a way to engage the technology in her head while she was free. She could pick a guard and walk out the front door of this place. She suddenly realized there was no "jump 'ware" in this man's head. How was she supposed to return?

The tech was in her head. She'd be leaving her body behind, without her having any way to jump out of the body she climbed into. That would be a hell of a thing. She wouldn't even be the right gender. However, if her options included torture at the hands of these people, and the high probability that she would die when the experiments were over, then escape was the only option.

It was two long hours before they decided that she had performed to their standards. They ended the session by giving her mental guidance to the way back. It worked a lot like body jumping initially, without firing up the 'ware to do it. She was certain she would be stuck in his body forever. When she finally slid back into her body, mentally exhausted, she was grateful. She offered no resistance as the orderlies came to take her back into her room. Even when one of them copped a feel, she had no energy to snap at him or even make a snide comment. She ate her dinner and promptly fell asleep, dreaming about strange men whom she wore like a glove.

The next day, out in the exercise yard, one of the other prisoners approached her. He was a big, musclebound man that didn't seem like the type to spend hours in front of code. He put his hand against the wall behind her and stared at her for a while before he spoke.

"Keep acting like you're not sure what's going on, and look for ways to get away from me." He said.

"Interesting way to start a conversation, since that's what I'm doing." Diane said, shrinking back from him.

"I hear you survived the test. Me too. I figure if we can get three of us to be able to do this thing, we can make it out of here. It won't be easy and one of us might even die, but it increases our chances. You in?" He lowered his head closer to hers.

She knew it could be a trap, could be a set up to catch the escapees early. The possibility that he simply didn't think he could escape without backup was valid, too. He could ditch her as soon as his use for her had ended. This all considered, she didn't have a plan for escape and she needed one. She nodded.

"First rule is that if we're seen talking too much they get involved. Messages will have to be short and direct. Don't approach me. Let them think that I'm harassing you. They aren't going to be as inclined to interrupt. I'll let you know who the third is, and I'll tell you the plan when we get to that point. For now, just keep acting usual, so they don't suspect anything." With that, he chucked her under her chin, and she stepped away and rubbed her chin, even though it hadn't hurt.

Survival. It's about survival, nothing more. Diane wondered what she had agreed to without knowing. She was desperate. Getting out was the only thing she cared about. She had to take a risk, or else she'd be stuck here, strapped to a table, trying to get an erection for a faceless voice that controlled her every minute.

THE OTHER SHOE

Carnelia woke on a white sand beach, sitting in a deck chair, staring out at a tropical blue ocean. Ice clinked in a glass off to her right. She looked down to see a stem glass full of what looked like iced sangria, perched on a small table precariously standing in the sand. The beach was shaped like half of a cantaloupe, and she was nestled in its center. She could hear the surf, smell the ocean's salt-and-decay scent, and feel the sun beat down on her skin. She blinked in surprise. It was her skin. Ocher with golden undertones, but something about this wasn't right. Wasn't her body dead?

Carnelia reached out her hand to touch her face. Her cheekbones, the gentle tilt to her eyes. She snagged a tuft of kinky black hair. It felt just like it always had.

Tears welled up in her eyes. She stood up on the beach. The sand was hot on her naked soles, but it felt invigorating. She dug her toes down deep, reaching the wet sand beneath the surface. She looked for any signs of civilization. There were no boats, no docks, no people walking their dogs or tanning on the beach. There weren't any visible buildings, except for a lighthouse positioned at the edge of the bowl. Carnelia hadn't gotten too deeply into math but she figured the lighthouse was several miles away from its size relative to her.

Am I dreaming? She wondered. The question was half pitched to Orochi, half in thought to herself. She missed Orochi, wished that he was here to help her. She couldn't remember what she'd been doing before she got to this beach. When she tried to reach out for the memory, it skittered away from her like a nervous kitten.

It was too late, she'd questioned the reality. Her mind started to reach for explanations. She came up with being in a virtual on the Web. She'd gone to many meetings portraying other people. Some people jumped in C-pods and never came out, until their muscles atrophied and they wasted away from lack of exercise. C-pods were capable of providing limbs with electric impulses to simulate motion, but thus far no one had been able to fully circumvent the human body's need for activity.

Holding a thought was like trying to scoop up seawater in her two hands. She could concentrate for a moment but then it was...

"Come in for a swim!" A girl shouted at her in English. Carnelia turned to look.

She was beautiful, with long blonde hair that streamed out behind her as she tread water. She had long eyelashes, beaded with seawater, looking like jewels in the sunlight. Her body was toned, obviously an athletic sort. Carnelia felt suspicion rise up her spine. Was she real, or a hallucination?

"I'm good." Carnelia half spoke, half shouted to make sure her voice carried. "Who are you?"

"I'm a local." She said.

"Deliberate vagueness makes me nervous," Carnelia said.

The girl laughed. It was a laugh out of a movie, a round, full-throated, delightful sound that made Carnelia envious. "You have every right to be! But that doesn't mean I'm not helpful. You're going to wake up soon, and it's not going to be pleasant."

Anxiety gripped Carn's stomach. "Where am I?"

"Don't panic. I know what I'm doing."

"What do you mean, don't panic?" Even as she heard the words, she started to panic. The last time she'd heard don't panic, an EMT was telling her that her mother was dead.

She had her hands curled around either side of her mouth, yelling as though it were some kind of cheer. "Wake up, Carnelia!"

Then she rose out of the water, making an arc with her body as she dove back into the placid depths of the ocean.

Carnelia watched as the line between skin and scale seamlessly melded, as her jewel green hindquarters revealed themselves to be a long, slender tail, like a fish.

The system glitched. Carnelia had no time to marvel at the realism of the mermaid avatar before she was in the water, which was considerably darker than it had been. She struggled to get out but the water sucked her down, pulling her shoulders and her head back. She tried to shake it off and stand, but something restrained her. Viscous fluid filled her mouth as she struggled. She tried to spit. More of the fluid flooded into her mouth, down her esophagus. She felt ill as the seawater reached her stomach. Wait, no, it was too thick to be water. She tried to reach up, to claw at her face. She couldn't breathe, she was drowning…

"Get it off of her!" English flooded her ears as the water had her lungs. Terse bursts of Nipponese followed.

She pushed up against sudden hands that restrained her. She pushed up against nylon straps and gasped for air, coughing and struggling. Her esophagus burned like she'd drunk lava instead of whatever that gunk was. The restraining hands wouldn't let her go and more nylon straps were cinched firmly in place. Something still choked her, she didn't feel like she was receiving enough air. The hands pushed her down by her shoulders. Two hands stabilized her head. She flailed, but had no leverage. The hands pried apart her jaw. Something plastic and cylindrical pushed against her lips, then into her mouth and down her throat.

Thrashing weakly against the barrage, she felt tears well in her eyes. Something was happening inside of her. She could feel it. She couldn't tell from the sensations what was happening. If they were killing her, this was a very strange method.

All at once, the techs holding her down let her go, and she sat up violently. Someone pulled a long, clear, flexible tube up out of her chest cavity, through her throat, and finally out of her mouth. She gagged, jerking her head, only to find that she was free.

She turned to her side and vomited up brackish fluid that tasted nothing like the sea. The technicians on either side of her continued their check of her body. As her body dried, it reacted to the cold air by bursting into goose bumps. She was next to the glass coffin. Somehow she'd imagined waking up would be a better experience. They had her on a stretcher, next to the submersion tank. The nylon straps pulled against her but she managed to sit forward and lean over the side. She vomited again for good measure, rejecting the fluid that made it into her stomach in her panic.

"You were going into shock." The woman's voice was measured and pleasant. "Our apologies for your rough treatment."

By her count there were four techs assigned to the task of handling her, as well as the fifth in front of her, who appeared to be a doctor. Her demeanor and the poker face she maintained gave that away.

"You were supposed to be asleep for this part," The woman explained with a calm voice, as though she were narrating for some unseen camera. "Decanting procedures are unpleasant, we prefer that you don't have to go through them consciously."

Carnelia wanted to kill this woman. Instead, she asked, "What went wrong?"

"I'm not sure how you became aware so early. We'll have to run a trace and find out if there were any anomalies with your transfer." She could have been discussing the weather.

Carnelia kept her face as expressionless as she could. Maybe Orochi had found her already...

"We're going to let you go, to see if you can stand. Will you please try?" The doctor asked.

Carnelia nodded miserably. Something seemed wrong. She looked down at her arms, and they were still that gold limned ocher that she recognized as her own. She glanced at her left thigh. There was no trace of the scar she'd had for four years now. There should be a long, pale scar that twined from her knee to halfway up her thigh. She'd sliced herself pretty badly crawling through a plate glass window before she was "promoted" to the Glass House. She hated that scar, hated how her skin was marred. Now, it was flawless.

"Stand up." The doctor urged.

It was easy to say it, but this body had virtually no muscle tone. Living at the Glass House, she'd worked out regularly for lack of anything better to do. This body didn't look like her body, but it did. She turned and caught a glimpse of her reflection in the dome of the glass coffin still pooled with fluid. The same skin, the same eyes, the same cheekbones. She looked as if she were a radiation victim or a chemo kid. Her hair was long, longer than she'd ever worn it in her life, and it slicked around her body as though hiding her nakedness.

When she didn't stand, she was jerked upwards, forcing her body into a position that didn't feel natural. She tried to protest but her throat was etched by bile and acid and lacerated by plastic. She couldn't make a sound.

"I'm sure you have questions," The woman said. "Right now we have to get you into fighting form. Real food, muscle stimulation, light therapy."

"Rehab." Carnelia croaked.

"That's right, rehab. Your throat will need rest, so just answer me by shaking your head or nodding. Are you in significant pain anywhere?" The woman reminded her of Pixru, although taller and older. Another woman proving that her beauty was merely a genetic accident.

Carnelia shook her head. She felt weak, she felt awful, but there weren't any sharp pains distracting her.

"Are your eyes working properly?" She pulled out a tiny LED light, and flicked it between Carnelia's eyes.

Carnelia squinted to protect her vision. Too late; purple tracers danced wherever she looked.

"They were." She rasped.

The woman chuckled. "Humor. That's a good sign."

The orderlies decided that Carnelia's hobbled gate wasn't quick enough, and despite her protests they swept her up and carried her to rehab.

Her first stop was the shower. Another mirror showed her hollowed cheeks, sunken eyes, and pallid undertone of her skin. She looked like an otherworldly creature from a horror movie. She stepped into the hot running water and let the heat soak into her bones. It was only then she realized how chilled she was. She started shaking as the visceral reality of what was happening to her hit home. Memory rushed in to fill in the gaps.

She gasped as the floor rushed up to meet her.

MACHINES WHAT HACK CODE

Taking the Tokyo subway was much like taking Seattle's hyperloop, except more crowded. Orochi ducked to step into the car, and stood away from the doors, trying to leave room for other people to enter. Many saw Orochi and opted to find a different car in which to sit. Nathan took advantage of this behavior and grabbed a seat on the bench.

"We're moving, aren't we?" Nathan asked.

"You didn't like that hotel anyway." Orochi said, pulling a cigarette out of his pack. He held the pack to his nose and inhaled the tobacco. He felt content and stuck the filter into his mouth, producing a lighter like magic.

"We don't have that kind of money anymore." Nathan said.

"As a matter of fact, we do. How do you think I got the plane?" Orochi asked.

"I thought those funds were frozen." Nathan tilted his head, curious.

"They need to hire better Savvy." Orochi said, a hint of self-satisfaction in his voice.

Nathan winced. "Is that smart?"

"The day Rascati's Savvy catch me is the day I voluntarily quit."

"Okay, so beyond learning that every interrogation room looks effectively the same, what did we get out of going to the police department?" Nathan asked.

"I met people. I think that Daizo is a very interesting young man, with an absolute passion for finding his partner. Which could come in useful to us. I also confirmed that Kasumi hasn't been seen since her last shift, which she ended abruptly. So, there's proof something is odd. I also think that Takeshi doesn't like me." Orochi shrugged.

"Imagine that." Nathan said wryly. "Much as usual, you get the bulk of the attention. They didn't seem to worry overmuch about me. The feeling is mutual though - I don't think Takeshi liked me much either."

"That's because they're idiots. I am going to need your help for this next bit. We have to take that information we borrowed and find the specific coordinates of those cameras so we can map the destination. Then we're going to find who lives there, and what kind of code they run." Orochi took a drag off of his cigarette, and blew a puff into the no smoking sign. "After you find us a hotel more to your liking."

Nathan leaned his head back, a sign that he was contacting his 'ware. Orochi waited until Nathan's eyes snapped open, finishing the cigarette and making faces at babies. He quit after the third child hid his head in his mother's shoulder rather than smile.

Orochi made it through two cigarettes by the time they made it off the subway.

Nathan led them to a skyrise eighty stories tall.

Orochi quirked an eyebrow at his friend. "Oh, yeah, that's not ostentatious."

Nathan shrugged. "It will have beds that you can sleep in."

"Sold." Orochi said, and followed his friend to get the keys.

Orochi made sure they were set up before hiking downstairs to hunt up some food. While there was no quaint cookie shop to be found, there was a promising sushi place, as well as a Cauc-friendly place selling fried fish. Orochi grabbed some sushi and then got back upstairs to get to work.

Nathan provided him with the white van's destination, and the two of them started rummaging through what was registered at that address.

Orochi looked through his visor, looking at the building's strange, bulging form of glass and steel. It was an inefficient design, made to look like a globe that was held in place by some kind of tower. There was something about the design that made Orochi distinctly uncomfortable.

"Are you ready to crack it?" Nathan asked.

Orochi grinned. "Little bunny foo foo..."

"They won't know what hit them." Nathan said.

While he waited for Nathan to retrieve the data, Orochi took out another cigarette. He let his thoughts meander for a little while. He realized how long it had been since he'd slept. He wasn't sure he'd sleep again until Carnelia was safe.

Nathan took a deep breath and blew it out slowly. "I can't even get a name. These guys make Pixru look incompetent."

Shaking his head, Orochi frowned. "You need backup?"

"I need more than what our machines can produce. The system has more ways to shut a guy down than a Goth girl on a Friday night." Nathan sounded frustrated.

"Let's try the best friend approach." Orochi said. "We have a name. It's Kasumi Yasutoro. Maybe she doesn't have anything on her computer about this place, but she's tied to it, and it'll be much easier to retrieve data off of her."

"Let's try." Nathan put his visor on and got cracking.

Orochi went out and got some beer from a vending machine. He brought it back up and smiled when he saw the pleased look on Nathan's face. "I've got the name."

"What is it?" Orochi asked.

"Typhon Inc." Nathan said. "Let's get some sleep, and some food, and then we can find out what they've done with Carnelia."

"This is taking too long, Carnelia's in danger!" Orochi said, crushing the can of beer.

Nathan gave Orochi a sympathetic look. "Other than you, when has Carn ever gotten stuck in a person?"

"Never." Orochi said.

"Right. Which means that these guys were fishing for something out of the ordinary. Maybe not Carn specifically, but certainly someone with unusual abilities." Nathan moved his hand, drifted over to one of the beds to sit.

"Lucky us." Orochi frowned. "Do you think they targeted Carn on purpose?"

"I think we should behave as though that's the case and act accordingly." Nathan said. "If they just got extraordinarily lucky and caught the one bodyjumper in the world by accident, it won't change much of what we're doing. They're not going to kill her. We have time to do something."

"I've got to go in." Orochi fiddled with his visor. "See what the landscape is like."

"I could get something huge and heavy and beat you over the head. Or, you could rack out for four hours and run your rescue attempt. Okay?" Nathan glowered.

"You're not going to bend on this, are you?" Orochi asked.

"You're going to hallucinate, and then you'll be no help to anyone. Four hours and I'll wake you." Nathan pointed to one of the beds.

"I'll sleep in the chair." Orochi headed over to the overstuffed chair. He felt a little surprise that he started drifting so quickly. Maybe he was tired...

He woke to Nathan shaking him. "Orochi! It's all right. You were dreaming."

"I was?" Orochi blinked. "What was it?"

"Did you turn on you dream recorder?" Nathan asked.

"Yeah, but I haven't had a chance to watch much footage. I've got other things to do." Orochi shrugged.

"Well, go look for Carn, and we'll deal with that later." Nathan suggested.

Orochi sat back, slipping his visor on. He had an address. They had good guards, but Orochi was better. He dove in, sending his mind into the code fields to Savvy an entrance.

He found the hole in the code and could see the work to close it up. He hurried and slipped through, then his world tilted and he felt distinctly like he was falling...

He stood on a white sand beach. There was a highball glass full of what appeared to be red sangria next to him, ice still in cubes in the glass. He could hear the sea, smell it, and when he looked up a crystalline blue-green plane of water sheared off at the sand and continued on to the horizon. A lighthouse was off to his left. This was well beyond the capacity of his visor.

"Carnelia!" He shouted. He tried to access the virtuality with his 'ware, strip the visual and bust down to the code, but the optical maintained resolution. He shouted again. "Carnelia!"

"She left." The voice came from the direction of the water. Orochi turned to see a beautiful woman from the torso up, bobbing gently in the ocean. Her long, blonde hair streamed behind her in the water. She had eyes the color of the sea surrounding her, and her cheeks were flushed pink. She was the kind of girl that would make a man's mouth go dry. She wore a cutesy bikini top shaped like clamshells. The water was so clear that he could make out that she had a magnificently rendered tail submerged beneath the surface.

Avatar.

"Will she be back?" He asked, hopeful.

The girl laughed. "It's hard to say yet."

"Who are you?" Orochi asked. "If you don't mind me asking."

"I'm Atargatis. And you're not supposed to be here." The mermaid gave him a sad smile. "Goodbye."

With her words, a strong wind blew in, and the sapphire sky turned black as he watched. The sea reflected the sky, the welcoming waves turning to pewter, with white caps rolling in. He could feel the sting of sand whipped up by the wind, and he looked around. The sangria had spilled out onto the white sand, leaving a red stain like blood.

"Can't we talk about this?" Orochi shouted against the wind.

From everywhere and nowhere, her voice replied, "No."

His visor returned him to the other side of the server code, where the hole he'd just entered closed up tight. He could see the code, and he could see the repairs. He wasn't about to give up, snotty mermaid notwithstanding. Orochi gripped the arms of the chair, and sent out programs to feel the edges of what he was up against. The security code was dense, constantly seeking out programming data that didn't correlate to what was already written.

Orochi grinned.

"Nathan." He said, to get his friend's attention. "I need a Ninth Roman Legion."

He could hear the smile in Nathan's voice. "Coming right up."

As they worked, he caught Nathan up to what he'd seen inside.

"Alt-real." Nathan said sagely. "Those are nasty."

"I've played with them before." Orochi said. "I made Carn rob a bank with an alt-real vault... although we weren't plugged in, it was all done with holograms."

"When you're dealing with security, the code correlates to something visual in the system. The mermaid is most likely the security program. The ocean is probably the information we're looking for. The beach is most likely a staging ground, but it probably houses some goodies for the mermaid to draw on when she needs it. Going in is not going to be easy." Nathan pulled off his visor.

"I think they've already shown that. What the hell wasp's nest did we step in?" Orochi took off his visor and put it on the side table. "This place has better protection than the Tokyo Police Department, and they're the best funded police force in the world. Parris's place wasn't this intense."

"Parris was an idiot. He had access to the best Savvy in Seattle and he didn't keep them on a leash. He was sloppy and got caught accordingly." Nathan wrinkled his nose in distaste. "That said, he kept everything under wraps for a while because he had dirty cops."

"And we've seen that Typhon doesn't seem to fear the cops, at least." Orochi pulled out a cigarette and lit it. "Which means that there's inside work going on."

"Okay, we can figure this out all day, but I need to make a Roman Legion for you, and you need to build some code that mimics their signature. You should order in, this is going to take time."

Orochi felt his jaw clench and unclenched it purposefully. "You can't cover every contingency, and you can't move once you're entrenched. That place might be secure, but it's only got so much security it can have before it crashes its own system. We just have to keep cracking at it."

"This would go faster with more machines." Nathan pointed out.

"Oh, they don't like me in this neck of the woods, I don't think we could get hired guns. We could get some MWHC's and barrage attack them."

Nathan raised his eyebrow. "The Ninth Roman Legion?"

Orochi made a face. "Sometimes old tricks are old tricks because they work."

"Fine, let's go buy some 'ware and get it up and running. It's going to take a lot of machines and a lot of time. Where are we going to put them all?" Nathan asked.

"We may not have to. I have a plan." He flicked on his visor.

"Is it a plan with bullets? Because we always seem to end up at the wrong end of bullets." Nathan pointed out.

ORIENTATION

The floor was hard and rough against her skin. She tried to push herself up. She felt her muscles buckle, but she forced herself on. It was no different than the last push-up in a workout, the one that feels the worst. Carnelia pushed hard, and then one by one disentangled her legs and forced them back under her. She pushed up, imagining it was just a long squat. Her knees wobbled but she managed. The input from her body was intense. The impact of the floor, the working of her muscles, this body wasn't ready to handle it.

Carnelia looked in the mirror, looking at the sag of the muscles that made her look like a zombie from a movie. *It really is a clone.*

Clones were illegal. With overpopulation being a significant issue, it was deemed that making additional people was counter-intuitive. Proponents argued that the humans were for medical purposes, to keep the original owner alive, but life extension had in general been curtailed. It was acceptable to save a twenty-year old who was in a car accident, but it was not acceptable to prolong life beyond the first century.

Humanity had had an on again, off again love affair with cloning, but during the Great Crisis, clone banks took off as law enforcement crashed under the weight of instability. The fact that the world was overpopulated, and that there weren't resources to care for everyone left the population feeling as though clones were an unreasonable way to extend life. Religions began whipping up their own Inquisitions, arguing that clones were soulless meat containers that shouldn't exist.

She looked at her arm, flexed her fingers one by one. Who would have thought that a soulless meat container would be exactly what she needed?

"Carnelia?" The woman doctor poked her head in. "It's Dr. Akamatsu. Are you all right?"

"Yeah." She said quickly. "This body has never walked before, I have to teach it."

"You are an unusual circumstance." She said. "Normally it takes a year to get up and rolling."

Clamping down on the thought that the brains needed as much time to click over as the bodies, she nodded politely. "I've heard that before."

Dr. Akamatsu straightened and took a breath. "You can talk, you can walk, it looks like you need some time to build muscle, and we can augment that with our equipment. We can get you up and running in no time. Are you hungry?"

She paused to think about the question. She knew there was nothing in her stomach, but she didn't feel any hunger signals. "No."

"That will take a while to develop as well. This body hasn't needed to use its stomach, so we'll go slow. You'll probably only want small meals as your body gets used to its new activity level." The doctor said matter-of-factly.

Carnelia nodded, and continued to nod as Dr. Akamatsu explained to her about the care and feeding of her own body. It felt surreal - this was *her* body, but it wasn't, it wasn't at all. From the lack of scars to the lack of muscle tone to the long hair, this was just a thing, a container, and not even a great container. She had wanted to spring into this body and take off running, but they had her for however long it would take to make this body independent. Disappointment seared her to the bone.

They walked through the dark part of the building. Unlike the glass coffins, which shed light everywhere, this part of the building had distant lighting so it seemed much darker. Plaster, paint, ceiling fixtures, it looked like an office, but it closed in on her. Knowing the purpose behind the structure added to the dark feel. Kaito was right; they were considerably different than Parris's crew. Parris had allowed Carnelia and the rest of them the liberty to go off and do what they wanted to do on their off time. Kaito kept them unconscious until he needed them.

Closing her eyes for a moment, Carnelia tried not to scream.

"Are you all right?" The doctor asked, putting her hand on Carnelia's shoulder to steady her. "Dizzy spell?"

"Yes." Carnelia lied, forcing her eyes open. "My balance isn't quite online."

"Do you need me to steady you?" The doctor asked earnestly.

"No." Carnelia shrugged off Dr. Akamatsu's hand. "I'm fine."

Dr. Akamatsu smiled approvingly. "That's the spirit. I've noticed your gait is improving already. I've been hoping to figure out how you do it so that we can bring others up to speed in less time."

Great. Now I'm a guinea pig. Carnelia shrugged. "I don't know how I do it."

Disappointment flashed across Dr. Akamatsu's features, and Carnelia felt it was a small victory.

They walked in silence until they got to Kaito's office. The stairs were a special hell, but Carnelia refused to accept help from the doctor. She gripped the rail and pulled herself forward. She was exhausted by the time they got to the top of the stairs.

Kaito looked up from his holoscreen when he saw the two women enter his office. He frowned when he saw what Carnelia wore. "Atargatis, note: Now that Carnelia is up, make an appointment for her to do a fitting."

There was an acknowledgment signal. Strange, Carnelia would have thought that a facility this complex would employ an AI.

Into the quiet, Carnelia said, "Unusual program designation. It sounds Greek."

"You'll be introduced. Atargatis runs many important systems and keeps Typhon rolling." Kaito said dismissively. "So, how are the new legs?"

"Weak." Carnelia said candidly. "Like it's been in mothballs for twenty-odd years."

"Nineteen. I believe the twentieth is coming up." Kaito said cheerfully. "Isn't that wonderful? You get to reset two years of your life!"

"If only that were true." Carnelia said without a trace of irony in her tone.

"Now, now. I gave you what you wanted, this is no time to turn into an ungrateful bitch." Kaito said, his voice taking an edge. "Nothing I said was incorrect."

"You didn't tell me I'd need months of rehabilitation!" She wanted to jump to her feet but her body wouldn't obey.

"Would that have changed your mind?" Kaito asked.

She looked at the floor.

"Exactly. A small price to pay to get your body back. Remember, I know you died back in Parris's house, we were aware of his movements for some time." Kaito stood from behind his desk, a modern-style twisted black metal display that looked more like art than anything functional. "If it weren't for me, you'd be trapped in someone else's body forever. And I can tell by how eager you were when you saw your body that you would do anything not to be looking at someone's face in the mirror the rest of your life. This body is an anchor - no matter how many people you jump in, you will always have a home waiting for you, so that you don't slowly feel your identity erode away. I know how important it is, so it is best if you remind yourself of the same. And always remember that Typhon gave your body back." He nodded sharply.

"Well, now that I'm in the family, as it were, will you tell me how you got my body? I've never been to anywhere in Panasia, never left Seattle's greendome before." Carnelia asked.

"You have your mother to thank." Kaito said crisply.

Carnelia felt the world ride up and threaten to overwhelm her. "I'm sorry, what?"

"Melinde Hargrove. She approached us and signed on for a family package. She wanted to make sure that if any of you got degenerative diseases, that you would have clones that you could access for replacement organs." Kaito smiled winningly, as though he were selling her on the idea rather than telling a story.

"Mom?" Carnelia's thoughts swam. She remembered her mother, a petite, beautiful woman with short black hair and beautiful golden skin. She didn't think her mom was capable of doing something outright illegal, something that was a violation of human rights. That didn't seem possible. "How could she?"

"She was a rich woman who was very protective of her family. She paid very good money to have clones made." Kaito reached over and hit a button on the side of his desk.

She wouldn't have just made them for me. Carnelia thought.

As if on cue, her brother walked into the room.

"Michael?" Carnelia rose to her feet unsteadily, staring at him. His hair was slicked back, and he wore a gray suit with a slight sheen, the familiar bulge at his hip that told her he was armed. Tears threatened to spill but she blinked them away, unwilling to let Kaito see his manipulation working.

"I go by Mikeru." Her brother said, his voice distant as the moon.

"How is this possible? Michael wasn't a bodyjumper, and he died..." The word hitched in her throat and she couldn't force herself to go on.

"Mikeru has been active for a while now." Kaito explained. "He's had time to acclimate."

How long? Carnelia looked at this self-confident, healthy, near perfect copy of her brother. His face didn't show any of the grayness or atrophy that her face had. And it took a while to build a personality, when there wasn't a template to start with like hers. *He's been awake while Michael was still alive.*

"Is he a drug addict?" The question slipped out before she could reign it in.

"Let me get something straight with you." Mikeru said, pointing a finger at her. "Just because we share mutual genetic history does not make you my sister. I am not Michael Hargrove, or Michael Cesnos either. I am Mikeru Hitochigai, and I do not want to have anything to do with you."

"Wow, you really do make clones accurately." Carnelia said, trying to sound unaffected. "My brother didn't want anything to do with me either."

"Mikeru!" Kaito's rebuke was sharp. "You step out of place."

Mikeru grunted as if punched. "Yes, Kaito."

"You will extend this employee every courtesy expected of a Typhon agent." Kaito's words were hard and well-defined. "If I assign you to back her up in a mission, that is what you are expected to do, to the full extent of your capabilities."

"Yes, Kaito." Mikeru's expression betrayed him, but his words were calm and measured.

"She is one of the most valued assets Typhon has, and you have the honor of being selected to assist her. If she dies in your care, you and all of your make will be discontinued." Kaito nodded, as though agreeing with himself that his point had been made.

Silent, brooding, Mikeru nodded to affirm what he'd heard.

"So, we're thieves." Carnelia guessed into the silence that followed.

"Mikeru is a thief, and one of the highest order. You, on the other hand, are something more. You are going to be an actress." Kaito's eyes glittered.

"Look." Carnelia sighed. "This is something that Parris was getting involved in, and it didn't work out for him so well. It brought his entire empire down on itself. I recommend that you try a different tactic, because this one has already been played out."

Kaito threw back his head and laughed. "Parris was an idiot. He was short sighted and didn't know what to do with the people that he thought he could take over. Our establishment has been working on ways to get your brand of bodyjumpers into our midst. We got a hold of your equipment, but none of the surgeries were successful."

Carnelia groaned. She realized that she was going to have to go through surgery again if she wanted to live. "What if it's your clones? What if there's something about them that can't take the tech? You could be counting your chickens before they hatch."

Kaito leaned on his desk. "We installed the tech inside your head ages ago. You survived, as you can see, so from now on you don't have that to worry about."

Something tickled the back of Carnelia's mind. Something wasn't right. Or needed more of her attention. She pushed it away as something that could come back when she wasn't talking to yet another madman.

"Don't be afraid, we've thought this through." Kaito said calmly. "It is not the mess that you're used to from Parris's stable."

"May I go?" Mikeru asked.

Kaito looked at Carnelia. "Do you want him to stay?"

"Not really. I don't want to make him do something he doesn't want to do." Carnelia said.

Mikeru looked at Kaito for confirmation. Kaito nodded dismissively, and Mikeru walked out of the office.

"I don't understand why you are doing this." She said once he was gone. "Why force him to work with me when it makes him unhappy? I'm sure you have others who would be more than willing to work with me."

"Mikeru is in the unique position of knowing about you." Kaito said. "He's been kept aware of the scenario in Seattle, whereas most of the others who work for us here don't have that clearance. He will come around once he accepts that he is doing the right thing for the corporation. And he would die first, despite his stated claim of distaste for you."

Carnelia sat back. She felt exhausted and all she had done was talk.

"We have a rebuild appointment scheduled in the afternoon, to help with the muscle weakness. I apologize that we couldn't have done one earlier, but we need someone conscious to determine the pain threshold of the body. We will discuss your itinerary once you've finished your session." Kaito waved a dismissal at her.

"Are you kidding? I haven't been in this body twenty-four hours." Carnelia tried to sit up and look indignant, but she couldn't summon the energy.

"We have a deadline to keep." Kaito said, smiling warmly. "Besides, once you've jumped out of your body you'll feel much better."

Carnelia glowered and sat up with effort. "Then I'm free to go?"

"Yes. Your personal assistant will be at the door, waiting to get you clothes and a room situated."

"Who's it going to be, my mother?" She said bitterly.

"No one you know." Kaito walked behind his desk and sat down, bringing up a holoscreen. "I thought that might be appreciated given your reception with your brother."

Arguing that he was not her brother seemed petty, and likely to draw out her conversation with Kaito even further. She turned and left without another word.

The girl on the other side of the door appeared to be the same age as Carnelia. She wore unrelieved red, from her hair (it was hard to tell if it was a wig or strong pigment dye) to her stiletto heels that made Carnelia's calves ache just looking at them. Her lipstick was the same vibrant shade as her hair. Her eye makeup tended towards dramatic, dark shades that left Carnelia wondering what she was doing here.

"I'm Yuuki." She said, eying Carnelia's wardrobe. "It's my job to get you set up at Typhon."

"Why do you work here?" Carnelia asked Yuuki's back as she had already started down the stairs from the mezzanine.

"Immortality." Yuuki said. "Of course, I just tell my parents that it's a side job to pay for my fashion."

"Right." Carnelia wished that someone would be normal for her, for just a few minutes.

"Atargatis set up a fitting for some clothes to get you started. Once you've had a chance to rehabilitate your body we'll get you another fitting. There's also a room for you in the executive suites. You're very lucky, those are reserved for corporate VIPs." Yuuki looked over her shoulder as though to assess what made Carnelia rate.

"What is Atargatis?" Carnelia asked, looking back towards the racks of glass coffins. They were heading towards an area that looked more like a normal building, although with a center section removed.

"Our AI." Yuuki said, appearing to not care. "She has multiple uses, scheduling, security, whatever needs to be handled."

"Do you have Savvy who run her systems?" Carnelia asked.

Yuuki laughed as if Carnelia had said something funny. "Atargatis is an all-inclusive system. She can stop Savvy attacks and keep all the clones alive at the same time."

"Sounds sophisticated." Carnelia followed the brilliant crimson through the dark hallways of Typhon's inner sanctum.

"It is." Yuuki said, obviously bored with the topic. "Let's take the elevator, I think the stairs might be too much for you right now."

"Thanks." Carnelia said, thinking that Yuuki's bonus structure might involve empathy towards the new employees.

The two women stepped out on the third floor, the doors opening up into a hallway that had doors to one side, and art hanging in regular intervals on the other.

The doors had numbers tooled in copper plaques on each one, numbered one through five.

"Six through ten are the next floor, and eleven through fifteen the next. You're in room three." Yuuki pointed. "It's keyed to you so just walk on through."

The room was large, looking like a studio apartment. There was a bathroom, a closet, and a bed area. A countertop hosted cabinets beneath, and there was a microwave and a miniature fridge installed as well. Carnelia expected to find an honor bar installed somewhere next to the fridge. There wasn't even a beer to be found. The fridge didn't hold anything, and neither did the cupboards.

"Don't worry, I can take care of that now that you're here." Yuuki said when she noticed Carnelia's search. "However, for the first few days you're on a protein shake diet, until your stomach is up to processing real food. We don't want you eating anything that your body can't tolerate. A doctor will bring you your meals, the next one should be up in thirty minutes."

Yuuki also showed Carnelia the operations for the screen in her room. It did not connect to the Web, but it would stream shows internally for her entertainment.

"And now I must go get some more things arranged for you. I'll be back for your scheduled appointments. In the meantime, get some rest, relax." Yuuki excused herself, and the door to the room slid shut.

Carnelia could hear the bolt mechanism slide home from where she sat.

NEW FACE

The hotel door burst open.

Orochi's eyes snapped open at the bang of the door. Hyde burst through the door, Stetson and all. Orochi reached for his Zerorez, drawing it in one smooth motion and aiming it at the cowboy.

Nathan saw the shotgun and rolled off the bed onto the floor. While he was covered he searched for his pistol.

"Good mornin', boys." Hyde said in a jovial tone, addressing the room. "Y'all poked around my girlfriend's computer last night, and I'm gonna have to kill you for that. No hard feelings, but you understand you had this comin'."

Orochi didn't waver. "You stole Carnelia, Hyde. We're just trying to get her back."

"I didn't steal her." Hyde corrected. He turned away from the bed and altered his aim to Orochi's head. "They didn't tell me they were fishin' for her. Hell, if I coulda warned her off, I may even have - that girl ain't nothin' but trouble."

131

"We'll take her off of your hands." Orochi offered. "We can all walk away from this."

"You ain't been nothin' but trouble either." Hyde's finger flexed on the trigger.

Two triggers clicked in unison, two shots going off at the same moment. Even feeling the breath-stopping sensation of a twelve gauge bullet slap his bulletproof jacket, Orochi tried to move out of the way. He flipped over the chair, sprawling on the carpet, trying to get his wind back. His jacket still worked but he figured he was pushing the limit of its spec.

Out of the corner of his eye Orochi caught a flash of movement; a woman in all black heading towards Hyde at ramming speed. Orochi's bullet hit the mark, flattening on Hyde's bulletproof duster and knocking him down. The woman wasted no time. She brandished black zip ties. Taking advantage of Hyde's position, she grabbed his arms, immobilizing him like a calf at a rodeo. She grabbed his shotgun and holstered it across her back behind a gearpack she wore.

"Orochi?" Nathan sprang up from behind the bed, pistol aimed at Hyde. "Are you okay?"

Orochi stood up over Hyde, feeling like he was walking up on a rattlesnake that had been irritated. He took his eyes off the threat, reasonably secure in seeing him bound up. He looked to the surprise rescue force. She was tall. He approved. "Do I know you?"

"No." She answered, and nudged Hyde with her foot. "Stand up."

"People don't do nice things for no reason. We'll talk after I end this piece of shit." He flexed his finger, pulling the trigger.

Before he could pull it completely, her hand was suddenly around his wrist, and she'd moved his arm to aim at the floor. Her grip felt like steel beams around his wrist. He looked at her, startled, and tried to break her hold. There was no way someone with her slim build could exert this kind of force. Or move that fast.

"I have my reasons, but you can't kill him." The woman said.

"You don't look like you can stop me." Orochi said, giving her the once over.

She squeezed her hand and the bones in his wrist rubbed together unpleasantly. "I don't look like it, no."

"Okay, okay, point made, I'll hear you out." Orochi retrieved his wrist and gave it a surreptitious rub. He did not put the Zerorez away.

"Did that just happen?" Nathan snorted.

"She's a cyborg." Orochi said. "Or maybe a really complex AI."

"An AI bounty hunter? Creative." She smirked. "Look, there's a bounty on this guy, and I don't get it if he's dead. I've got him out of your hair, let me out of here with him, we'll all win."

"I'm pretty easy to defeat, being that I have access to the reasoning portion of my brain. Hyde, on the other hand, will fillet that ninja suit off your flesh and then bake you and serve you in a port wine reduction. Which is actually making me hungry, but we won't go there. We'll just go with the idea that he's going to kill you while you back is turned, and I can't allow that."

He turned and fired, aiming for Hyde's head. The bullet came full stop against the crown of the Stetson. It was askew, but it was protection enough. Hyde's head snapped back, and his eyes rolled up in his head, unconscious.

"You may have access to the reasoning portion of your brain, but you sure don't use it." She snapped.

"It's like she knows you." Nathan commented.

"We have to leave now. Three shots have been fired in this room. Do you think you have time to get away before the police come? Do you know what the penalty for having guns in Tokyo is?" She shook her head.

Nathan and Orochi exchanged glances. There was no time to discuss why their weapons hadn't been confiscated earlier, but they mutually agreed to consider that later.

"Here." She pulled out a black business card. In raised white lettering, the card read, "Emi," plus a Tokyo phone number. "Go, I'll distract the cops and get my bounty. Call me later today, if you like. We can talk about this guy and about your clumsy attempt to catch him."

"Orochi, why is she rescuing us?" Nathan asked out of the corner of his mouth.

"Gift horses and free pizza, my friend." Orochi said sagely. "Never question either."

Orochi let himself be dragged out of the hotel room, after making a quick stop to gather their gear. He held up the card. "We'll talk."

"I can't wait." Emi gave him a broad wink and a big smile. She moved Hyde to the chair like she was handling a small child. His Stetson rolled on the floor where she'd left it.

Orochi clenched his hand on his gun, before slipping it back into its holster and out of the way.

"I hate this town." Orochi grumbled as they sprinted down the hallway to the stairs.

"We're going to have chijo no ashi on us as soon as we hit the street." Nathan said. "If we can make it to the subway we can head to a different section of town."

"What about towards the Shinjuku area?" Orochi suggested. "Get up in their front yard."

"Just head to Typhon? Their security isn't just going to be that mermaid." Nathan reminded him. "They're going to have armed guards, and you didn't think to take Hyde's hat with you."

A white exoskeleton became visible as it walked down the sidewalk, people scattering from its path.

"That's our cue," Orochi said, hurrying his step. "Let's go!"

The sight of them fleeing towards a subway station caught the exoskeleton's attention, and it twisted down the block and towards them. It babbled at them in Nipponese - Orochi translated it to 'Stop, in the name of the law, or we'll take your Zerorez and your best friend!"

The exoskeleton was fast, and made great strides to catch up to them, but there were civilians in the way that prevented it from hitting its maximum speed. This greatly assisted Orochi and Nathan in their efforts to get away while the getting was good. They bolted through the subway entrance and got many looks from locals just making a day of it.

"And now we have a new player." Orochi followed Nathan through the turnstiles to get into the subway. A flock of school children in red and gray uniforms eyed them curiously as they made it through the stiles and into the train. "Who is this Emi person? Who does she represent? Why is she getting involved in Hyde's business? Is she a potential ally, or just another pain in the ass?"

"Time was you would have asked for her phone number, rather than her offering it to you." Nathan teased.

"Saves time when they offer," Orochi rallied.

Orochi stood, ignoring the many cocked heads trying to gauge his height. He'd learned to ignore that on the Hyperloop back home years ago. He also resisted the urge to make Godzilla roars.

"Back to what we were saying before we were so rudely interrupted," Nathan said with a forced lightness, "that you don't seem as interested in Emi as you would be before."

Orochi frowned. "If she's an independent worker, I'd love to have her on our side. Local talent is always the best help. It's just that when bodyjumpers are involved, you can't always trust what's behind those eyes."

Nathan shrugged. "You say that like you can trust what's behind anyone's eyes."

Orochi glared at Nathan. "You know what I mean."

"You told me a long time ago not to let you start seeing bodyjumpers where they didn't exist. I haven't forgotten." Nathan sat when a transit goer left her spot. "Too much suspicion is as dangerous as not enough."

"Fine, I'm approaching too paranoid. I just can't shake the feeling that those in charge have a long game in mind, not just taking advantage of some happenstance. Hyde's a dog that needs a master, he's not interested in running his own game. If he's involved somehow, than it stands to reason that there's a Parris running around telling him what to do. And whoever it is, they're not interested in learning about me before taking me out. They just want me tied up and shipped off

to the crematorium. The game is afoot, or so they say."
Orochi's hand brushed his shirt pocket, frowned when he
had no pack to draw from.

"Listen. We've got to come up with our own plan. I
know you're in a rush because Carn is in danger, but why
would they kill her if they know what they have?"
Nathan said.

"Are you trying to raise my spirits? Because you're a
goddamn natural, allow me to assure you." Orochi
glowered.

"Okay, fine. First, we need to pick a spot to work
from that isn't our spot for sleeping. We need more
machines, and better stuff than we carried over the
water. Next, you're pushing yourself on four hours of
sleep a night, and that's going to end up with you folding
at crunch time. This isn't sustainable. Stop pushing so
hard and save some of that strength for when we need
you." Nathan's eyes flicked at the various advertisements
along the top of the doors, watching the pictures, still
and live action, advertise exotic items.

"Fine, be reasonable, see if I care." Orochi said
flippantly.

Nathan accepted his win gracefully by smirking at
his friend.

SHIROI USAGI

"Let's get off at the next stop." Orochi said.

"Why?" Nathan asked, looking around.

"Because it's much harder to predict opponents who behave randomly." Orochi let go of the pole when the doors slid open, and grabbed his stuff. Nathan followed along behind him, watching another part of Tokyo reveal itself to them as they walked up the stairs. They were far enough away that they couldn't make out their old hotel in the skyline. Cherry trees lined the road, although it was the wrong season for them to be in blossom. The clouds were gathering, promising a late afternoon rain shower. Cars crept by, bumper to bumper as they drove down the main roads. Many people chose to walk, and the subways had no lack of traffic either. Seattle felt more spacious, more open. These were a people who had long suffered under the scourge of overpopulation, and had become at ease with its downsides and solutions.

Orochi kept an eye out for white exoskeletons, but none showed themselves. He doubted they could be very sneaky in their tin can armor, but everything that was painted white caught his eye until he'd identified it.

"What are we looking for?" Nathan asked.

"I think we just found it." Orochi said, pointing ahead and to the left.

A painted white rabbit nibbled on a clover flower above the entryway for what looked like a gallery. Beneath the white rabbit sign, there were signs posted in several languages. "C-pod Rentals," "Hourly Rates," "All currency welcome" were readable. A larger sign read, Shiroi Usagi.

The whole place was dilapidated and looked as though it were a rain shower away from collapse. Given the clouds, that didn't look like it would hold out much longer.

"Oh, you always take me to the nicest places," Nathan joked.

"Yes, well, we aren't ruining any reputable businesses by walking in." Orochi smiled grimly. "How nice of us."

The inside of the Shiroi Usagi wasn't much better than the outside boasted. The walls were covered in peeling paper, and there were many more empty C-pods than ones in service. Music floated in from the main hall, located behind the counter, where the proprietor sat playing some kind of card game by herself.

She was an elderly woman with her hair tied neatly in a steel gray bun. Her eyes were lost to the the lines in her face; it was difficult to tell if she squinted to keep the light out or simply shut her eyes to keep from looking at what her life had become. She frowned upon their entrance, and Orochi wondered for a moment if she was in on the bodyjumper plot as well. If she wasn't, then she'd be the only person in Tokyo who wasn't.

She eyed Orochi up and down as though he were a tree suddenly sprouted in her foyer. "No English."

"Translator." Orochi pulled out a small, square machine with a speaker and a microphone. The little machine echoed mechanically, "Hon'yaku-sha."

"Nansensu no kotoba." The old woman said.

"Nonsense words." The translator said tonelessly.

"What a shame." Nathan said. "If only there was some way to tell her that we have a lot of money that we'd like to give her for using her C-pods."

The translator translated, and the old woman perked up. She looked between the two of them. "How much money?"

Orochi grinned. "Lots of money, No English. We want all of your C-pods for two days."

"What for?" She asked in English, caution warring with avarice.

"A big party." Orochi said. "A big ExcavatorTrade party."

Her eyes narrowed with suspicion. "You are doing something shady."

"No ma'am. That would be illegal." Orochi said, holding up his hand in a scout's honor gesture.

They haggled over money for an hour, the proprietress giving no quarter for what her C-pods were worth. They finally settled accounts and paid her up front. She didn't kick out those using her machines but she agreed to take no further business until they had concluded theirs. She also wouldn't extend any contracts during their stay.

Not wanting to waste any time, Orochi and Nathan walked around the C-Pods, investigating the set-up and determining if they had everything they needed or if they would have to shop for what she didn't have.

"Are they linked?" Orochi asked as he watched Koharu turn back to her game with a satisfied look on her face.

"You let her fleece us." Nathan said as he checked out the tech.

"It'll make her feel better when the police are swarming all over her establishment. Now, are they linked?" Orochi leaned down to eye the control boxes for the C-pods.

"More or less. There's toggle switches to join parties up. It looks like the most that can be linked at the same time is ten, but I can do blocks of ten, that's around five blocks. And then we can link those with a little more work. Nothing I can't pull off." Nathan said, cracking open the other control boxes.

"Yeah, but how long will it take you?" Orochi asked. "This is bound to attract some attention."

"I'm sure they're closely watching all the sketchy C-pod places for this type of maneuver. Then they might be half as paranoid as you." Nathan grabbed out some pliers and started pulling wires. "This will take me a few hours. Why don't you go scope out the area and find some food. We can trade off when I'm done with this part."

Orochi left the Shiroi Usagi and stepped out into the foot traffic, looking for what the neighborhood had to offer. The walkers spread out to avoid him. It wasn't something he thought they were aware they were doing. He felt Emi's card in his pocket. He wasn't sure how to categorize her. On the one hand, she could have just been sent to stop Hyde from doing something stupid. Parris would never do something like that, but he liked to think that over here, things were different. On the other hand, Hyde was a well-known bad guy, and it was entirely possible that some other entity had ideas of their own.

He looked into windows. Big glass panes, smaller sections that were joined by wood or metal, cloudy plastic, mirrored surface. He could smell food smells, even if he couldn't see any restaurants nearby. He followed his nose to try to find food he could haul back to Nathan.

After a few blocks his mind flickered back to Emi. If she was a plant, she just took Hyde back to his superiors at Typhon, and neither the worse for wear. If not, who was she working for? If there was another group involved in this circus, who the hell would they be and what would they want?

He brought back some ramen for Nathan and himself. They worked separately on their projects, occasionally breaking the silence with a thoughtful grunt or a quizzical cough. Orochi gave up on his project and started helping Nathan with his. They bundled cords in silence.

"I think this is what we can do with the equipment we have." Orochi said. "When do we want to kick this off?"

"Tomorrow morning." Nathan suggested. "Bad guys sleep late, they're bound to miss what's going on for the first little while."

RECONSTITUTED

Yuuki led Carnelia up to the fifth floor of Typhon Inc. The hallway opened out to view the glass coffins, glowing softly in the darkness. Carnelia could make out dark shapes of bodies floating in the clear suspension fluid. Analogies for birth and death wrapped up in one container. She shivered because it was too accurate.

She felt winded up the stairs, and cursed this body's weakness. The door to the office was open, and Carnelia sunk down in a chair for a few minutes while she waited for her body to catch up. Yuuki didn't say a word, just patiently waited for Carnelia to catch her breath. She went to find the tech assigned for the service.

Carnelia forced herself to her feet. Ignoring her unsteady legs, she walked further into the room to discover an M-pod. The tech joined them, following Yuuki. He wore scrubs, a mask, and a hair cover. Almost none of him was visible.

Yuuki shut the door behind them. "This is Saburo, he's a trained tech and will be helping you with this procedure."

"How many of these has he done?" Carnelia asked.

"None. However, we brought him on because he has the skills to do this." Yuuki assured her.

"Charming." Carnelia let acid etch her tone. "I thought you were professionals."

"The joys of being the elite of the elite, I suppose. We don't always have the cutting edge materials in place to cater to your every whim." Yuuki's expression was a mask of servility.

"Are we going to do this?" Carnelia sighed.

"The next step to do is to take your clothes off." Yuuki ordered. "Then get in the pod."

Carnelia stiffened. She did not want to do anything this woman said, but she wasn't in any state to put up a fight. They would just strip her down and toss her in, and that would be humiliating. This way she got to retain at least a smidgen of her dignity. She couldn't take the clothes off quickly, because her equilibrium was still in doubt, but she was at least capable of getting up into the M-pod and pulling the door closed.

After she lay down and settled in, the tech walked over to the control panel and dialed in a few commands. He said something to Yuuki in their language.

"Commencing reconstruction," Yuuki said blandly.

A needle stung her, high on her hip. It was a thin needle, thinner than a hypodermic, so thin she almost didn't feel it after initial contact. Then she was swarmed by thin needles, stabbing her everywhere. Her back, neck, shoulders, arms, legs, torso. The needles penetrated at various lengths, depending on the depth of the muscle.

She would have expected it to hurt to be a human porcupine, but instead it ached fiercely. She blinked back tears, unwilling to cry in front of Yuuki. She summoned up her courage. "That wasn't so bad..."

"Commencing stage two." Yuuki said formally.

All of her weakened muscles contracted together in waves across her body.

"The full session runs half an hour. I am going to go sit down and read a magazine. If you need anything, just yell for me." Yuuki waved cheerfully and walked away from view.

Her muscles began to contract in alternating sections. First her right front quarter would contract, then her left back quarter would contract. The muscles ached as they worked. Carnelia was shaking from effort, biting down on the urge to scream.

She heard of this style of rehabilitation. It was commonly abused by gamers and other types who didn't want to put effort into keeping their body in shape. This was an M-pod mod, not something that came standard. It was against all of her beliefs about how to keep a body healthy, but she didn't have a lot of choice.

The contractions slowly stopped feeling painful. They almost felt normal.

Then they stopped.

"Is it done?" Carnelia asked.

Yuuki appeared in the view port as if by magic. "Oh, no, it's not done. Now you sit for twenty minutes and let the chemical component operate."

"Chemical component?" Carnelia echoed.

"Don't worry, they've laced it with painkillers. They should be kicking in now." Yuuki smiled.

A wave of relaxation passed through Carnelia, and she fought to keep her eyes open. "On cue."

"It'll take the edge off." She said brightly.

Inside her skin, Carnelia felt as though her muscles had been set on fire. Every muscle in her body, including the muscles in her face and muscles in very intimate locations, felt as though they were burning and melting into each other. She knew the painkillers were working, but if that was the case she needed something much stronger. Her fingers splayed out and gripped on the plastic sides of the M-pod as her body bucked from the pain assaulting her muscles.

"Yuuki!" She yelled. "I need more painkillers!"

Yuuki appeared in the view port, looking concerned. "That's the highest dose your body can tolerate at your weight and health level. We can give you more in twenty minutes."

Carnelia willed herself to murder Yuuki through the glass. Yuuki seemed to take it as a sign she was done talking and went back to her magazine.

She closed her eyes, and suddenly she was on a sandy beach. There was no sangria this time, just beach chairs, aimed out at the ocean. She looked out into the white crests of the water, and saw a form jump. Blonde hair, green tail. It was the mermaid.

The mermaid swam towards her, jumping every so often as though to show Carnelia her progress. She came out to the shallows, but had to stop before making it to the edge of the beach.

Carnelia shrugged. She knew where she was in the real world and she had no interest in being there. Maybe the mermaid would be better company. She stepped out into the water, walking out until the water covered her knees. "Who are you?"

"I'm Atargatis." The mermaid said. "And you're Carnelia."

"You're the system AI?" Carnelia asked, looking around the beach again.

"In a manner of speaking." She said. "I'm the systems operator."

"You're human?" Carnelia asked.

"You must not be familiar with alt-reals." Atargatis approached the sand. She pushed herself up on her arms.

"I've dealt with one in person." Carnelia said, recalling her bank caper with Orochi. "Not like this."

"Then you know that alt-reals are a system where the visual output is the UI. The sand, the water, everything has a correlation, but if you're not familiar with the system it's very disorienting. It adds an extra layer of protection." Atargatis explained.

"Because any system given enough time and motivation is doomed to fail." Carnelia quoted Orochi's creed.

Atargatis nodded. "I do everything around here. I keep the lights on, and I order supplies, and I hack video feeds and wipe traces of people's activities away. I'm quite good if I do say so myself."

Questions flooded Carnelia's thoughts, questions about whether she'd seen any work from a Savvy named Orochi. But she didn't dare, not until she determined the loyalty of this strange creature.

"Why do I keep ending up in this place?" Carnelia asked. "This is tech based, and I haven't touched my 'ware since I got here. I'm not even sure this body *has* ware, outside of the jump stuff."

"I invited you." Atargatis said.

"I don't remember getting an invite." Carnelia looked at the mermaid quizzically.

"Well, I think you're unconscious in your body, so you wouldn't." Atargatis folded her arms and leaned on them as the crystal clear ocean lapped around her. "You should come in, the water's nice."

"What's the ocean stand for?" Carnelia asked, suddenly aware of how deep she already was in it.

"Oh, just data. Don't worry, just because it's a visual analog, it doesn't stop working just because you know what it is... and you said yourself that you're not Savvy. It's just going to feel like water." Atargatis encouraged.

It did feel like water, but somehow Carnelia felt edgy about in getting in deeper. She was reminded of the story of the woman who ate six seeds and earned a life in Hell six months out of the year.

Atargatis pushed off of the sand, flipping backwards to encourage Carnelia to join her. "You'll wake up dry, you don't have anything to worry about."

Carnelia noticed that her body looked different here. She saw her scar on her thigh, one that wasn't on the body she currently had. There were other little scars from mishaps. Her thighs were muscled, with very good tone. The tone she remembered having when she lived in the Glass House.

"I look like me." She said, wonderingly.

"Residual body image." Atargatis said. "Your mind and your body are one, and your mind remembers what your body has survived."

"That's a complex avatar generator they have here." Carnelia said. "Picking up on mind cues."

"It's the most sophisticated in the world." Atargatis said proudly. "I can use it to do almost anything."

Carnelia paused. "You don't get out much, do you?"

Atargatis blushed, her porcelain cheeks offering no cover from the stain. "I don't get out ever."

Carnelia looked at her feet in the sand. At first she thought the sand had covered them, but then she realized that they were turning clear. "Uh, Atargatis..."

The mermaid had noticed. "Look for me when you get a chance."

"How?" Carnelia asked, watching with fascination as her body turned as clear as glass. As it inched up her body, she could no longer see herself in the clear waters of the ocean. The process wasn't painful, simply persistent.

"Quiet your mind." Atargatis said, and dived back into the water.

Carnelia's eyes snapped open, and she groaned. Her muscles felt sore, all six hundred and forty of them. No, not all. Her heart didn't hurt. Her lungs didn't. The organ muscles didn't burn. It was all the other muscles, but still there were an outstanding array to choose from.

Yuuki's face popped into view. "Need a cocktail?"

The cheer in her tone made Carnelia want to slap her, but Yuuki wasn't her personal assistant, she was her jailer. She had to remember that no one was on her side here.

No one, except maybe Atargatis. She seemed lonely. She was also the systems admin for this clone factory. Having Atargatis on her side could help her get out of here. Even if she had to take Atargatis with her, having the head of security should be an asset.

"C'mon. I'll help you back to your room." Yuuki said, misreading Carnelia's pause.

Carnelia listened to the M-pod seal release with a small hiss, and then the tech and Yuuki's arms were under her, helping her up to sitting. Yuuki handed her a cup with a lid and a straw. "I hope you like chocolate."

She took a sip. It tasted like chalk. "You've got half of it right."

"Protein for the girl who hasn't eaten in twenty years. It'll help the soreness." Yuuki explained.

"I can't imagine that's true." Carnelia said, but she obediently took another sip. Three more sips and she was full.

"It'll take time, building that up. No magic bullet." Yuuki explained, helping Carnelia up off of the M-pod.

Carnelia sighed. "Well, this magic bullet could use some improvement."

After she'd dressed, the walk from the medical area to her room was torture. The bottoms of her feet were just as sore as the rest of her, and walking took focused concentration and willpower not to yell. She sat gratefully on her bed, knowing her room was a prison but also knowing she was as weak as a kitten.

"How long will it take for me to recover?" Carnelia asked. "I just want to die right now."

Yuuki giggled as though Carnelia had made a joke. "I'm told the effects take eight hours to set. Now's the time to lay back and get a good night's sleep, and then tomorrow I'll take you to your fitting and we'll get you some new clothes. Don't worry, there shouldn't be anything but a little residual soreness. I'm told it's like a good workout. You've had something to eat, that should carry you through to tomorrow morning, and by then you may be ready for a real breakfast. I'll have both options for you, depending on how adventurous you feel."

"I'm not a clothes person. Will you help me find good ones?" Carnelia asked. *I guess I don't have to be so surly, she's at least trying to be pleasant.*

A spark lit behind Yuuki's eyes and she clapped her hands together. "That would be wonderful! We'll have so much fun, and then we can get you into something proper for your station here. Don't worry, I have the best taste! You'll love it, it'll be great."

Carnelia smiled warmly. She didn't trust Yuuki as far as she could throw her, but there was no harm in making her feel confident that Carnelia was acclimating to her new position in the 'company.' Having as many ways out as possible made it more likely that one of the ways would work.

AQUAMAN

It was early morning; so early, that only the barest glow of the rising sun stained the clouds red. The shutters across the business's windows were drawn, occluding what took place inside.

"Are the Ninth ready?" Orochi asked, putting the final touches on the wiring.

Nathan nodded. "Awaiting orders."

Orochi held up his hand. "They will know glory on this day!"

Nathan laughed and shook his head. "Okay, Titus Aurelius, you need to go get suited up for your deep sea dive."

A C-pod that could accommodate Orochi's bulk had been buried in the back of the office. It was broken, but the fix had been a pleasantly simple challenge. Nathan made disparaging comments about what a C-pod that big got used for, but Orochi didn't care. Love bed or no, it would be his chariot into the depths of Typhon's secrets. He pulled the lid shut and activated the C-pod's instruments. "Online."

"I'm switching on the Legion." Nathan said, and Orochi heard the whine of electricity in the background. "How long do you want them gone for before you jump in?"

"I want to give them thirty seconds to stir up the sand and then I'll dive in." Orochi said.

"Okay, start your timer." Nathan said. "And be careful, I don't have a way to fix your brain if you fry it."

"I'll be back for supper." Orochi grinned and waved from his perch.

Nathan grunted and started watching holomonitors. "You'd better."

Even expecting the cold, he gasped with shock as the water enclosed over his head. He concentrated.

>*run Merman*

Changing avatars was as easy as playing with modeling clay. Most Savvy started when they were young, and spent hours crafting the "perfect avatar." It was easier to project a mind's eye version of yourself, even if it wasn't always entirely accurate to the true form. Not that it mattered. Whether the avatar was a six year old with a lollipop or a hulking three meter long bug, all avatars had standard abilities. It was a sign of a good Savvy that they could project a pixel and make themselves effectively invisible, or give themselves the strength to flip a bus. Anyone smart was cautious about avatars. They gave away everything and nothing at the same time.

Feeling his "legs" fuse together made him shiver, but as he unfurled his tail fin he found he could jet forward at a good clip. His tail was a virulent green, and since he was modding his avatar he gave himself his mohawk as well. As the avatar was just a light projection, the mohawk held fast despite the laws of reality that would break down the styling product and leave it flat against his head. He knew he didn't have long before security found him, so he started swimming faster, keeping his eye open for unusual things. He didn't know what exactly he was looking for. It could be as subtle as a fishing hook or as obvious as a floating monitor. Analogy savvy ended up being a lot of guesswork, which was why bigger corporations preferred it. It was so much easier to keep your data safe if your server looked like a chicken in a digital barnyard. It would take a Savvy hours to go through the pigs, cows, goats, and sheep before they even got to what they were looking for.

What he wanted to find was the girl. She wasn't some digital copy. He'd seen breathtaking AI that were complex and self-aware, but they tended to have a logic pattern they lived by. He hadn't seen enough of the mermaid to ascertain if she had a definable logic pattern, but what little he'd seen suggested that she didn't. He wasn't surprised. With a company that had access to so many people, it made sense to use a person instead of AI where they could. What he couldn't figure out was why she was a Cauc when they were in Nippon.

He looked behind him. A dark shape cruised towards him. Currents shifted behind him and he pushed forward just in time to avoid the snapping jaws of a great white shark. He put on a burst of speed, but the shark had him in its sights and it mirrored each of his movements. It seemed as though he'd found the security system. Great.

The shark's jaw hinged wide open, and it thrust forward though the water like a torpedo. Orochi jerked sideways at the last second, feeling the force of the current as its jaws snapped shut. He felt a snag, and looked back. Hooked onto his tail was a two foot long remora - a suckerfish that rode along with sharks. Orochi swished his tail back and forth, trying to dislodge the remora, but it clamped on even harder. Virus alarms sounded in his head as his avatar was breached. Damn it, he had misdiagnosed the threat levels of these creatures, and it had cost him. Great.

The shark kept pace with him. He knew it was fast enough to catch him, so he figured that it probably meant that it was programmed to wait until the target stopped moving and then eject any and all files associated with the avatar. He wasn't about to let that happen.

Pain trailed up his tail and into his torso. Pain emitters were a cheap and easy way to get rid of Savvy. They could always abandon their avatars to escape, which is what most of them did. Orochi refused to be dealt with so easily. He gritted his teeth and kept swimming, trying to make gains on the great white. The pain felt as though someone had lined his nerves with thermite and set his tail on fire. He grabbed at the remora to pull it off forcibly. It was stuck to the fine webbing of his fin, suckered on so hard it dented the tail on the other side. The shark noticed him slowing, and turned back towards him.

This is why these fuckers set up these alt-reals, Orochi thought to himself as he struggled again with the suckerfish. *If this was pure code I'd be having a margarita by now.*

His antivirals blared at him again. He knew the remora was responsible, but could only juggle so much. The shark was going to eat him. He needed to swim out but he needed to find Carn first. Worse, this was all the 'bot sentinels of this place, he hadn't glimpsed the mermaid once. He couldn't reason with viruses or disruptors. He could talk to the girl. The only thing he could think was that the Ninth were doing their job and keeping her distracted. If that was the case, did that mean she was the only Savvy they employed?

Orochi looked around for the shark, but it was gone. He spun around in a circle, trying to get a lock on it. He looked down to see a giant, dark hole ringed in jagged white triangles, heading up in his direction. Orochi swam up, at least, he hoped it was up, and felt a shock of cold air as he breached the surface. The remora created drag on his fin, and then the dark surrounded him, teeth cutting out the sun as he was swallowed whole by the bot. The interior was too dark to see, and the water collected in swallowing him churned in the great stomach of the beast.

Having no intention of finding out how digestion worked here, Orochi reached down and brought his tail up, getting a firm grasp on the remora. It struggled in his grip. He yanked, feeling the threat to his tailfin if he continued. Orochi grinned. It was an avatar, after all, and while he kept pain sensors on as fair warning for incoming danger, he could afford a ripped tail to get the virus puker off of him. The pain was fierce as he pulled, twisting the remora in his grip to rid himself of the thing. As seconds passed and he realized it wasn't working, he closed his eyes and summoned an avatar adjustment. A six-inch long spike jutted up from his tail, spearing the remora in the head, and breaking its suction. The suckerfish slipped off of his tail, and Orochi grabbed it up. The remora immediately began to try to attach its mouth to something. Orochi was happy to oblige, slapping the remora against the interior wall of the shark.

He'd been inside for too long. He started looking for a handhold, something to help him climb out. He could feel the motion, feel the shark swimming with the classic swipes of its tail. The inside appeared to be not quite modeled after animal anatomy. The walls were slick.

Orochi struck out, but his fists simply bounced off of the material. He took his spike, prepared for pain, and snapped it off. Turning it around, he stabbed at the slick walls. The spike rebounded without making a dent.

Fine. Orochi took the spike, and held it above the meat of his left palm. He punctured his hand, letting his blood mix with the water. *You want to play 'Who has the baddest virus?' You get to play with mine.*

The shark started jerking violently. It threw Orochi around, sloshing him against walls. Against the black, green code began scrolling rapidly, lighting everything with a garish glow. Dropping the spike, Orochi hoisted himself up towards the jagged exit. He could barely make it out, but the glow helped. He wanted to read the code, but he stopped as soon as he saw that it was garbage.

Orochi sighed. *How am I going to make it out of this thing without being bitten in half?*

The teeth clamped shut and swung wide, then clamped shut again. Orochi shuddered. Leaving half an avatar was as bad as losing the whole thing. There was information that Atargatis could retrieve later, and that wouldn't be good for him. He waited a short distance from the entrance, floating freely to try to follow the motion of the beast. He watched the water pour in from the open mouth, and then he heard the snap of the teeth as they crashed closed.

The mouth opened again, and with the water, a tiny figure flowed into the cavernous maw. Orochi looked at it. It was two figures, really, one a fuzzy-despite-circumstances monkey, the other a rather cartoonish and oversized sea horse. The monkey squeaked when it identified Orochi, and offered him a salute with his tiny sword.

"About time you showed up," Orochi said.

A CURIOUS GIFT

The windows were filthy.

This close to the edge of the dome, the wind kicked up more, and it left particulate wherever it passed. Their house was a tiny rectangle in a residential area surrounded by other rectangles. They were as wide apart as space would allow. It was a tiny community that lived by the axiom "Leave well enough alone." She'd met two people she liked to have coffee with but otherwise the rest of them were a mystery.

Today, the dirt was about to have a reckoning. For too many days now her depression reminded her of the futility of cleaning. Diane didn't want to live in a dirt pit, and her son was coming along in a month or two. She had to get the place spruced up for his arrival.

Humming to herself, Diane felt a little like Cinderella, scrubbing the windows and singing to mice. The difference was that she had her Prince Charming already. They would never be the King and Queen of anything, but they had done it; they'd survived.

A knock on the door stopped her cold. She looked outside to see a brown truck with a yellow stripe, looming on her driveway. She frowned. Sometimes bandits dressed up in legit logos to lure women out of their houses so they could steal. Then again, this was the back half of nowhere, and it was evident that this house didn't have much in the way of finery.

The knock came again, and Diane drifted towards the door. She wished John were home. Then again, it may just be gifts for the baby. She put her hand protectively over her belly and opened the door.

"Package for you ma'am." He held out a device with a stylus attached. "Sign here please."

Letting out a breath she didn't realize she was holding, she laughed to herself as she signed for the package. "Thank you."

"Thank you." He handed her the package, about the size of a loaf of bread, and took his device back. He stepped lively back to his truck and slid back in the driver's seat. The truck rumbled to life and backed out of the driveway.

Diane shut the door behind her and looked at the package. The return address looked like it had ripped in transit; she couldn't see who it was from. That bothered her, but she figured she could open it and find out who it was from, so she could get a thank you letter out.

Inside the cardboard box was a smaller box, wrapped in baby blue paper and white ribbon. There was a card with a teddy bear on it, and the inside read, "It's okay to open this before the shower. -J"

J? Who could J be? It couldn't be John, that wasn't his handwriting. Unless he'd gotten someone to write the card for him, just to throw her off the track. Maybe he'd ordered it over the phone.

She'd never know if she didn't open it. She pulled off the blue and white packaging and uncovered a wooden box. It wasn't very big, maybe big enough to hold a deck of cards. Curious, she used her thumb to slide the lid backwards, and yelped as something stung her.

Dropping the box, she looked at her thumb to see a small dot of blood welling up. Her heart sank as she realized this was something else. She looked at the box, tumbled on its side. There was a hooded snake peeking up from the inside of the box, carved out of the same wood the box was made from. It was cleverly made to snap up when the top slid open.

What had it dosed her with?

Panicking, she picked up the snake-box and looked around it for clues. Was there a card saying who J was? Who was J? She didn't know anyone who was named J, or started with J, except for John...

She felt dizzy. Diane walked to the couch, and sat down. She needed to call John, to tell him what happened. She was too far out to get emergency services, and she feared the dizziness was only going to get worse. She connected with her comm 'ware to reach John.

"Operator, this is Diane speaking. I'm horribly fucked, can you help me?" A voice rang through her comm system and into her ears. A familiar voice. And in that moment, she knew who J was.

"Did you miss me?" Janus asked. "I sure missed you!"

Her eyes rolled back in her head. She saw the face of the man she'd worked with to escape the compound. A big, meaty man with a wide nose and a prominent brow, with the mind of a genius prowling inside.

"You fucked me," he said. "I was getting us out."

She couldn't think of anything to say. She was terrified, and for some reason her belly hurt.

Wrapping her arms around her middle, Diane came out of her hallucination to find that whatever this stuff was, it was inducing labor. She needed to call John. How could she when her comm ware wasn't working?

A biovirus. She gasped, feeling a contraction tighten down on her middle. *How am I going to deactivate a biovirus?*

"By now, you're probably thinking, what on Earth has this awful man done to me?" Janus's voice was warm in her ears. "Hopefully for you, you can figure it out on your own."

"Shut up!" She yelled, scrambling to sit up on the couch. "You're a vile person and you deserved what you got!"

Janus tsked. "Such language, and in front of your son."

"I got out, you got out. That was years ago. Why are you doing this?" Diane begged.

"I know you hate me, but think about how much I hate you." Janus jibed. "It's so much worse than you think!"

It's a recording. Diane relaxed. She had to concentrate now. She ignored Janus's patter and took herself gingerly to her bedroom. She opened the second drawer of her nightstand, and moved a scattering of pictures and bric-a-brac out of the way of the glass case.

Tears sprang to her eyes. The dizziness came back, worse than before. She could feel Jack kick inside her. She put a quieting hand on her belly. "I'm sorry, Jack. No one is coming to save us. We have to save ourselves."

Janus's voice cut off abruptly as his biovirus took out her comms system.

Pain lanced up her back, and into her head. Of course. He was targeting the jump 'ware, what else would he pick?

Think, Diane. She winced at the contraction that locked the muscles in her belly. "If I were Janus, what would I target a jumper with?"

The answer came to her in stark realization. That son of a bitch had hit her and her son with lycanthropy! Lycanthropy was capable of ruining hardware in certain kinds of technology - and Diane was willing to bet that he meant it to scramble her internal 'ware.

She pulled herself on to their bed, trying to remember when John said he'd be home. She tried to remember her neighbor's home number. The numbers started to flip as she watched, as the lycanthropy played with the systems she had active in her head. Her antivirus flared to life and was slapped to death in nanoseconds.

Tears streamed down her face as she started losing track of time. The pain of childbirth and the pain of the biovirus fused into a miserable mass. She rubbed her hands over her belly.

"Little bunny foo-foo," she sang to her unborn son. "Hoppin' through the forest..."

9TH LEGION

The monkey looked around the shark, tapping the side with its sword. The shark made a hollow belling noise.

"Yeah, that's the problem. That's the exit." Orochi pointed at the rapidly chomping teeth. The light flowed in and was cut off by the mouth closing, until it made a kind of strobe effect.

The monkey babbled at Orochi.

Orochi shrugged. "Wait for the lycanthropy to kill it, I guess. It would have been nice if you'd brought some of your friends, you know."

Looking affronted, the not-wet monkey crossed its arms across its tiny chest. Then, the monkey dove down, deep into the shark's midsection.

The shark avatar jerked. Orochi looked for his companion and the seahorse, when he felt the shark jerk again. Orochi smiled broadly. The shark opened his jaws and ripped itself in half, peeling apart like a cartoon. It deposited Orochi back in the ocean.

Astride his mount, the little monkey crossed its arms across its chest again, looking triumphant.

Orochi clapped. "Well done. I think I've got it from here."

The monkey babbled something incoherent and dove into the ocean without delay.

Orochi looked around, wondering where the star attraction could be found.

"I told you to go away!" A melodious voice crossed the ocean, and he smiled. *Right on cue.* He was not surprised to see the blonde mermaid.

"So did your shark!" He jerked his thumb back at what was left of it. "I don't abandon my friends just because I'm told to."

"Your friend?" The mermaid closed some of the distance between them, while keeping out of his reach.

Orochi wondered what was making her so cautious. He swum forward, just to keep her off balance. "Yeah. Carnelia. Beautiful girl. Some people stole her from me and I want her back." Orochi kept an eye on her, and an eye on the shark, and wished he had two extra eyes to find the code he wanted. He noticed a piece of driftwood floating towards him. His heart rate edged up a notch.

"She's with us now." The mermaid asserted. If she noticed the driftwood she gave no sign.

"I'll share, sweetheart, but I don't give people to other people. My friend is either free to go, or I'm going to make sure she's free to go." Orochi swam back a couple of feet, to line up better with the floating wood. It looked like it was about a foot long, and about four inches wide.

"She thinks it's better on the outside..." Her expression betrayed her mixed feelings.

"I don't think she's confused." Orochi felt a pain flare in his side and tried not to swear. He wasn't going to be able to stay as long as he thought.

She looked sad. "You sent those monkey-things, didn't you? You shouldn't have done that, I have orders to kill you now."

"That's the Ninth legion. They are full of shenanigans." Orochi winked at her. "So you're the one who clevered the box van into oblivion and hid my friend's kidnapping. Tsk, tsk, Atargatis. I mean, well done on a professional level but I'm afraid be the one to tell you, you made a very large mistake."

"You are a threat to the system, and I am bound to protect it." Said Atargatis, ignoring his words.

"Or you could come with me." Orochi offered.

"You don't understand, I can't leave here..." She covered her mouth with her hands, her blue eyes going wide.

"Yes, you can." Orochi said. "They need you more than you need them. You're their Savvy, you're the one who does the cleanup when they mess up. They depend on you but I am willing to bet they never give you the appreciation you deserve."

She paused. "I get... stuff..."

"I'd be more than happy to rescue you." Orochi said, making a flourish with his hand and snatching up the piece of driftwood. "You can come with Carn and spend time with her in the sun. My name's Orochi. Pleasure to meet you."

Atargatis shook her head. "It's impossible, you don't understand."

Pain flared and Orochi almost cried out. He saw that it was going to take more work than he had time for.

"Atargatis, do you know what I did to that shark over there?" He asked.

She shook her head.

"I released a biovirus into it. You don't happen to have any biological agents in this alt-real, do you? Because lycanthropy's a dirty bitch to mitigate..."

"What?" She swam backwards, distancing herself from the shark. "You did what?"

"I'd recommend you unplug and have a complete system sweep before you log in again." Orochi waved at her. "Have a nice day."

With that, he disincorporated his avatar.

Nathan was there to greet him. "You disincorporated in the sea? Why don't you just hand them your home address and shoe size?"

"I have about fifty thousand viruses that I have to clean before I get to justifying myself to you," Orochi said, rubbing his eyes. "They got dosed with lycanthropy, they're going to flash fry everything in that alt-real."

"Then why didn't you discorporate in the shark? It would have saved you some time." Nathan asked.

"Then I wouldn't have gotten the driftwood." Orochi explained as he focused on virus removal.

"It was just a piece of driftwood. I don't see why you bothered." Nathan said.

"When I hack it, it's going to have key algorithms I need to get behind the curtain." Orochi said. "No more bullshit alt-reals, nothing but pure code."

"I'll believe it when I see it." Nathan said.

"What about you?" Orochi asked, reading the anti-virals as they reported in the numbers. "How did the Ninth Legion fare?"

Nathan smiled. "I'm pleased. Hooking up those C-pods allowed me to feed in a program that replicated and sent itself out to the other 'pods until they were all ready. I didn't have a lot to work with but fortunately I had a few things I could cobble together. They had one mission - search and destroy. If they ran into enemy code, they had to dispatch it. The fact that they were cute little monkeys was just what I had on hand already. The seahorses were a nice touch, I thought."

Orochi nodded. "They did good work. Not much got through their screen to attack me, and I handled it."

"They kept Atargatis busy for a good chunk of the time. They have a lot of redundant systems to catch anything that makes it beyond the first layer. These guys thrive on paranoia. That being said, they do have their weak points, as well. Atargatis is good but she's one mind. They have all kinds of canned answers to a Savvy attack, but those answers aren't manned by AI, so they have no logic stream to follow. They don't work together." Nathan reported, flipping switches in the C-pod to access local scrub systems. "I don't think they have as many people on the payroll as they'd like us to believe."

"Just really, really important ones." Orochi said. "I feel like we should go back in while they're dealing with lycanthropy shutting down their systems."

"If you want to make a hole be my guest. But I warn you, my legion are all just soldiers and they don't get ideas of their own." Nathan said. "They are not prepared to improvise."

"Well, they're all hands on deck now. I'm sure we made their lives hell but I doubt that it's crashing the system completely, or I wouldn't have needed you to whip up the Ninth. They'll know what they're dealing with in a couple of hours." Orochi shrugged and kept working on his decontamination procedures.

"Were you able to find her?" Nathan asked.

"No." Orochi's expression darkened. "But they're going to keep her as far away from the tech side of things as they can manage. When I decode the data that I managed to grab while I was talking to Atargatis, that should give me a better insight into how their system works, and with luck, where they're holding."

"It could be anything." Nathan said. "That's a lot to hang on a discarded program."

"You're right, it could be. But for Carnelia's sake, this better be a goddamn treasure map or she may be in her eighties when we get her out of there." Orochi said, fishing for his pack of cigarettes and frowning when he remembered he was out.

BACK IN BUSINESS

"I told you this didn't work out for Parris, didn't I?" Carnelia looked at her ashen gray hands as Kaito explained to her what he expected as they sat in his office. The fine muscles between the tiny bones in her hands were sore. Every muscle ached, but she couldn't remember a day where her hands had felt sore from being worked too hard. It was a novelty.

"You did. But Parris is an idiot, you and I both know this. He was forcing you to do something distasteful. I am asking you to go put in a vote. You will only need her body for a couple of hours, and then you can come back." Kaito smoothed his perfectly straight tie.

"What happens if I get stuck?" Carnelia asked. "You set up traps, that means other people can set traps. What happens if reporters ask me questions I don't know the answers to? What happens if I get accosted by someone who says they know me? I imagine politicians get that ploy all the time, but I won't know if it's true or not. There are a lot of factors here I don't think you've taken into account."

Kaito's expression darkened as she went on. "Your concerns are based in fear, and prior improper treatment. You will say, 'No Comment' to the journalists. You will stay with your aide at all times. You will get back to the C-pod as fast as you can when the vote is over. Don't give any speeches. It doesn't matter what the politician would normally do, it matters what you do. Don't draw undue attention to yourself."

"I could stay and not come back. Then I'd be in a powerful politician's body, and you wouldn't be able to reach me." Carnelia said.

"You could do that." Kaito said. "No question. But you want your body too badly to settle for someone else's."

Carnelia closed her eyes. He had her there, dead to rights. There was no walking away from this so soon after she got it back, even in the shitty condition she was in. "I'll do it."

Kaito grinned. "I knew you would. Get something to eat, the report down to the C-pod bay, and we'll get you dialed in to your target."

Carnelia got up and walked out quickly. She didn't want anything to eat, but it was probably in her best interest to eat something if she wanted to keep her body functional.

She didn't remember her body being this much work before. It was a part of the plan, body and spirit as one. Now she had to deal with problems she couldn't even fathom. No wonder Parris had a twenty-four hour policy. It was to keep his bodyjumpers reigned in, but it was also to keep them sane.

Frowning, she replayed the conversation with Kaito in her mind. There was no way out. He had done his research. She could dance out of here with another woman's body, however, she'd barely been in this body for twenty-four hours and it felt like home. Given the last couple of months with Pixru, she couldn't go through the rest of her life in a foreign body. It solved the problem of being pregnant with her brother's kid, too.

The door to the C-pod bay was open, and Mikeru stood inside with a clipboard, startling her. "Are you ready to get started?"

"What are you doing here?" She managed. "This isn't what you're supposed to be doing."

"You don't tell me what I'm supposed to be doing." Mikeru said bitterly. "Kaito does."

"Well, Kaito is stupid. You're a thief, there's no thief required for this job." Carn grumbled.

"I'm the fixer." Mikeru straightened up.

"You make a poor fixer. You stand out like a sore thumb in a crowd, no one is going to forget seeing you." Carn pointed out.

"Are you always this difficult to work with before we even get rolling?" Mikeru snapped.

"I'm demanding because being good requires being demanding. I know you don't like me but if you still do the work then we're good. If you get rattled because I'm pointing out flaws before we get started, then you should get Kaito to reassign you because I don't work with dead weight." Her chin was up, her eyes focused on his, her every gesture as familiar as if she'd been born in this body. She approved. She realized she was chewing on Mikeru the way she would on Michael, and then shrugged. She didn't trust him yet, she needed to double-check his work until she knew if he was solid.

"You aren't going to need much for this run, it's only two hours long." Mikeru's chest was puffed out, a signal to Carn that she'd achieved her goal of punching him in the pride. "We've got our security amidst their security, and I need to run the comms to make sure to keep people away from you. I'm not going to be anywhere visible."

"Anything I need to know?"

"You're the face. Your only job is to be a convincing politician. Avoid getting in deep conversations. Don't get cornered by journalists. Glower and look unwelcoming. Your entire mission is to vote 'no' on the referendum being brought to the table. You don't have to get fancy, don't have to get speechy. Just vote and leave. We'll pick you up outside of the grounds, and we'll have a C-pod on hand. Transporting Nakemura back to the place is our problem, and we already have a plan for it. You'll be back at base, so you won't have to deal with it." Mikeru outlined for her. "Got it?"

Carnelia nodded thoughtfully. "Well, aren't you prepared for your debut? Let's hope that fuzzy part in the middle works out for you."

"I'd be more worried about yourself." Mikeru growled.

Carnelia felt a pang as she observed her brother in action. Genetic brother, at any rate. She wasn't going to get picky, it was already too confusing. In her mind she saw him lying face down in a pool of blood, shot by Hyde. She pushed the image away. "That'd make one of us. When are we rolling?"

"When you get your ass in the C-pod." Mikeru pointed to the room behind him. "Anytime you're ready, Miss Cesnos."

"That's Nakemura." She said, sauntering off to the C-pod room.

Ready for her debut, she wore a tank top, and short, tight-fitting shorts. It was what she commonly wore on jumps. At least at the Glass House there were protocols.

Those who live in glass houses.

She shook off the concern and felt the kiss of the hypodermic needle, the press of electrodes across her forehead. This wasn't her idea of a good time, but this was her new way to make a living, and her other options weren't too great. She hoped Orochi would rescue her, but as the time passed she began to think that he couldn't get to her. Even if he could, she still had to stall until he got here.

She felt a familiar tilting sensation. Opening her eyes, she saw that she was in a different C-pod than she'd left from, a higher quality model. She looked down and saw her arms, golden in color. She sighed. She wondered how Pixru was surviving without her. Had she come back to the surface? Or was she still in the bento box? At least her ethics dilemma had been resolved.

"Muneo?" A voice filtered through the plastic and metal cage of the C-pod. "The people are asking for you."

"I didn't realize the time." She said, cracking the seal on the 'pod. She climbed out with the practiced ease of someone who worked in C-pods consistently. She looked at the person to whom the voice belonged.

He was a small man, impeccably dressed in a maroon dress shirt, black suit pants, and a tie that married the two colors together. He had a round, friendly face and a clipboard. She thought his name was Iha Hiroyasu, but seeing someone's face on a two by three dossier photo and seeing someone standing in front of you and smiling made the match a little more difficult than she'd first thought.

This did not fill her with confidence.

VOTE

"Saito called this morning." Iha said as they walked down the hall towards the conference. "He wants to know if he's still fired."

"Oh, Iha, you shouldn't have to run interference between us." Carnelia said contritely. "Let me handle him after this is over."

He gave her a surprised look. "Thank you, Muneo."

Carnelia was glad that Muneo wasn't prone to smirking. It was easier to keep her features schooled. The woman was quite healthy, a fact that drove home what poor shape her body was in. The treatments had done their job, though. She felt at least fifty percent better than she had upon awakening. Walking across her room's space didn't make her feel exhausted like it had the day before.

"...expects you to make a statement after the vote." Iha's voice floated back into her mind.

"Oh, that's fine, but I have to make a quick stop at the C-pod before I do that." Carnelia said.

Iha blinked at her. "Your last call of the day was over as I came to get you."

Carnelia searched for a plausible excuse. "I wasn't done with that call, I just knew I had to come out to make the vote. I had to wrap in the middle and I promised I would finish details right afterwards."

"The press are going to want to see you." Iha looked unhappy. "They're going to want you to show your strength against Typhon."

Carnelia tried not to wince. She was certainly complicating Muneo Nakamura's life, all right. "It won't take long, it'll give the journalists time to swarm around other politicians and get their statements first."

Iha looked disappointed. "Our time is now, Muneo! If you want to be taken seriously as a politician, you have to make a speech after the vote."

"I will." Carnelia lied. "After I make the call."

They stepped into the Grand Hall, the room as white as snow, pillars reaching up to the vaulted ceilings, and flags hanging from niches in the wall. There were most likely two thousand people in the building, from politicians to their staff to the staff of the Grand Hall to the janitors. Most of the people in the building were embroiled in politics.

The noise of conversation murmured loudly when she stepped into the room, and Carnelia could see people pointing at her. The timbre of the voices changed, and she could tell that people were talking about her now. Flashes went off from cameras. Her stomach clenched. She'd never been a famous person, never had to pretend she was a target to more than shop clerks and valets. This was what Parris forced her into, but there was no way she could have pulled it off.

How was she going to pull this off? She didn't know enough about Muneo to make even the most casual conversation without being suspicious. One person with an axe to grind or a story to post could catch her off-guard, leaving telltale marks that Muneo wasn't herself. Kaito was an idiot, thinking that she could pull this off in such a short time.

But I'm the one here to bear the brunt of it. Carnelia took a deep breath and smiled at the pointing journalists.

"Are you ready?" Iha asked.

Carnelia nodded.

"Follow me." He said, and led her past the upper echelon, where there was a table full of food, and many people standing around it grazing off of the trays. Some people greeted her, but none tried to stop her as she followed Iha to the voting booths.

"Listen." Iha said as they approached. "I know you and Saito have your arrangement, but I think you should hire a new head of security. He's too close to you, and he doesn't make the best choices. I think you'd be better off leaving him fired and not mix business with pleasure."

Carnelia blinked in surprise. "Everything is going to change after this vote. I say we table this conversation until after I get a few things out of the way first."

Iha looked as though Carnelia had slapped him. The penny dropped. Iha saw an opening and wanted a chance to take it, and Saito stood in his way. "Yes, Muneo."

She stood outside the curtain for a moment. "I'll give what you said some thought."

His smile was brilliant, and she knew she'd read him correctly. She felt a pang that she had set this scenario in motion but she'd lived too long by being who she was expected to be to worry about the damage that it did. This was her survival, and he and his boss were impinging on it.

No, this was her survival until Orochi rescued her.

She stepped into the voting booth.

The voting mechanism was simple. There was a screen, and an electronic pen, and the referendum numbers. She'd been given the list of what to vote for or against. There were only five items on the docket today, nothing someone couldn't memorize in twenty minutes.

Muneo Nakamura was just one vote. She couldn't swing the entire vote with one twitch of her pen.

Then there was the small amount of information Carnelia had overheard Kaito discussing over the comms while Carnelia was marched down to the C-pod. Muneo was the most vocal politician in Tokyo regarding Typhon Inc. She called for their release of documentation regarding the type of business they ran.

Kaito had also mentioned that Muneo Nakamura's father lay among the number of the glass coffins. He had died in a car accident outside Typhon's awareness until it was too late to arrange a rescue attempt without giving away their position. Kaito tried to convince whoever was on the other line that Nakamura Senior should be woken up to control Muneo. He wasn't getting his way.

The plan was to discredit her using her own plan to bring Typhon down. If she spent all of her time shouting "Vote Yes" and then voted no, no one would ever trust her as a politician again. Her constituents would dry up and blow away, leaving her career in flames.

Carnelia stared at the screen. There was no guarantee that her vote would win or lose the called for investigation. Typhon had deep pockets and many politicians would sit back and accept those yen and vote no and call Muneo out as a radical or a hysterical woman or whatever they wanted to label her with.

There was, however, a guarantee that a vote of 'no' would break this woman's career and possibly the woman with it.

She couldn't stop Kaito from targeting Muneo in other ways. She could only take a stand, and show Kaito that his arrangement was bullshit and that Carnelia wasn't going to work for people like him anymore. Whether or not it brought down the hammer on her, she had to show that she wasn't going to lay down for this kind of treatment anymore.

On the screen, she ticked off the opposite of everything she'd been told to do. It took less than thirty seconds.

Less than thirty seconds to ruin her life instead of Muneo's.

She stepped out of the voting booth, feeling shaky. Iha stood waiting for her, his face painted with concern. "Are you all right?"

"It's a big moment, standing up to a big corporation." She said, giving him a tremulous smile. "Think you can sneak me back to the C-pod?"

"That's not as important as this speech!" Iha flushed with frustration.

She put a hand on his cheek, caressing it gently and feeling the heat as he flushed again. "I'm sorry this frustrates you, but I need to do this. You have no idea how much better my career will be for it."

"Follow me." Iha said quietly, showing her the access tunnels that led to the downstairs C-pod area.

She slid inside a C-pod, and sighed. Nothing left to do but take her lumps. Except, there was one thing that she could do for Muneo before she left. "Call Saito."

"What do you want?" A grumpy male baritone growled in her ear.

"You were right." Carnelia said, hoping that was true. "Typhon has it out for me and they have access to tech we don't fully understand."

"Finally, some sense." Saito's voice held a note of satisfaction.

"You're rehired, but you need to get here fast, because there are Typhon agents here and I'm barely keeping them held off." She crossed her fingers.

"I'm a block away, keep out of sight and I'll be there." He promised.

"Listen, here's an important thing that I can't explain." She said, looking at the chronometer. She'd give herself a few more seconds then jump. "If I don't act like myself, if I can't answer questions I should be able to easily, or if any of our team acts that way - Iha, anybody - assume Typhon has gotten to them."

"Got it." He paused. "What were you wearing the night we first kissed?"

"I have to go." Carnelia saw someone moving towards the C-pod, and hoped it was Iha.

"Muneo!" Saito's voice was insistent.

She flipped the switch to jump back to her body.

DRIFTWOOD

Back at the hotel, Nathan looked unimpressed. "That's what you got?"

"Yeah." Orochi grinned, looking pleased with himself.

"Go out and get dinner. I'll have something for us when you get back." Orochi slipped his visor on, and changed the view from the alt-real configuration to raw code.

"Fine, but don't expect much." Nathan turned to leave.

Orochi was already buried in code. "What did you break off from? Please be off of something good... something connected to big secrets."

It took twenty minutes and there were still translation gaps, but Orochi sat down to legible code. "That's right, reveal your secrets."

The code was multi-layered, data blended with operation codes mixed with security strata. It was like peeling an orange; the first layer wasn't so hard, but there was always pith to pluck and unexpected seeds, and pressing too hard would ruin the whole thing. Orochi worked fastidiously, knowing this was his one shot at Typhon's sensitive bits.

There were numbers, one through two hundred and fifty-six, and each one corresponded with a name. Number 117 was sectioned off into 117.1, 117.2, all the way to 117.5. There were no others like it, and it corresponded to a name, Charlotte Hargrove. Number 116 was named Michael Hargrove, and number 115 was Melinde Hargrove.

Nathan walked in and the smell of food summoned Orochi from his work. "Ah, ramen."

"To ramen." Nathan said and tossed Orochi chopsticks.

"To ramen." Orochi responded. "And I think you got here about ten minutes too early."

"Nah, I love when I'm here and I hear you yell triumphantly." Nathan chuckled. "You're like a school kid."

Orochi grabbed his container of noodles and mock growled at Nathan. "I can't be big bad all the time."

They hurried through their dinner so they could see what Orochi had cracked.

Nathan looked over his shoulder and whistled. "That was on the driftwood?"

"Not quite so unimpressive now, is it?" Orochi asked smugly.

"Walk me through it, I can't read half of it." Nathan urged.

"First, there's this set of curiosities. They have five of this girl." Orochi points out. "Same name, just different designator."

"That's got to be significant, there aren't any other ones like that." Nathan said after a quick scan of the records.

"What would let you have five of the same person?" Orochi asked Nathan.

"You can't be serious." Nathan looked again. "Clones?"

"Looks that way." Orochi said. "I have a couple other important things here. The first is a loop of their security tasks, which will come in handy to develop a 'ware that stops them in their tracks. We can model off of this and experiment. I've already got my team on it."

"Hey, I thought I was your sec team." Nathan frowned.

"Oh, come on now. My bots are good for quick iteration but they're nothing compared to what you can do once you get to work." Orochi's conciliatory tone made both of them laugh.

"This isn't the best part though. There was definitely a creamy center. There are definite links that Typhon is a split group off of the original bodyjumping group." Orochi pointed to a spot on his screen.

"Woah! Well then, why don't they have any jump 'ware?" Nathan asked.

"Sadly, the driftwood is tantalizing, but it doesn't answer a lot of questions. However, this demands a full scale attack. I was already pissed at them for stealing Carn, but now stealing Carn AND being an offshoot of this bunch of body slavers is more than I can stand. We have to shut these guys down cold." Orochi set his noodles down and stood up. "It's going to take more than we have, resource-wise."

"What about Rascati?" Nathan asked. "Now that you've got proof, this is pretty much what your little subdivision of non-existent government lives to investigate."

Orochi frowned. "I don't know if I want to hear him bitch and then gloat."

Nathan blinked. "Eaten by alt-real sharks is okay, but a few negative words from a geezer makes you tremble? What the fuck, I'm taking away your man card."

"What? No way. My man card stays where it is. You like Rascati so much, you call him."

"I don't work for him. Look, Orochi, you may have done exactly what he expected you to do, and that's why he's given you this much leeway, so you can do all the legwork and he has plausible deniability. He's probably surprised that you haven't tried to contact him. So just swallow some of that inflated pride of yours and call him. It's hard to say what help they can be a greendome away, but there's no sense not finding out."

"Fine." Orochi acquiesced. "Why do you have to be so right all the time?"

"Easy. I don't get to be the seven foot two lead, so I have to have some redeeming quality." Nathan grinned.

"This is not a movie." Orochi grumbled.

"Call your superior officer, cadet." Nathan pointed to his visor.

"Jeeze, what the hell time of day is it anyway?" Orochi looked at his visor. "Looks like it would be 7 am there. Too bad, I was hoping it would be an inconvenient time for him."

"No time like the present." Nathan stared at him.

"Fine!" Orochi slipped his visor on. "Commence humiliating comm."

The comm beep went off twice before Rascati's face filled up Orochi's visor. "Enjoying Tokyo?"

"It's lovely this time of the year. You should see it." Orochi kept his voice level.

"I'm afraid I can't but I've sent help." Rascati said blandly. "You've met her... she introduced herself by pulling your ass out of the fire..."

"Emi?" Orochi blurted.

"She'll be hurt that she didn't get to play that card herself but you don't have time to play trust games. She's local help but we have an arrangement with her company." Rascati explained.

"That's all we get? Your premier bodyjumper is kidnapped, her partner is the only one who helps?" Orochi sounded tired to his own ears.

"And all this time I thought you were paying attention when we talked about words like jurisdiction. Not to mention that travel between greendomes is awful, as I suspect you learned the hard way when you flew out. I want to send more help but I'm not authorized to. Emi's an augment, she'll worth at least three people, and I know you flew out with your Savvy friend. You almost have the whole band." Rascati's face wore creases of worry, and Orochi knew that he wasn't being fully forthcoming.

"I just found out that Typhon is related to the Orochi Group." Orochi said.

"So we have a name for our kidnappers. That will be of some help. Any other tidbits you're willing to share?"

"They're a clone bank, not a bodyjumper place the way Parris had. We think that's why they're so keen after Carnelia, because she has the 'ware and the way."

"Hmm..." Rascati said. "She doesn't have the 'ware if she's not in Pixru. How does that work exactly? If only we could get some experiments going..."

"We wondered the same thing. It's possible, but we don't have any stats on how long it would take a clone to be viable. That may be all they're doing with her, we have no way to know. Their security is top of the line. They have a full time security Savvy just like Parris had, and the canned stuff is alt-real, so it's confusing and hard to integrate. Nathan and I managed to steal a piece of intel from them, but the only way I got away was by unleashing lycanthropy on them. No one has come to kill us yet so I'm guessing it messed up their tracking system, but with their resources all we can do is stay on the move."

Rascati nodded. "Call Emi. She has contacts, they may be willing to be hired. We want Carn out of their hands as fast as possible. It's nice to know that we may have a few days yet before she's active, but we can't rely on that. They're clone experts, so there's no doubt that they have some kind of augment-slave knock off that lets them get clones active faster. Also keep in mind that they have people to choose from, Carn could look like anybody, even men."

"Thanks, I might have forgotten about that part." Orochi said drily. "I'll contact Emi."

"I'm sorry I can't do anything more directly. Let's just say the heads of this operation have learned a valuable lesson about where they send their investigation." Rascati looked contrite.

"We'll get her back." Orochi said, and cut the connection.

"How did it go?" Nathan asked.

"We have an addition to our team." Orochi winced.

Nathan grunted. "Their generosity knows no bounds."

"It's Emi."

Nathan choked. "Are you serious?"

"She's local help but apparently she has contacts back to secret international agencies that technically don't exist." Orochi pulled his visor off of his head and played with it between his fingers.

"They're not flying anyone out?" Nathan asked.

"It's outside of their jurisdiction. If they did, everything would get taken, before they even made it off the tarmac. They probably didn't catch us because I went rogue and had no marks on me." Orochi sighed. "Which makes me wonder if this was their contingency plan in the first place."

"Doesn't matter if it was, there's no way we're leaving Carn in these people's hands. No one I know deserves what these people do." Nathan shivered. "Making your own stable of thieves.. ugh. Did the driftwood say how they harvest their blueprints?"

"There wasn't much, but it looked like a basic insurance scam. "Buy your body so you can harvest its organs when you're fucked. That kind of thing." Orochi looked grim.

"Yeah, these guys are all basically the lowest form of human. That's okay, it helps me sleep at night to know we're taking them out." Nathan walked over to his gear. "Upload the security strand to me, I'll work on it while you're making connections with Emi."

Orochi smiled. "Nathan, you are the best friend a guy could ask for."

Nathan returned his smile with one of his own. "Let's burn them down."

In a matter of minutes everything was uploaded. Orochi pulled out Emi's card and turned it over in his hands. He couldn't help but wonder what he'd be getting into bringing her on board, but at the moment, the clock was screaming in his ears, and he was willing to take any help he could get.

"Hi, this is Orochi." Orochi bit his cheek in thought. What was he going to say to this woman?

"Oh, hi there." She said, sounding cheerful. "What can I help you with?"

"You'd be amazed." Orochi said, then wished he hadn't. "You caught us off guard with your Hyde hunt."

"Looked like you needed the extra help." Emi said generously.

"Maybe. It's not every day that you're facing down the barrel of a gun when a random woman shows up and takes the gunman down." Orochi briefly wondered if he sounded like an asshole.

"It's my job." Emi said. "Hunting folk down."

"We may be in the market." Orochi said. "Typically it's nice to know more before you hire though."

"Fair enough." Emi said. "I'm an augment, free agent, typically work for bounty but sometimes for cash. I'm good at the physical tasks - shooting, fighting, climbing, you get the idea. I can do basic tech shit if it's not too sophisticated."

"I'm not familiar with the term augment." Orochi said.

Emi laughed. "I should have slowed down a bit there. Augments are physically augmented humans. Muscles are medically hopped up to be faster, stronger, etc. Truth is, most people have augmentation - meniscus, or traps, or maybe even an entire muscle group. Augments take it a step further, and have all their muscles enhanced so that they are stronger and faster than the average person."

"Sounds painful." Orochi joked.

"Only when it's getting installed, and the year or two it takes to settle." Emi said dismissively. "We're popular in Nippon, lots of people hire them as status symbols."

"Oh, this wouldn't be a status thing." Orochi promised. "So, what do you think about taking white hat jobs?"

"They rarely pay as well." Emi said. "Still, there's a do-right feeling you get that tends to make that not so bad."

"I guess that would put us as more of a gray hat job, then." Orochi said. "We're not exactly the good guys but the people we're after are definitely the bad guys."

"Good guys, bad guys, I'm kind of a 'who signs my checks' guy." Emi admitted.

"Yeah, well, these guys could definitely outbid us if it came to that." Orochi said, feeling his jaw tighten. "Do you stay on your side?"

"I do." Emi said. "A merc who flips sides is a merc that doesn't find jobs."

"Okay, now that I know what you would have said had I called, let me tell you that I called Rascati twenty minutes ago and he ratted you out. I know you're supposed to be a member of this elite force tasked with rescuing Carnelia, and that you aren't part of my division but somehow you rate." Orochi said.

"You asshole! You led me on." Emi sounded peeved.

"You're the one who came under false pretenses. You could have told us who you were when you were escorting Hyde away. So, now that we've brushed all that bullshit away, I want to know who I'm going to be rescuing my partner with."

Emi paused. "I work for an agency partnered with the Bureau. I'm just a grunt, they never tell me much. I know that the target is a very important person, and that it's possible that she's in trouble even now. So, we have to move fast. I'm a feet on the ground type - I do a lot of physical damage with weapons and without, and I am good at blowing things up when things get too hot. I have a present for the bad guys once we make it inside their complex."

"See, now, I think we can work together." Orochi said. "I think I like you already."

GIRL TALK

She jumped back into her body and immediately felt hands seize her arms and legs. She put up no resistance; they manhandled her to the ground. She was on her knees, head forced down, in obeisance to Kaito. She would have collapsed if they didn't hold her up, so she took her win where she could and waited for the storm to start.

"You had one job." Kaito's tightly controlled voice was focused like a laser beam. He radiated anger from the core of his being. He strode up to her and slapped her. Carnelia's head rocked back, but she didn't cry out. She was tougher than one backhanded slap. "You did exactly the opposite of what I asked!"

Carnelia didn't reply.

"I am trying to think. Why would Carnelia do the opposite of what I asked? Did I not provide you with your body? Did I not give you living accommodations and clothes to wear? Was this not an amiable working situation?" Kaito's voice rose a notch with every question.

"No." Carnelia said. She lifted her head up to meet Kaito's gaze.

"What?" Kaito looked like he would slap her again.

"I'm not free to go. I am being held against my will. You are in fact enslaving me. This is not an amiable working arrangement. This is illegal, immoral, and wrong. I see no need to participate in your plans." Carnelia held her head high.

Kaito looked at her, and then laughed. He clapped, slowly, each clap a counterpoint to the quiet in the room. "Oh, look who has thoughts about how she should be used. Look at who thinks that I care about her feelings. I *own* you, Carnelia. I have a contract that I could bring to the courts. You are a producer, and you stay alive only if you produce."

"If you kill me, you kill your golden goose." Carnelia pointed out. *Not to mention your contract would never hold up in court.*

Kaito sobered. "There is an unfortunate truth to what you say. However, there are ways to get our point across without harming the goose."

The two security men who dragged her out of the C-pod pulled her to her feet. They took her down the stairs, to the base of the glass coffins, where the eerie glow lit up their ornate tattoos that coiled up the full length of their arms.

Carnelia took a deep breath. *Whatever they dish out, it's nothing Parris hasn't done to me already.*

Two more men appeared, their muscles evident beneath their suits. They escorted a third man, and when Carnelia saw him, she gasped.

Mikeru.

The two guards forced her into a headlock. She tried to extricate herself but even with newly renovated musculature she was no match for their strength.

The same action was taken by the two men escorting Mikeru. They had him pinned, with his arms behind his back, incapable of moving.

He's not my brother he's not my brother he's not my brother... Carnelia clung to the idea as she watched Kaito swing and connect with Mikeru's midsection. She heard him grunt, and gritted her teeth. Even if he weren't her brother and just her fixer... no, that wasn't true. Kaito was hurting her brother, and she was forced to watch.

Kaito swung and this time connected with Mikeru's jaw. Mikeru's head snapped back with the impact, but he righted himself and readied himself for the next hit.

"It wasn't his fault!" Carnelia yelled, willing the next hit to not land.

It landed, this time in Mikeru's middle.

Kaito turned back to her and grinned. "Oh, no, he didn't do anything wrong. Except he lost control over you. This is what happens when you don't do your job!"

Lashing out with a kick, Kaito's blow hit Mikeru in the knee. Mikeru cried out, and the two guards fought to keep him standing.

Carnelia watched as each blow landed. Kaito didn't look like a strong man, however he was relentless and seemed to know where to punch or kick to do the maximum amount of damage. Mikeru stood for a while, but eventually he sagged to his knees. The security guards adjusted their grip and kept holding on.

A thin trickle of sweat rolled down Kaito's forehead, and he came around with a kick that clipped Mikeru in the temple. Mikeru's eyes rolled up and the two guards dropped him to the ground like a sack of meat.

Holding back the tears, Carnelia stared at her unconscious brother. He may have been only a clone, but she was a clone too. That didn't make either of them any less human. She stared as the chance she had to win him to her side fractured and dissolved.

"Golden goose or not, I don't feel as though I've driven the point home enough." Kaito said, walking towards her. He snapped a punch, catching Carnelia on the cheek. The pain exploded up the side of her face and down, and she twisted in her guards grip to get away. He kicked her in the stomach, and the pain was so intense that she sagged immediately. She knew she'd withstood worse, but this body hadn't, and this body was still in the process of becoming.

She cried out as he kicked her twice more, and the guards let her go. She held herself up on knees and elbows, wondering if she would ever be able to eat again. It was worse because she knew the beating she took was a fraction of the damage Mikeru had been subjected to.

"Get her up, put her in her room. One of you stay on door duty. No one is allowed in but Yuuki. She's allowed food and water but no perks. Go." Kaito walked away before he'd finished issuing his orders.

She looked over her shoulder and saw Mikeru trying to pick himself up off the floor. He spit, and a red gob hit the smooth concrete floor. He pushed himself up to his knees, and then he looked over to where Carnelia was being dragged off. His expression was unreadable.

Carnelia wanted to throw up, but considering her non-functional stomach, she was fairly certain that wasn't physically possible. She didn't fight against the guards as they hauled her to her feet. She didn't help them either. She knew dead weight was a pain to carry. The two guards did not complain at her passivity, they simply wrestled her onto the elevator. When the elevator reached her floor, the doors opened and they pushed her out. The doors looked like the doors of prison cells, and she wondered why she hadn't noticed that before.

Once she was in her room, Carnelia immediately went for her bed and curled up on it. She was sore. She'd have nasty bruises, but she wasn't too concerned. Everyone would know why she got them, anyway. Now, she was after larger fish. The mermaid, specifically. She'd spoken to Atargatis twice now, both times when she was unconscious. She wasn't sure that she could create that state in herself, but what if she could get most of the way there, and jump off? It was worth experimenting. It seemed like the worst thing that could happen was that she'd get a nap in.

Lying on the bed, Carnelia slowed her breathing. It was one of those little tricks she learned while jumping. Slow breathing and counting to thirty helped her calm her mind. She always felt stupid until number fifteen, when the whole thing seemed to start taking effect.

For a moment, she saw the beach.

Carnelia's eyes snapped open, and then she cursed and closed her eyes again. It took time for the beach to resolve, and for her not to think about it hard enough to burst it like a bubble. She had to accept the reality as it was, not criticize it.

It was then that she realized that something was wrong with the beach.

The sand was wrong somehow. When Carn stepped into it it felt boggy. There was a seahorse washed up on shore, but it looked cartoonish, with ballooned characteristics. It didn't fit in with this reality at all.

"Carnelia?" Atargatis' voice sounded quakey.

"Atargatis, is that you?" Carnelia stood on the beach and looked for the blonde mermaid. She couldn't see her.

"I heard Kaito say he was going to kill you." Atargatis sounded scared. Her voice. Was it coming from the seahorse? "He wouldn't listen to me."

"You tried to stop him?" Approval colored her voice. "Aw, Atargatis, that was kind. Why can't I see you?"

"They all treat me like I'm some stupid AI. They don't talk to me unless they want something. They don't bring me things, they don't even tell me how their day went unless they're just talking to each other and I overhear them." Atargatis' voice was coming from the seahorse, Carnelia was sure of it. She walked over to the strange seahorse, struggling through the boggy sand.

"You're not stupid. But why are you a seahorse? What happened?" Carnelia asked.

"Orochi unleashed lycanthropy on the system." Atargatis said. "I've been trying to fix my avatar, but he wreaked a lot of havoc."

Carnelia remembered her brush with lycanthropy. She shuddered. "You're lucky to be alive."

"Am I?" Atargatis asked. Storm clouds gathered across the sky.

"You are." Carnelia said. "Lycanthropy can kill you."

"Not me." Atargatis said confidently. "That version is out of date. It's causing issues because any virus will, but there's a known cure."

Carnelia hadn't had access to a cure when she'd been infected. She'd only had time to introduce a new strain of lycanthropy into Orochi's body. She wasn't entirely sure that Atargatis' confidence was well founded.

"Would you put me into the ocean?" Atargatis asked.

"Sure." Carnelia gently picked up the cartoon seahorse and walked through the boggy sand to the ocean. She gently lowered it in.

She watched the seahorse for a while, crossing her fingers. As she watched, the seahorse struggled, its shape bulging and stretching. Two fins unfurled from the skinny end of the tail, which thickened and lengthened and turned into an emerald cascade. The body lengthened and became a torso, complete with clamshell top and Atargatis' winning smile.

"You did it!" Carnelia clapped her hands together.

"A lot of the attack didn't permanently disable anything." Atargatis frowned. "It was a distraction."

The mermaid's words gave her glee but she couldn't show it yet. "If you can change your avatar's shape, why don't you change it to give you legs?" Carnelia asked. "Come out here with me."

Atargatis blushed. "I don't know how to walk."

"You don't need to know how to walk to make a walking algorithm." Carnelia said before the words sank in.

Atargatis frowned. "They have me in a tank. Being plugged in to the Web takes me away from my body. I'm their Savvy. They don't want me wandering too far so they have controls on my avatar's shape."

Carnelia's heart went out to Atargatis. Trapped as a servant to a nest of thieves who ignored her and didn't appreciate what she did at all. Anger blossomed in her heart, anger she hadn't even felt for her own incarceration. "Do you have jumpware?"

"They won't install it." Atargatis' voice trembled. "Even without it, I have tried. I know it can be done, but I have never seen it done until you got here."

This gave Carnelia pause. When she'd jumped into Orochi she hadn't been in a C-pod, but she had the 'ware in her head. Then Hyde managed to jump into a new person to get himself to Tokyo. Could it be that the jumpware was another of Parris's lies?

"Did you see me?" Carnelia asked. "Earlier today, when I had to go out to the politician?"

"I watched." Atargatis said. "But I didn't understand."

Carnelia made a decision. "If there's a way to teach you to jump, we'll find it. I'm going to make sure you get out no matter what."

Atargatis smiled. "Will I meet Orochi?"

"You sure will."

"I like him." Atargatis announced.

Carnelia sat down on the beach to be on the level with the mermaid. It felt like sand should, again, rather than the boggy mess it had been. "I'm glad to hear that."

"When will he come back?" Atargatis asked.

"I think Orochi is coming here to save us." Carnelia assured her. "You may have to stop being so efficient for a little while. In fact, I think you should leave Orochi's distraction running, and not cure the lycanthropy."

"Oh, I get it." Atargatis nodded, bobbing in the waves.

"Good." Carnelia felt a flood of relief. Having Typhon's Savvy on their side would make rescue much easier.

"What if I can't learn to jump, Carnelia?" Her voice was pitched low, a little girl afraid of the dark. "What will happen then?"

"Show me where they keep you." Carnelia said, reaching out her hand. "We'll pull you out and carry you if we have to. You won't be trapped here anymore. You will be free to go, and you can stay with people who care about you."

Tentatively, the mermaid reached out and took Carnelia's hand. Her gaze dropped beneath the surface of the water. "I don't know how to work sub-optimally."

Carnelia cursed. If she had been acting as a software analog for many years, it may just be that she couldn't switch off her subroutines. She thought frantically. She didn't want to hurt Atargatis. She'd seen enough hurt today. A thought sparked in her mind and she realized what she could do.

Taking Atargatis' other hand, Carnelia pulled the mermaid in close. Her wide blue eyes blinked in confusion as Carnelia leaned in and gave the mermaid a gentle kiss. Atargatis stiffened in surprise, but then softened and put her arms around Carnelia, holding her tight.

Carnelia slowly broke contact. "Did that stop you from running optimally?"

Atargatis thought about the question. "I think I went offline."

Carnelia laughed. "I'll take that as a yes."

"That was very nice, but you can't stay here with me all the time." Atargatis said pragmatically. "You have to wake up sometime."

"Do you think you can just remember?" Carnelia asked.

Atargatis giggled. "I'll never forget!"

FOUND

On the concrete by their house, Jack balanced on a hoverboard. It rocked back and forth wildly, nearly causing her son to tip onto the ground beneath him. Diane watched from her kitchen window. She didn't want to be a helicopter mom, but watching Jack do something that could get him hurt wasn't something she could help. She wanted to make sure that if he did hurt himself, she could go right to him to take care of the problem.

A large truck drove up to the front of the house. Jack jumped off his hoverboard and ran straight towards the house. He looked like an ordinary twelve-year-old, except that he had just turned eight. The lycanthropy had done something to his body's metabolism, and no amount of testing had shown what or how to reduce the change. Diane saw the three men get out of the truck, and she almost dropped the dish she'd been drying. The man in the middle wore a cowboy hat, a duster and cowboy boots. Her blood turned to ice inside her veins.

She heard Jack slam the door. "Mom! We've got to go!"

She knew they weren't there for Jack. "Okay, baby, you need to go hide like we talked about."

"What about you?" He demanded.

"I can't hide where you hide, you know that. Go now!" She pushed him forward, up the staircase of their home. There was a small access panel that led up to a crawlspace almost too small for Jack to fit into anymore. They'd grown complacent. She prayed that he could hide.

She knew John would be home soon. She knew that she could hide, but all that would do was to put Jack in danger of being found. If she could convince them their job was done, maybe they would leave and John and Jack would be safe.

Hyde stepped into the front door without knocking. "Chimera! It's been so long!"

"Doesn't Emilio have anything better to do?" She couldn't control the hiss in her voice. "It's been what, ten years? Why don't you just let it go? Don't you think I would have said something by now?"

Hyde walked in, looking around the house. He motioned to the other two men, assigning them to either side of the door. "Now, that's cute and all, but you and Cerberus are what we call loose ends... you and your boy, Jack. You've been living on our extended charity because we quite simply had better things to do than worry about y'all. If you went talking about what you'd seen and heard, the media would laugh you out of their offices. Now, however, it's a different story. Emilio is close to achieving his goal, and the loose ends gotta be tied up."

Diane looked around the room for something she could use as a weapon. There were kitchen knives, and she could probably reach for one, but Hyde had a sawed off shotgun he let her glimpse, and she couldn't move faster than he could draw.

"So, what's it going to be?" Hyde asked dramatically. "You going to come back with us quiet-like and agree to work for Emilio as a jumper, or are you going to be a rather unfortunate stain on your kitchen linoleum?"

For a moment Diane was speechless. She hadn't expected an offer to come back and work for Emilio and his ilk. She had never been a thief or a con artist, she was a Savvy who got kidnapped and forcibly experimented on. She remembered her time in the military compound, the only female for miles, constantly afraid of what might befall her. She was not interested in going back to that life. Not that it was a life. Jack couldn't be raised to be a part of this. Doubtless they'd want to put the 'ware in his brain as soon as he was old enough, and he'd never think anything more about it. It would be a day in the office for him.

"I remember you before you decided on the cowboy look." She said calmly. "You were scared, like we all were, terrified of what they were doing and the surgeries they were trying on us and what was going to happen next. You were nice to me, when no one else was. Then one day your number was called, and you went into the C-pod and came out this different person. Your name was Carl."

"We're acquainted." Hyde said, snapping up his sawed off shotgun and pulling the trigger.

Diane staggered back from the blast, which she could feel ripping through her dress and lodging in her body. Pain that clustered like stars in a galaxy spiraled through her body.

"Where's Cerberus?" Hyde asked, casually reloading.

"You're a big, multinational corporation and you can't find a single man?" Diane coughed. She felt blood trickle from the corner of her mouth. "For shame."

"We'll find your husband, just like we found your son." Diane hadn't noticed when the goon had gone upstairs, but she heard her son putting up a fight.

"Jack!" She yelled, her heart breaking. "Run, fight, get away from these men, do what you have to honey!"

"That's enough." Hyde kicked her leg, but it was more of a cuff than a kick.

Jack came into view, trying to free his arm from Hyde's goon. When he saw her, he screamed. "Mom!"

She didn't mean to do it. She just couldn't let him die. He was too young to know what to do. She felt herself slip free of her body. No, she couldn't. Couldn't take him over. He had to live his own life.

Diane could see the spot where the conscious and the subconscious joined, and she dove into the subconscious level of Jack's mind. She could feel Jack kick the goon, feel him running. She wanted to shut her eyes but they weren't her eyes, and the visions she could see were dimming. Somehow he was out the front door and running, they had clear shots but they weren't taking them.

They had to take Jack alive.

Honey, can you hear me? Diane asked.

No response came back to her, for he was focused on finding a place to hide.

She couldn't see. She could hear his breath, coming quickly, and his heart beat fast as he ran for his life.

Jack, find your father. I love you.

A feeling of numbness overtook her, as input from her son's mind grew more tenuous, and less cohesive. She was in his subconscious mind. This was the place of dreams, the place of stray thoughts. She felt incredible sadness well up as she realized there was no one to jump to, and her thoughts were fading out. Would she live here? Or would she be absorbed by her son's psyche?

I'll always be with you, Jack.

SCALE MODEL

Orochi sat hunched over his coffee mug when Nathan emerged from the hotel room's water closet. He sat on the bed, which was too short, but so was every other piece of furniture.

Nathan snorted. "Oh, my, I haven't seen you brood like that since Parris."

"My dreams are getting stranger." Orochi said.

Nathan grabbed a mug and poured some coffee for himself. "Have you tried the recorder?"

Orochi looked thoughtfully out the window, at the people and the buildings jutting up behind them. "Yeah, but it doesn't record anything viable. I am remembering more though. It's like I'm hearing echoes of my mom's psyche."

Sitting down next to his friend, Nathan blew on his coffee. "Echoes?"

"Must be." Orochi said. "It was like I was there, watching what happened, but I couldn't talk and I couldn't interact. Last night I dreamed about her murder. I never knew what happened because she sent me up to hide, but I knew someone killed her. I never got a good look. Last night, I saw. It was Hyde."

"Ouch. Well, now you know." Nathan said quietly. "Finding him is going to be a task."

"I'm not going to let that distract me. If I see any cowboys on my way to Typhon, I'll shoot them, but I can't let that distract me from saving Carn." Orochi took a sip of his coffee.

Nathan looked relieved. "Did you learn anything else?"

Orochi smiled. "I got a name."

"A name?" Nathan scooted forward. "Whose name?"

"Emilio." Orochi said triumphantly. "I looked it up in the Orochi Group files Mom left for me. Emilio Sanchez is listed, but it was buried pretty deep."

"Who is he?" Nathan asked.

"His family is notorious for being a part of La Eme. It looks like the family deliberately shielded him from the life, and sent him to school to be a lawyer to take care of family troubles. He also had a gift for money, and soon was investing not only his wealth, but the ill-gotten gains of the rest of his family. He built up a portfolio that was as clean as filtered water, and then he started investing in psychological experiments." Orochi said.

"That doesn't seem very investment savvy." Nathan noted.

"No, not compared to what he had been doing. Anyway, I can follow his money, but it's a shell game. He has multiple accounts, multiple businesses, accounts in names other than his, the whole works. I do have money that puts him at Typhon, and I do have money that puts him in Las Vegas, back in the Ex-States." Orochi said. "I've only just gotten started."

"Stretch goal?" Nathan asked.

"Entirely new project." Orochi corrected. "He's on my list, but I can't go worrying about it until I'm sure Carn is out of his grasp."

"Speaking of that, how's this project going?" Nathan eyed Orochi's workspace.

The little model was pieced together with scotch tape and hope. The central area was a basketball, with sections taped to the bottom to give it stability, and a tower up the side. Different colored lines were drawn on the cardboard, indicating believed power, water, sewer, and fiber optic cable that entered the building.

"They use way more energy a month than a big hollow building might generally need." Nathan confirmed from his visor. "The amount of water they use is more consistent with a tenant building rather than a business office. Data's off the chart too but that's consistent with what we've seen."

"They house the clones there." Orochi said thoughtfully.

Nathan paled. "What are we going to do about them?"

"We may not be able to do anything about them." Orochi said. "We don't know what their wake-up routines are, and I'm sure those are on strict lockdown. If it's a complicated system, or it needs some of that data that we're going to be stopping, or who knows... the water... I'm not saying let's shoot them all in the head, but I think we should just crack Typhon open and let the local authorities deal with the clones."

Nathan gave him a hard look. "Leave the clones in the hands of Panasia, an entity known both for its hard limits on procreation and its policies on no angel rescue?

They'll cut the power and say, 'Too bad none of them could survive on their own.'"

Orochi threw up his hands. "What do you want from me, Nathan? We don't know how many clones there are. Would you like me to give them all piggy-back rides to safety, while we're getting shot at, and trying to find Carnelia? What if taking them out of their tanks prematurely killed them? What if they got shot because the bad guys were trying to kill me? What if we only had three people going inside to cover that enormous property?"

"It'd be nice if you gave it some thought instead of just dismissing it out of hand." Nathan grumbled.

"I have!" Orochi gripped the back of a chair, his knuckles turning white under the pressure. "I've ran logistics on every way to rescue an unknown number of clones plus Carnelia, and it just can't be done. If we had more manpower, sure. If we had more Savvy, maybe. But with a crew of three people, we can't aim for stretch goals. We have to do what we came to do and gtfo."

Nathan frowned. "I just can't believe..."

Lifting his hands, and clenching and unclenching them to regain blood flow, Orochi shook his head. "If you can come up with a master plan that will save all the innocents while still making room for Carnelia's rescue and our getaway, by all means."

"We could talk to Atargatis." Nathan said hopefully.

"Atargatis runs their security system." Orochi said.

"She has access to everything. She'd know how the wake-up procedures worked, and what we could plan for." Nathan's blue eyes glittered. "It's a place to start."

"She'd know what our plans were. You're putting a lot of trust in the hands of the 'ware that wants to keep us out." Orochi cautioned.

"You said she's a human operator. What if she's trapped? What if we include her in our rescue?" Nathan suggested.

"What if she's acting coy because she wants to draw us in and find out everything about our plans before handing us over to the leaders?" Orochi asked flatly. "I already offered to rescue her, but then I deployed lycanthropy into her alt-real so I doubt she is inclined to listen to anything I have to say."

"Orochi, I know you're pathologically incapable of something as simple as an apology, but that may be all it takes. 'Sorry, I didn't realize you were human when I dosed you with lycanthropy, hope you weren't too hurt in the fallout.'" Nathan stood up from his perch o the bed, staring at his friend. "'Can I make it up to you?'"

"What if she doesn't want me to?" Orochi asked.

Nathan shrugged. "Then we would know that we tried every avenue that we could, and we'd know for certain if we could rescue the clones are not."

"Do you think we could get them all white armor with black joins?" Orochi asked. "With blaster pistols and the like?"

"Oh, I'm sure that wouldn't be insulting at all." Nathan chuckled.

"Well, it wouldn't be for a while, anyway... until they saw the movie..." Orochi grinned.

"Get in your hole and go talk to the mermaid." Nathan stretched out his hand. "We don't have time for your ego."

Rather than answer, Orochi grabbed his visor and pulled it down over his eyes.

The connection was terrible. Orochi tried to smooth it out but whatever generated the interference was outside his control. He chuckled to himself. The lycanthropy was still impeding parts of the system. This was good to see. Inconvenient, but he knew how to navigate a biovirus. He'd been living with it all his life.

He found himself on a sandy beach. The sky was steel gray and the waves rolling in were dark with white caps. The beach was bare of everything but a fire pit, with the coals still smoldering. The sky had no birds. This told Orochi that the health of the alt-real was suffering. He tried not to look smug.

"You're late!" Atargatis rose out of the water, and folded her arms beneath her shell-covered breasts. "I am to leave this and you are taking your own time."

Orochi blinked. "What?"

"You are to rescue, are you not? That is why you continue to visit this place." Atargatis demanded.

"Well... I wasn't sure if you wanted to be rescued." Orochi said dully.

"Why would I not want to be rescued? However, it will be difficult, my body is..." She paused, looking for a word. "fully integrated."

"Fully integrated into what?" Orochi asked, afraid to know.

"The system, of course." Atargatis dove under the water and resurfaced. "I am installed."

Orochi tried to visualize what a full installation meant, and decided he'd better just ask. "Would it kill you to uninstall you?"

Atargatis shrugged. "Possibly. It is all right though. Carnelia is going to teach me body jumping."

Orochi frowned. "I thought her body jumping magic required technology."

Atargatis laughed, liquid delight bubbling up from her middle. "The tech is not important. Waking up the body is what is important. It will be difficult to sneak away in a new clone."

"About that." Orochi said, holding up a hand. "How many clones are there?"

"Two hundred and fifty six." She said. "Sixty four are active, the rest are in hibernation."

"How long does it take to activate a clone?" He asked.

"A week." She said. "They start at zero and have to do a lot of catching up."

Shit. "How long does it take for them to be mobile? Where they could be moved safely?" Orochi asked.

"It takes twelve hours for them to be off of the life support systems." Atargatis tilted her head, obviously wondering what Orochi was thinking.

"Can you activate them without being noticed?" Orochi asked.

Atargatis looked up at the clouds, thinking. "There are panel lights."

"Can you somehow dampen or leave the panel lights off while still running the systems necessary to wake them up?" Orochi asked.

"Possibly. I have had a lot of difficulty since the lycanthropy virus." She gave Orochi a dirty look.

"You haven't been able to flush it out?" Orochi asked, surprised.

"Carnelia thought that it was to facilitate our escape and asked me not to defeat it." Atargatis looked at the sand. "I am perfectly capable of ending your virus on my own."

Orochi fought a grin for such a confident Savvy. "It helps us with our plan, but if you need to end it to activate the clones, do so."

"Do you want me to start up their activation?" Atargatis asked.

"No, I think we need more than twelve hours. I'm going to need more people." Orochi wondered briefly how he was going to pull this off. "I will tell you when to start the activation."

"More than twelve hours of lycanthropy in the system? Kaito is going to realize something is wrong." Atargatis warned.

"Hmmmm. You're right. Let's make use of it. Tell me, does he have any important documents or archived information that is very valuable to him?" Orochi asked.

"Yes." Atargatis said.

"Let's target it with the lycanthropy. They already know it's floating in the system, let's say you just can't get a hold on it, and then target his stash." Orochi grinned.

Atargatis looked solemn. "Is it the only way?"

"You may have some lingering feelings of loyalty, but trust me, you're better off with me and Carn and Nathan. You're not a device, you're a person, and we know that." Orochi said, giving her a warm smile.

Atargatis planted her fists on her scaled hips. "You are not the first people to say these things! You are not the only ones who promised to take Atargatis. I am forgettable! I am convenient! And you will throw me in the trash, and I will be hurt by Kaito for my deeds."

"Did Carnelia tell you where she was from before she came here?" Orochi asked.

"No..." Atargatis paused.

"Let me show you." Orochi summoned a globe. "She started here."

A red 'x' hovered over Seattle.

"You're over here." Another red 'x' appeared, this time over Tokyo. "Do you know what the world is like outside of a greendome?"

"No." Atargatis shook her head.

"Allow me to show you." Focusing, he boosted the wind in the alt-real, making the water choppy and white. Storms rolled in across the sky, with lightning shooting between cloud banks.

"Stop!" Atargatis threw out her hands, and suddenly the lagoon was transformed into a crystal clear inlet with skies of blue.

"I was just getting started." Orochi said calmly. "We hadn't even reached the height of it."

"So what, that it is stormy?" Atargatis asked, folding her arms across her chest.

"I took a plane and flew forty thousand feet above the ground in those weather conditions to save Carnelia." Orochi explained. "I risked my life and my best friend's life to come here. What I'm saying is, when I say I'm your friend, I will go to lengths to prove it. I'm sure others have tried to manipulate you but that's where this is different. I'm not manipulating you. I'm asking for your help."

She frowned. "You're saving Carnelia and me."

"Is there anyone else that needs saving?" Orochi asked, hating himself for opening that particular door.

"You are saving the clones, yes? I thought that was what you asked earlier." Atargatis said.

"If we can save them we will. I'm still getting a handle on if we can." Orochi said.

To his relief, Atargatis nodded. "It will be tricky to save them all. You will need much help."

"Know any good Savvy?" Orochi asked.

"One that is not you." Atargatis swam in a little circle, ducking under the water and pushing her hair from her eyes when she surfaced.

"What's their name?" Orochi asked. He hoped it was no one he'd ever heard of.

"Pixru." Atargatis said, smiling. "She's been very anxious to discover what you are doing here."

BROTHER DEAREST

They brought her dinner, which distracted from Carnelia going back and looking for Atargatis. For a jail cell, Carnelia had to admit that it was a nice one. She even had food and booze. In her last cell she had to put up with Lizbet coming into her room and stealing her things. She even had company if she could figure out how she kept making contact with Atargatis.

What was it that Atargatis had been trying to tell her? Psy what? The only word Carnelia could think of was psychic, but that didn't make any sense. No one was psychic. Sure, Carn could do weird shit that was off the grid, but that was because of the tech in her brain, right?

She walked back over to the bed, flopping sullenly. She closed her eyes.

At first, it felt like she was floating off the bed. She put her hands out to be sure, but everything felt normal, right down to the sheets. She closed her eyes again, and tried to reach out with her mind. After all, what did she have to lose?

The room was a swirl of lights, some dim, some bright. Uncertain of what she was seeing, she headed towards the brightest light in the entire building. There, she found a woman sleeping in a glass coffin. It was definitely a woman from the waist up, encased in breathing apparatus. From the waist down, there was little but stumps where legs had been amputated.

Fearing the worst, that this woman's amputation was to keep her installed, Carnelia felt angry. There were ways to resolve body issues such as hers. And in a clone bank, one should be able to do so easily. Why would they leave her this way?

Carnelia wanted to burn the building to the ground. She'd rescue Atargatis first, but this place was going down like Parris's had.

About to take action, Carnelia heard a knock on her jail door, and she snapped awake. She was just about to give someone a piece of her mind.

Anyone but Mikeru.

"I imagine you're getting bored." He said, looking around the room. "Would you like company?"

"I thought you hated me." Carnelia sat up.

"I thought I hated you too." Mikeru stepped inside. The door slid closed with a soft click. He walked in and sat down, as though invited.

"Care to explain?" She asked, wondering if she could trust him.

"I've been alive for five years." Mikeru said. "They woke me up and put me to work. I knew my original was running around, but he was running around in Seattle, so it's not like we'd bump into each other."

"Was there a me running around?" Carnelia was pretty sure she knew the answer.

"There were some Charlotte Hargroves active since I've been activated." Mikeru said. "I never saw them."

"Multiple..." Carnelia couldn't finish the thought.

"I'd hear about them being defrosted." Mikeru shrugged. "They were strong-willed, like you."

"What were they..."

"I don't know!" Mikeru erupted to his feet. "It wasn't good, but I wasn't told. The one time I asked, they threatened to kill me. I knew better than to ask again."

Carnelia held her flight instinct in check. He hadn't advanced on her. She watched him closely, looking out for any further temper flares. "I've worked for men like that."

"You work for men like that." Mikeru corrected, rubbing a bruise forming on his temple.

"You got brought up that way." Carnelia pointed out. "They're all you've ever known. I worked for a completely different outfit. You may not know this, but I brought that outfit to the ground."

"Not alone." Mikeru pointed out. "You were with them until Orochi showed up."

"You've heard of him." Carnelia smiled. "How much did they tell you about me?"

"Everything." Mikeru said. "I'm supposed to befriend you. They wanted me to know as much as there was to know."

"So, how am I to trust you when you go and tell me that this is in a ploy to get me to trust you?" Carnelia asked.

"I don't expect you to trust me. I just... I'm just a thief, I've never been a con artist. I don't make people trust me for a living. That's what you do." Mikeru rubbed his hands slowly back and forth, looking around the room.

"I've changed." Carnelia said, and realized she'd meant it. "I used to be okay with incarceration and right impingement and doing what I'm told. I had a big reset on my life, and I don't blindly obey the rules anymore. They are going to kill me for that, but that's not going to change who I am."

Mikeru's eyes widened at her bravado. "You are some kind of crazy."

"You're right about that." Carnelia assured him.

"They're going to order you on another job, and if you don't do as you're told they are going to kill you." Mikeru said, urgency coloring his tone. He sounded so much like Michael that she ached for her fallen brother.

"Then I hope they don't have another job lined up for me very soon." Carnelia said.

"You know, when they had those other yous awake, I always... I wished that we were brother and sister. There are a few families here together, but none of them are awake. Just floating together, one big happy family." Mikeru looked away, ashamed.

"That is the only way for a family to be happy and together forever. In cold storage." Carnelia said bitterly.

"No." He shook his head in denial. "I believe that you can have a happy family. I do!"

In that moment, she believed him. "Can I tell you a secret?"

He looked up.

"I didn't tell anyone... because it's rather awkward. The body I was living in, before I jumped into this mess... well... this didn't happen with me in the body but she's pregnant with my brother's kid. Now Michael's dead, and

Pixru isn't conscious. She's in a prolonged coma and we're not sure if she can wake up." Carnelia said. "It shouldn't be like that. She should have woken up after I left. I don't know what's causing her to be stuck..."

"Why are you telling me this?" Mikeru asked her, voice trembling.

"Because there's a little person outside of this messed up world who needs you, and is floating in cold storage, waiting to be a happy family." Carnelia explained.

"No, I mean... if you know you're going to die in here, and leave me alone, why would you tell me about a baby I have no chance of finding?" Mikeru looked miserable.

"To give you hope of something better than this." Carnelia spread her hands to include all of Typhon.

"So that it can be taken away when you die?" Mikeru paced along the floor. His hands shook.

"You'd better make sure that doesn't happen then, right?" Carnelia asked. "You're invested in this now."

He rounded on her. "You'd better do what they ask you to do tomorrow, or I'll be the one pulling the trigger myself."

She watched him storm out of the room, a dark expression on his face. So far, for having no plan, she was shaping something up. She lay down so she could continue talking to Atargatis.

The beach was warm and welcome, and Atargatis showed up quickly. "That was fast."

"Mikeru visited me. I have a few questions for you, but I also wanted to ask you to delete any recorded audio from that conversation. I wasn't thinking about being

recorded when I talked to Mikeru... sloppy of me."
Carnelia said.

"It is done." Atargatis grinned. "That was an easy
task. What are your questions?"

"I want to know more about the file for Charlotte
Hargrove." Carnelia remembered the four empty glass
coffins that surrounded her when she came to in her
body. "I want to know when they were activated, and
why, and how many."

"Those files are confidential." Atargatis said, putting
her hand in front of her mouth. "I need to deconstruct
some security before they may be opened."

Carnelia waited impatiently for her friend to crack
the file.

"First instance of active in the year 2286. Second
activation 2287. Third activation 2287. Fourth and last
activation, 2289." Atargatis read for her friend. "It
appears as though there were a set of trials. They are
odd trials. They do not involve any technology being
installed."

"What were they?" Carnelia asked.

Atargatis blinked. "This is what I tried to tell you,
that you are a psychic. They are psychic trials."

Sudden pain ripped at Carnelia's core, and she
screamed as Atargatis dissolved in a swirl of emerald
and gold.

HAT TRICK

Orochi thought he may have apologized to Nathan at least six times before jacking in and looking for Pixru on the Web. He knew it shouldn't be possible, but he wasn't sure he got to determine what was possible anymore.

He was in a chat, which was a simple interface. He always imagined the voice of the person he was speaking with, even though he couldn't hear them. Chats weren't popular with many people, who preferred alt-reals. He thought about Pixru having her own alt-real to manipulate. That was terrifying. He decided to initiate contact with her in this format and be glad that things weren't more complicated.

"Good morning, Princess." Orochi greeted her genially.

"Just like you to try to decrease my stature online." Pixru sounded tetchy. "I'm not a princess, I'm a Savvy."

"Oooh, someone woke up on the wrong side of the M-pod." Orochi teased. "Shouldn't you just be glad that you're awake?"

"Not finding the state my body is in." Pixru snapped.

"Oh, come on, Carn has taken care of your body. She couldn't have put on more than a couple extra pounds." Orochi said.

"Oh, she put on extra pounds all right. Because I'm pregnant!" She hissed angrily.

Orochi blinked behind his visor. So much for uncomplicated. "Oh."

Silence was her only reply.

Orochi rallied. "That can't possibly be her fault. We've been in intensive training and she only had Rascati or I to choose from, and Rascati's barely half a step up from a robot. It certainly wasn't me..."

"I know it wasn't her, but that doesn't mean it couldn't have been you." She said pointedly.

Orochi fell silent at that. Memories of his brief affair with Pixru flashed behind his eyes, and he could feel himself flushing scarlet. "But... we... careful..."

"Don't be so concerned, I'm reasonably sure it was Michael." Her cold demeanor leached out any sympathy from her assurance.

Biting back a caustic, "That's a relief," Orochi felt waves of emotion pass through him. The fear of a near miss. The huge wave of what-if scenarios. Mostly he was angry, angry enough to stop talking to her, but right now he needed her more than he needed to start up their private war.

"Cat got your tongue twice? That's a new record." Pixru commented.

"So, why aren't you out there, yelling at Rascati about all of this?" Orochi said, yanking the conversation towards safer territory.

"I can't wake up enough to operate my body. I'm stuck in the Web. I could contact Rascati and tell him what's going on, but he'd have every reason to doubt my credibility. My best hope is to talk to you and convince him." She sounded so reasonable.

Orochi let out a sigh of relief. "I'm not sure what we can do for you if you can't wake up to your own body."

"I'll figure it out." She said. "But I'm taking over my body, whether Carnelia likes it or not."

"Carnelia has her own problems." Orochi said, not wanting to discuss them in too much depth. Pixru didn't like Carnelia and he was certain wearing her skin for a couple of months had made her even less inclined to help her.

"When doesn't she?" Pixru asked. "But at least she's out of my body, which I think is why I'm awake at all. Which is why she cannot come back."

Shit. Orochi hadn't realized that Pixru could wake up. Carnelia had sworn that she couldn't contact Pixru at all. He believed her, but what if leaving had triggered some kind of reawakening in Pixru's psyche? Where was he going to put her when this was all over? Why did everything have to be so complicated?

"It would go a long way if you would help me out with what I'm doing." Orochi suggested, realizing she was waiting for a reply.

"I was wondering when we'd get to this part." Despite the tonelessness of text, Orochi could hear her tone sliding into superiority. "As I am stuck in this twilight state, I could dedicate some time to projects. As long as you worked towards getting the goon squad to wake me up."

"You know what I have to work with." He said.

"You are the one eyed man." She snapped. "Make it happen."

"Your wish," he said, but didn't finish the line. Instead, he outlined what she could do to help.

"How did it go?" Nathan interrupted him as Orochi went back over the conversation with a fine-toothed comb.

"Better than expected, which of course means I screwed something up." Orochi said. "I'll figure out what it was later."

"When it's too late." Nathan muttered.

"She's over a barrel. She can't wake up and..." Orochi trailed off.

"If she can talk to you, what keeps her from talking to Rascati?" Nathan asked as though he hadn't noticed Orochi's pause.

"Nothing. But what makes Rascati open to her story? He's the head of security, how's he going to sell a comatose Savvy wandering the Web because she can't wake up?" Orochi considered his next move. Pixru was going to make things a lot easier for him. If he could overcome the fact that he hated her guts right now...

"Next step, now that we've made that call, we need to pull up stakes." Orochi said, pacing the confines of the hotel room. "We've got to move, so that Typhon doesn't send people on us, and I cannot look at this wallpaper any longer."

"I thought the wallpaper was soothing." Nathan chimed in.

"Things designed to soothe people grate on my nerves." Orochi said. "Let's pack our stuff and find a new hotel. Preferably in a different part of town."

"Lead on, Orochi." Nathan said, already breaking down his gear.

They were set to leave, and Orochi opened the door to find that a cleaning cart blocked their path. Orochi frowned. "Excuse me?"

An older man looked at him, surprised.

"Can you move this? We've got to get..." his last words were bitten off as the old man drew a pistol from under his hotel uniform.

Orochi fell backwards, hearing the roar of the gunshot as he landed. "Shit!"

By the bed, Nathan reached into his gear bag to draw his gun. "We should have listened to this advice yesterday."

"True." Orochi nodded his agreement. He jumped to his feet, then crouched low to stay behind the cleaning cart. "The cart cuts us off but it gives us cover. Let me see if I can kill this little pissant."

Drawing his Zerorez, Orochi stood to his full height and peeked up over the edge of the cart. The little old man grinned as though he'd been expecting that and took another shot. Orochi heard something whiz past his head. Already in a foul mood, it only took a moment to squeeze off a round of his own. The old man was surprisingly fit, and scrambled backwards, towards a hotel room door that was left ajar. Orochi revised his assumption and decided it was the floor's utility room.

"That's got to have summoned some attention." Nathan said, edging behind Orochi.

"Undoubtedly. I want you to grab the edge of the cart and push it towards the right. It should give us some cover down the hall."

"Some cover." Nathan scoffed.

"I pick some cover over no cover any day." Orochi said. "You go first, I'll be right behind you."

Nathan tried to roll the cart. "The wheels are locked."

Orochi slid down the wall and unlocked the wheel mechanisms, keeping an eye out for the geezer. "He's going to start shooting as soon as you move it, so keep to the far right corner as much as you can."

"Thanks." Nathan said with scathing sarcasm, and then started pushing.

A shot rang out, and Orochi popped up to take another shot at the old man. The old man moved with surprising speed. He aimed down the hall as Orochi pulled the trigger, and both of them squeezed off shots.

A bullet hit Orochi just beneath the collarbone.

Orochi slid to the floor, eyes rolling. "That never stops hurting!"

"You hit?" Nathan asked, concern writ across his features.

"He hit the coat, I'll be fine. Let's run now, I think I may have got him too." Orochi didn't chance a glance backwards, but ran for the exit away from the utility room.

"They're going to try to stop us at the front door," Nathan pointed out.

"That's why I'm going first." Orochi said, holstering his Zerorez. "Don't stop, just run."

"Aren't we the good guys here?" Nathan demanded.

"Yes, but we're also the Caucs in Panasia that had the nice cops tell us they were looking for any excuse to cold ship us back to Seattle. I'd rather not meet up with Inspector Shin again."

There was a crowd in the downstairs of the hotel, and they all looked up when they saw Orochi and Nathan exit the stairs. When they saw Orochi, some of them began to applaud.

"Oh my god." Nathan said under his breath. "This isn't happening."

"RUN!" Orochi yelled in English, then in Panasian.

If anything, the crowd applauded harder. Many had their recording devices out, aimed at Orochi and Nathan. Orochi made note of it, but there was no stopping videos that went viral.

When they didn't make a hole, Orochi charged into the crowd, forcing people to give way to his greater bulk. Many of the crowd were younger, students ranging from middle school to college age, and they kept filming, as Orochi pushed people out of his way. "There's a man with a gun chasing me. You need to get away!"

To this end, the man with the gun appeared at the top of the stairs, and took a shot at Orochi.

Pandemonium erupted as the onlookers turned into a churning mess of self-preservation. Orochi saw some kids grab smaller kids to hold in front of them. Others turned to run, tripped over those behind them, and knocked them over or were knocked over, to be trampled by the rest of the crowd.

Orochi seized a crying little girl away from the coward hiding behind her, and ran with her shielded by his body until he got to the door. Then he pushed her towards a huge potted plant, wishing he knew Nipponese for 'hide.' She seemed to understand, or at least to see the opportunity, and ducked behind the plant.

He looked over his shoulder. Nathan was right behind him, waving his gun to clear a path. They headed for the doors, trying to get away from people as quickly as possible.

Nathan looked stricken. "We can't just leave them!"

"Leaving them is the best thing to do." Orochi said, looking grim. "We're the target, he's not going to waste bullets on civilians."

Nathan looked back over his shoulder, his expression unreadable. "Fine."

Orochi's eyes flicked to the potted plant. He couldn't see her, but he was certain she was still there. "I know."

They ran.

Orochi noticed that there were people pointing at them, some bringing their devices up, all of them looking around for movie cameras or the like. Orochi didn't care. He'd seen this before, and as long as the old man didn't start firing into the crowd, they'd be fine. As soon as he found an entrance, they ran down into the subway, losing themselves in the chaos.

BREAKING POINT

Carnelia shuddered awake, and gasped for air. The air smelled stale, with a bite of plastic. Something covered her face. Her eyes were open, but the substance that she saw through was cloudy, and she couldn't make out where she was.

It wasn't a C-pod, although she felt like it could have been. Her fingers hit two flat, long walls. She gasped. It was a glass coffin. They'd reinstalled her into the clone tanks!

She reached up. Her arms floated slowly in the viscous fluid they used. She reached out and found the dimensions of the tank, and pounded on the glass. She made a fist and hit as hard as she could. She gave up after only a few hits. It might as well have been hardened steel.

"Awake then?" Kaito's voice sounded brisk. It was coming from inside her ear. Some internal comm unit they installed during her surgery, no doubt. Nothing she could do about it now. "I'm so glad. I have something special ready for you, something you need to see."

She couldn't answer with the air mask covering her face, but she knew he wouldn't care what she said anyway. She wondered how he was going to 'show' her, and tried not to range too far afield of what this man was capable of.

"You may have noticed that you were surrounded by empty tanks when you woke up. At the time I'm sure it was not important, but it may be of more importance to know that you are not the first version of you that was up and walking. We made five Charlotte Hargroves - one for your mother's request, and four because of an order from the founder of Typhon Inc." Kaito's voice felt intimately close, and Carnelia squirmed to get away.

Her mind latched on to the question. *Who was the founder of Typhon?*

"Do you want to know what happened to them?" Kaito's voice purred in her ear, interrupting her thoughts. "It's a very interesting story."

"Fuck off, Kaito." She snapped, the noises muffled by the breathing apparatus, unable to help herself. She probed the corners of the glass, trying to find a weak spot in the join for her to manipulate.

"Oh, you say that now, but wait until you see what I have to show you." Kaito said, his voice drifting away.

Without warning, she was standing. She stood in a room, naked, shivering, the room full of an array of medical equipment. An M-pod dominated one corner. She blinked, trying to figure out how she'd gotten here. She looked down. Her body looked right, smooth dark skin with a golden undertone, hands shaped the way she knew. Her knees were knobbier, and she hadn't filled out fully yet. She'd estimate this body as a young teen, with small budding breasts that she struggled not to cover.

She hated the embarrassment and vulnerability of being naked but she knew they were using it to psychologically weaken her.

"Charlotte, come here." A brusque male voice demanded. Without willing it, she turned in the direction of the voice, and she could see a doctor in a white coat and glasses. He looked blase about having a naked pubescent female in the room. "We are going to start with pain transference. Have we tried this one before?"

Carnelia willed this young body to say, "Fuck you," but she just stammered a tremulous no instead. Dread creeped up Carnelia's spine as the penny dropped. She was going to experience what this girl experienced, and she knew for a fact that none of the girls survived much more than a year apiece. She tried to block it out, tried to separate her personality from Charlotte's... but she couldn't. Something had her stuck here, and it wasn't anything she'd ever encountered before.

Charlotte stepped into the M-pod and climbed inside but the doctor didn't lower the lid. Instead, he brought out several implements that made Carnelia's stomach feel queasy. Needles, pliers, a scalpel, a spirit lamp. Long curved metal pieces that could be heated up by the spirit lamp and pressed against her flesh. Carnelia tried not to think about what was coming next.

"The subject is in another room, close by." The doctor explained as he drew his hand over the tools of his trade. "They do not know what I am using, or where. Your job is to project the pain so that you do not feel it yourself, only the subject should feel it."

Charlotte nodded. Inside her head, Carnelia screamed to be let out.

The first incision didn't hurt as much as she expected, but as the scalpel traced down her flesh pain flared.

"Focus on sending the pain away," The doctor said, instructions bland as milk.

Carnelia could feel the girl focusing. *Stop, you're doing what they want, you can't give in they never stop...*

Charlotte concentrated.

The doctor straightened as though he were receiving a comm. "It's not working. We'll have to try something else..."

Each new element hurt worse than the last. Charlotte whimpered. Carnelia swore. The doctor lit the spirit lamp and heated a metal-tipped probe until it turned red. Carnelia tried to grab a hold of one of Charlotte's arms, to make it knock his tools away from her, but it was impossible. This wasn't some psychic impression.

This was a memory, and Carnelia was reliving it.

The probe burned and Charlotte screamed, Carnelia along with her. The pain was everything, and Carnelia felt Charlotte's resolve shatter like glass as she howled in pain.

The doctor slapped her. "Concentrate!"

Charlotte looked at him, and Carnelia could feel it. Something moved behind the child's eyes, and she glared daggers at the doctor.

Suddenly the doctor began screaming, fell down clutching at his leg. Charlotte sat up as well as she could in the M-pod, staring hatred at him. The doctor pulled his pant leg up and to Carnelia's surprise, blood leaked from thin incisions and a burn mark showed livid red against his skin. He stood up, strode across the room and

240

slapped Charlotte hard enough to rattle her teeth. "That was *not* what you were told to do!"

The pain was gone, and she was back in her glass coffin, fuming at the memory.

"I like to think of this as a morality play." Kaito said as the vision faded around her. "The moral being, if you don't do what you're told, you will relive scenes that happened to your previous incarnations. There were four of them, if you didn't know. Each of them had to go through their own trials. All four of them are dead. I can kill you four different ways before I even get to killing you. I can't help but think that you didn't know who you were fucking with when you tried to make a stand. So, here I give you a little taste of what goes on here. I have plenty more where that came from, but you're a smart girl. I don't think you need more to know what you're looking forward to. Unless you do, in which case I am happy to oblige."

"What do you want, Kaito?" Carnelia asked, her words tinny in her ears. She wasn't sure he'd understand her.

Apparently he could hear her. "You are only with us for a short while, and then you're being transferred. During the time that I have you, I need you to do one more jump. This time, you are going to complete this job successfully, or I am going to show you all four of the girl's deaths, on a loop, until you leave here."

He can't kill me. Carnelia realized. Something about that knowledge made her feel a little braver, but she didn't want him to catch on. "What is it?"

"You're going to jump back into Muneo Nakamura, and you are going to facilitate her suicide." Kaito responded.

"The vote is over, Kaito. Why don't you just leave her alone?" Carnelia forced herself not to panic. He didn't know about Atargatis; she could still get out.

"She's not going to stop harping on Typhon, and I want to make an example of her." Kaito said. "Would you care to question me further or shall I turn on the loop?"

"No, not that." She looked around her sarcophagus, and at the dimly viewable world outside. "Are you going to leave me in here?"

"I should." Kaito's tone was dark. "You don't need your body for anything else right now, and I can monitor everything from where you are."

Shit. "I don't know if I can jump, this isn't a C-pod."

"If I get one speck of resistance from you on this job, it will be your permanent address. Am I clear?" There was an audible click of disconnection.

The fluid began to drain, like a bathtub. She descended, feeling contact with the cool, hard glass beneath her. The fluid felt thick on her skin, and she moved to take the breathing apparatus off of her face as techs cracked open the top to fish her out.

AUGMENTS

"What if he wasn't working alone?" Nathan asked, still breathing hard from their run. The subway was full of travelers, who all had the collective sense to ignore the Caucs riding the subway with them.

"I think we should just operate with that assumption." Orochi said. "It's more paranoid that way."

"Who did he work for?" Nathan asked, sitting down on the subway seat.

"I'm going to call Emi and find out. Keep a watch out for me, in case anybody draws weapons down here." Orochi closed his eyes and called Emi.

"Emi." She said, clear and direct.

"There was a shooting at the Shiodome." Orochi informed her.

"That was you?" Emi sounded surprised.

"Oh, it's almost always me. We got away before the chijo no ashi arrived, but they're no doubt going to ID us and start hunting us down." Orochi sighed. "We're going to have to move faster than we thought."

"Who was shooting at you?" Emi asked.

"Old guy. We'd never seen him before." Orochi said. "He could have been working for anybody."

Emi sighed. "Hyde got away. It might have been him."

"I'm sorry, what did you say?" Orochi felt a twitch start at the back of his jaw.

"Apparently his ability to jump does not require being in line of sight of a person, as opposed to what our intelligence told us. He stole a man but I didn't realize he'd made the switch until it was too late. Somewhere out there Hyde is at large and has an unlimited number of people he could take over." Emi sounded upset.

"Never be too paranoid where these guys are concerned." Orochi said. "Carn could jump into me without her support tech. We don't know what else they can do. They may not even know what they can do."

"We're ready to assault on them, right?" Emi asked.

"We're going to have to. The trouble is, we only have you, me, and Nathan. Except... how many people do you have on your team? I thought you were a solo."

"I have two people to call on. Kasshoku is all in, and I don't think it would be hard to get Sumisu to come with us. It's a small strike team, but if we're just going in to rescue Carn and blow the place up, it should be plenty."

"We have another girl to rescue." Orochi said. "Look, this is getting insane. Is there a place we can meet?"

"Where are you?" Emi asked.

"I'm just passing Shin-Ukachimachi." He said.

"Subway?" She asked.

"Currently." Orochi responded.

"Get off at Ryogoku. I'll be there to meet you." Emi said, and the link disconnected.

Orochi's eyes opened. He saw Nathan's eyes scanning back and forth, reading. He looked up when Orochi moved. "What do we have?"

"A cowboy on the loose and local help on the way." Orochi said.

"I'm sorry, I thought that detail was tied up." Nathan said, looking a little bit green.

"Apparently he's a Houdini. Let that keep you up at night." Orochi said. "Meanwhile we've got some help, and it looks like our timeline has been bumped up significantly."

"Good." Nathan said. "I can't actually believe that I'm saying this, but I can't wait for the flight home."

"That reminds me, I need to send a note to McCune. See if he's still in the area." Orochi sent it off with a thought.

When they arrived at the Ryogoku station, they saw Emi flanked by two men. The three of them stood out; dressed in black leather, they looked more like they belonged with Orochi than the rest of the people walking around the station. Children in school uniforms pointed and giggled behind their hands. When they met up, Emi said nothing, but they all followed her into a large van and climbed inside.

"We can talk here, and we're on our way somewhere safe." Emi explained.

"That Hyde doesn't know about?" Nathan asked.

Emi shot him a look. "He left behind his hat. We took it apart and found that it had serious bulletproofing, but nothing else of note."

"What about the man Hyde left behind?" Orochi asked. "How's he faring?"

"He's..." Emi searched for the words. "He can't talk. He doesn't understand us. We can get him to eat, and to drink, but that's about it. He's picking things up quickly, but he doesn't have it to start with."

"That sounds like a clone." Orochi assessed.

"Before we get into that," Emi interrupted, "This is Sumisu and Kasshoku. They're part of my team."

Orochi nodded in acknowledgment. "Emi, what's your connection to your country's government?"

"Officially we don't exist. Unofficially we have some say." Emi sighed. "Not enough to do anything."

"Oh, you say that, but you'd be amazed what you can do with a tall nut with a gun running interference. The reason I ask is there are about two hundred clones in storage in Typhon. I've got a way to wake them in twelve hours, once I give the word."

"Are you crazy?" Emi asked abruptly. "I've been ordered to demolish the place once you get Carnelia out. And didn't you say you had another girl to save? There's no way we could rescue two hundred additional people!"

"You're asking about the systems operator." Orochi said smoothly over her objections. "She'll be helping us from the inside, on the condition that we don't leave her behind."

She pursed her lips. "One person we can manage. Two hundred plus is quite another matter."

"Give it time, the idea will grow on you." Orochi looked around the van. "So, what were you thinking about our advance on the enemy?"

Emi straightened her shoulders. "All three of us are augments. We could slip in at night, set the charges, find the needles in the haystack, grab them and blow the place behind us."

Nathan frowned. "And leave all the people *in potentia* to die in a fire."

Sumisu looked back and turned around to watch traffic. "They should not exist."

"They do exist." Nathan fired back. "You can't kill someone because they weren't intentional, that'd be half the planet's population."

"We'd be better off with half of the people dying off and leaving resources for the rest of us." Sumisu said sourly.

"We can't do this. Trying to rescue a group that large would ensure our failure for our objectives. They aren't functional people, they're *in potentia* as you said, and we wouldn't have the time to get them to safety before..." Emi trailed off.

"You're awfully keen on the idea of blowing up the building." Nathan observed. "Usually arsons and demolitions experts are more intent on widespread destruction, and you seem a little tightly wound to me."

Emi sighed. "They would keep using clones illegally. They'd keep making clones illegally. They would have the resources to shore themselves up when a politician they couldn't buy off came calling. I'm under direct orders that this place will be blown up. I can't do anything about them."

Nathan threw his head back. "Soldiers! You're all alike, hiding behind orders rather than do the right thing."

"Nathan." Orochi said patiently. "Could you explain to us a way to get the clones out?"

"Of course!" Nathan said. "Have Atargatis activate them, and walk them out to some waiting emergency vehicles, and then the hospitals can rehabilitate them."

"Who would educate them? How would they live in a world where they were mentally newborn in twenty year old bodies? Who would pay for their care?" Orochi asked. "What if their donors are still around? What if there were suddenly two yous walking around, one of which was you and the other was a total dependent?"

Nathan paused. "That doesn't matter, they are still living beings."

"They are." Orochi agreed. "Human beings who won't have any advocates, who won't have any way to defend themselves, and may have people actively wanting to have them killed."

Nathan frowned. "You flipped on what you told Atargatis awfully..."

"This is why it might be kinder to end things here, where they won't ever be awake." Orochi put his hand on Nathan's shoulder and gave him a significant look.

"It's not right." Nathan said quietly, eyes downcast.

"Then again.." Orochi began. "What if we could use them as a distraction?"

Emi perked up. "A distraction?"

Nathan winced. "Throw them under the bus?"

"A distraction." Orochi repeated. "Think about it. People swarming the clone banks, trying to figure out why they were activated, trying to stop the activation sequence, dealing with people getting up and helping themselves out the door... It would be easy, Atargatis said she could do it with twelve hours' notice."

"Twelve hours' notice?" Emi looked at Sumisu and Kasshoku, who were exchanging looks at each other. "You'd better tell her now, then."

ALLIES

Back in her room, Carnelia took the time to shower the tank solution off of her skin, trying to scrub away the feel of scalpels severing her flesh. Whatever it was Kaito had forced on her, it felt as real as if she had been there herself. She wondered if he had tapes of her memories since she'd gotten here, and if he watched them. He could know about Atargatis. She wished she knew more about the mechanism that made the memory feed work.

Her next step was talking to Atargatis. Carnelia flopped down on her bed and sighed. They needed to be ready to leave at a moment's notice. She had to find out how to teach Atargatis how to body jump, when she didn't know what she was doing herself. She took some calming breaths, and tried to focus on the beach.

The beach resolved quickly for her.

"What are you doing here?" Atargatis asked, swimming up to the shoreline. "Kaito told you to go to Muneo's!"

"Atargatis, I order you to stop prioritizing Kaito's commands." Carnelia said.

"You don't have override access." She frowned, sad. "Thank you though."

"If it helps, I am going to the C-pod, but I didn't have any clothes and I just wasn't going to walk through here naked, I don't care what Kaito thinks about the subject." Carnelia looked out at the ocean. It was crystal blue close up but there were patches of gray clouds in the sky and the water turned murky farther out. "I thought you weren't curing the lycanthropy?"

"Orochi has given me orders." She rose as far out of the water as she could. "He will rescue us."

"When?" Carnelia asked, feeling hope swell in her chest.

"Soon. He is to call me when they are near." Atargatis said. "I will tell you when he contacts me."

"Do you know what their plans are?" Carnelia asked, suddenly wondering if how long she could put off her excursion to murder Muneo.

"I think they are still making them." Atargatis said apologetically.

"I have to find a way to put off my jump. I can't be out when they're here, they'll never get me back together again." Carnelia bit her lip.

"I will tell you." Atargatis said.

"I won't be in my body, that won't work." Carnelia frowned.

"I will wake you." Atargatis said, more forcefully.

Carnelia smiled. "I hope that you can."

"Tell me about the body jump. I must know it so that I can practice." Atargatis said.

"Start by closing your eyes." Carnelia watched as Atargatis closed her eyes, then immediately peeked to watch her. "Let me tell you the steps, then we try it."

"Okay." Atargatis swum closer to the shallows.

"Close your eyes, then take deep breaths, like you're about to go on a dive. Then, after three deep breaths, imagine yourself jumping out of your skin, and into another person. The hard part, of course, is getting your consciousness to follow along with you." Carnelia said.

Atargartis nodded. "I will try this."

"We need to find you someone to jump you into." Carnelia said. "Someone we can find. We can't send you into a clone, they aren't ready to go. We need someone awake, and someone in a C-pod at the moment."

Atargatis' head tilted as she scanned the likely targets. "Dr. Akamatsu."

"Perfect." She thought rapidly. "You're going to be missed if you do this, so make your way to my room and escort me out as quickly as you can. It will be weird, trading this alt-real for a real body, but you won't have time to reflect, just get to me and we can teach you all about your new gift."

Could this work? Carnelia felt a rush of hope.

The mermaid quieted, closing her eyes and folding her hands together in a type of prayer. Carnelia could see her eyes moving under the lids, as though she were dreaming. She floated, sinking into the water until only her head remained floating half in, half out of the ocean. Her frown of concentration was so serious that Carnelia almost laughed, but she knew she couldn't. It would distract her, and it was already hard enough work.

Five minutes passed this way and Atargatis opened her eyes. She looked sorrowful. "I cannot!"

Carnelia schooled the disappointment off of her face. "That was your first try. Don't give up yet. I didn't jump my first try either."

Which wasn't true, she had succeeded her first try, but she'd had the tech and experienced teachers and a frame of reference. Atargatis had a poor teacher, and no context. It was much more difficult under her circumstances.

It's not a psychic gift. It's the tech. Carnelia thought. *But if that's true Atargatis is doomed.*

"Atargatis, let's stop for now. Tell me where you're located so that we can rescue you when the time comes." Carnelia said.

"Look in the water." Atargatis said, her tone alarming Carnelia.

Even as Carnelia looked, the water swirled into a vision of Typhon's racks of stacked glass coffins. Carnelia frowned. She wished there was a way to save them all. Their only crime was their donor's greed and wealth, and desire to continue living. It didn't seem right to punish them for crimes committed by others. Hovering to the side of the stacks was a much larger coffin, about the size of two of any of the others put together. Floating upright in the tank was a...

Carnelia choked. "That's you?"

Atargatis nodded. The being in the floating tank was more wire than girl. She had arms that terminated in stumps before the wrist. She wore the same face mask providing oxygen that any of the other clones did. Her hair floated in pale clouds around her face. She seemed incomplete. Carnelia had seen her before, and it didn't stop it from being horrific. She felt a surge of anger that they would keep her this way, and no small suspicion that they had made her that way on purpose.

"If we wake you, will you live?" Carnelia asked, shock curling at the edges of her awareness.

"I don't know." Atargatis said. "I think I would live a while at least."

"There is better medicine out there. Some way to give you hands and feet. The trick will be you surviving until we get to that kind of medical help." Carnelia turned to her friend. "Could you live out of that machine for an hour or two?"

"At least that long." Atargatis smiled, and it was hard for Carnelia to tell if she was being brave or simply unaware of the risk.

"I should wake up." Carnelia said. "Do what Orochi wants, and let me know when you know the plan. We'll practice on jumping again soon."

"Okay!" Atargatis dove into the water.

Carnelia woke up, and sensed someone was in her room with her.

She spun, looking around, when she saw Mikeru sitting on one of the chairs in the room. "You scared me to death!"

"Sorry." Mikeru said, sounding unapologetic. "In another few minutes I was going to wake you. What are you doing, anyway?"

"Pretending that I'm not here." Carnelia said. "Same as you, only in a different way."

"I don't pretend that I'm not here." Mikeru stiffened.

"You steal shit on behalf of guys who keep people like racks of meat hanging in a meat locker. You know that what they do is the basest level of evil but you don't protest or even stop doing what you're doing. You pretend that you're not involved in this spectacular shit show." She sat up and made eye contact. "Am I wrong?"

"You of all people ought to know what the penalty is for doing what you're not supposed to do. I'm sorry that I'm not volunteering for a life of torture." Mikeru glowered at her.

"Not volunteering for a life of torture is literally the least you can do." Carnelia chided.

"They killed four of you in very messy ways, it will mean nothing of them to do it a fifth time." Mikeru balled his fists.

Carnelia sighed. "I'm sorry, you didn't come here to pick a fight with me. What do you want?"

"I'm not sure that I do, anymore." Mikeru stood up.

"No, don't go. You obviously pulled some strings to get in here, so what do you want to say?" Carnelia walked over to him. She could see the energy thrumming through him, in his stiff hands, his straight back, and his corded neck.

"I want to know more about Pixru." Mikeru sat heavily on the bed. "What kind of woman is she?"

Fighting to keep back a laugh, Carnelia sat down near him. "She's a strong woman, with very traditional views when it comes to the Nipponese. She's a Savvy, the best I've ever heard of. She is financially stable, she is smart, and she is currently in a coma."

Mikeru winced. "Why?"

"The doctors haven't isolated the cause. They may have had some time to since I've been walkabout." Carnelia said.

"You've... been inside her?" Mikeru asked querulously.

"I had to, to survive." Carnelia said, feeling suddenly embarrassed. "She's not responsive, but her body is fully functional."

"And... you kept the baby?" Mikeru asked. "Knowing it was your brother's?"

"It's not like we... you know. The baby was already in residence. I hadn't decided what I should do. I didn't know who to talk to about it. Most people would get hung up on the 'not my kid' or the 'brother's dead' thing and not really hear the part where its my family." Carnelia felt deeply uncomfortable.

"Could you jump... you know, into the baby? Is their brain developed enough?" Mikeru asked.

Carnelia's eyes flew wide. "Oh, no, you can't ever jump into a kid. Maybe an older kid, like thirteen, but I wouldn't risk it. Kid's brains are really elastic and their neurons are developing pathways, and a bodyjumper's thought matrix would dissolve like salt in water."

"Oh." He reached out and put his hand over hers. "In any case, I'm glad you're still stewing on what to do. I think you'll decide what's best."

With that, he got up and started walking towards the exit.

"That's it?" Carnelia asked.

Mikeru looked to the corners of the room. Carnelia knew there were cameras, she just hadn't found them. "No. I'm to escort you to the C-pod so you can perform your next job."

SAVVY GIRLS

On their way back, Orochi closed his eyes and contacted Atargatis.

"You need to hurry up." Atargatis said as she surfaced from the lagoon. "Kaito is hurting her."

Orochi pressed his lips together in a line. "Is he hurting her now?"

"No." She confirmed.

"Is Carnelia all right?" Orochi asked, fearing the answer.

"At present." Atargatis smiled weakly.

Orochi frowned. "Atargatis... Can I call you Gatis?"

She giggled. "I've never had a short name before."

"Gatis, how's the initiation going?" Orochi asked.

"I turned off notifications from main operators. They could see the lights of the equipment as it activates, but they are small and not blinky lights, so they may attract no attention at all." Atargatis said.

"So, there is a chance that it could gain attention." Orochi said.

"Yes, there are operational lights that turn on. However someone would have to be in the clone bank, and know the significance of that particular light. I think maybe three people would be able to notice, if they were in the clone bank."

"Is there a way to close the clone bank so that people won't walk through it while you're activating?" Orochi asked.

"Yes but I think more people would notice than just three." Atargatis pointed out.

"You're our resident expert. If you think you can do it, we'll run with that." Orochi said. "Can you get a message to Carnelia?"

"She's in a C-pod right now, I can't connect with her."

Orochi froze. "She's out on a job?"

"Yes." Atargatis sounded shy.

"Okay, is she still using Kasumi as her base? Who's in the C-pod? I need to know which person to save when I get in Typhon." Orochi's mind whirred on this particular complication.

Atargatis gave him a look. "She is shorter than you, with long black hair, dark eyes, and beautiful skin."

"Can you show me?" Orochi asked.

"I can." She swirled around some lagoon water with her hand, and in a moment Carnelia's face resolved.

Orochi caught his breath. "That's not funny."

"I've been told I do not have a sense of humor. I do, but they do not understand. What do you not understand, Orochi?" Atargatis' head tilted in curiosity.

"That's.. that's Carnelia. Carnelia's dead, that can't be her." Orochi said, trying not to babble.

"That is her!" Atargatis assured him. "Her mother ordered her a clone body a long time ago. There were five made. The first four activated clones are now inoperable."

He signaled her to stop. "I want to come back to this conversation, but I need to know about you now. Where are you and what do you look like?"

"I am ugly." Atargatis said, hiding her face.

"I doubt that." Orochi said sincerely. "We can't save you if we don't know what you look like."

Reluctantly Atargatis swirled the water again, breaking up Carnelia's face. A large glass construction overtook the view, and inside a partially mechanical girl floated, suspended inside.

"How long can you live outside of your life support system?" Orochi asked. He felt his heart break at the thought of this cheerful, bright spirit caged and used by men who most probably did not see her, who ignored her unless they needed something. He hoped her answer was something he could work with.

"A day, perhaps." Atargatis said.

"That's long enough for us to get you out of there and get you set up." Orochi said.

"I'm going to body jump!" Atargatis informed him.

"You know how to body jump?" Orochi asked. He crouched down to get closer to her height.

"Not yet, but Carnelia is teaching me." Atargatis said.

"Well, let's plan on rescuing this body in case you don't learn how in time. Carnelia can still teach you how to jump later." Orochi said.

"Okay, that sounds.." She paused. Her eyes widened. "I must go!"

The alt-real dissolved into motes of gold and blue, and Orochi widened his eyes. "We have to go now!"

"You said it takes twelve hours to wake those clones up." Emi said. "If there's a hope of rescuing them..."

Nathan's head swiveled around to look at Orochi.

"Carnelia's out bodyjumping, and we have to bring her back now. They had clones of her body, and four of them have been killed. Something is going on that is way deeper than what we thought, and if we don't move now, they could kill her too. We can't let that happen, they'll get whatever it is they want from her, and we'll be left with no intel on these guys." He looked over at his friend. "I'm sorry. We tried to do this your way, but we just didn't do it fast enough."

Nathan nodded, but looked away without saying anything.

Sumisu exited the freeway and started driving towards Typhon.

"Do we have everything we need?" Emi asked.

Kasshoku shrugged. "We'd better."

Nathan shifted in his seat and looked out his window, not speaking. Sumisu concentrated on driving. Kasshoku and Emi chatted, but Orochi didn't have the heart for it. He had been so sure they wouldn't hurt her because of her unique abilities. She was a rare commodity, you didn't injure rare commodities. Then again, if Carn had been herself, there was no doubt that she was causing trouble, and no doubt driving people crazy. It was her best and least favorite trait all in one package.

You just need to stay alive a little longer, Carn. Then I can rescue you and get you back to Seattle's greendome, where you belong. He checked his messages, and saw one from McCune. He was ready to leave given half an hour's notice. Orochi knew it'd be longer than that, but he didn't know when he'd be able to message him again. "Be ready to fly at 0300 hours. Extra pay for the lousy hours."

"So, Orochi, what do you know about Typhon?" Emi asked when the conversation petered out. "Let's pool our resources."

"Technologically they are advanced." Orochi said. "Maybe pre-Crisis advanced. When all the toys worked before everyone devolved into tribal feuding. Their sysadmin is a human, rather than an AI, who is locked into the computer by virtue of her dependence on their systems. She says she can live for a day off of the system but I don't want to push that envelope. She's high-pri, because once we uninstall her, she's going to take a lot of that system down with it. It will cause all kinds of havoc, which will only be good for us."

Emi nodded. "Okay, so we have two girls to save. Where are they going to be?"

"Atargatis - Gatis for short - is going to be in the clone banks, which is in the big bubble part of the building. Carnelia could unfortunately be anywhere. The upside is that Nathan and I both know what she looks like, so unless they do some kind of weird switch, she's going to be easily identified." He showed them a picture that he had on file for her. "Her hair's longer and she probably looks a bit beaten up, but that's the general idea."

Nathan choked. "That's not funny, Orochi."

"You're telling me." Orochi said. "Gatis says she's had clones for years. Want to know more? So do I. We have to save the girl to find out."

Nathan leaned back. "Just when shit can't get any weirder…"

"I also have a Savvy who is very good at what she does, and needs to be updated about the change of the situation. She can alert us to how many people are in the system, who is doing what, and can crash the system when we're ready for that. Atargatis is integral to the system, but my Savvy will be able to continue operating after Gatis is uninstalled."

"We'll be there in twenty minutes." Sumisu informed them. "Maybe thirty depending on traffic."

"That should be enough time to contact my Savvy and let her know what we're up to." Orochi said. "See if there's anything we're missing, or if we can still save those clones."

Nathan looked over at him and smiled weakly. "Thanks."

"We are in a shitty situation." Orochi said. "We'll do the best we can, like we always do."

"We should talk about finding Hyde." Emi said. "I mean, how do you detect someone who hops bodies?"

Orochi shrugged. "There isn't a marker or indicator, if that's what you mean. Hyde is… well, his affectations make him unique. I've only seen him without the hat the one time, and that was when he was deliberately hiding from us. He has a specific way of talking, which is also concealable but he's so arrogant that he doesn't try to. They aren't particularly obvious, and the hat one may be off the table for a while, so there are no guarantees. I would just say if you run into a guy wearing a cowboy hat and drawling, you can feel reasonably safe putting a bullet in his heart."

There was a pause in the van as everyone digested the facts. Orochi said, "I'm going to call my contact, don't bother me unless it's urgent."

He paused before he contacted Pixru. He wasn't sure what he wanted to tell her, or what he would find out from her. He'd asked for a fairly long list. She would no doubt berate him for not giving her enough time.

"Pixru." He finally said.

She didn't immediately respond. Given what she was engaged in, that didn't surprise him, although he did worry that she could be hurt or lost. With her body not responsive, for her to get hurt so far distant would probably destroy any hope she had of getting back to one piece.

"Orochi." She startled him.

"Our situation has changed." He began. "Carnelia's in trouble."

Pixru chuckled. "Carnelia was *born* in trouble. I can't tell you how many times I had to listen to Michael complain about her..."

"I can't imagine you complaining about her yourself, with your sweet temperament." Orochi said dryly.

"I miss him so much." Pixru said, ignoring his comment.

"Pixru?" Orochi asked. "Are you having trouble concentrating?"

"No!" Pixru snapped. "I'm perfectly fine."

Orochi gave his chat log a side-eye before continuing. "Okay, let's get down to business then, Miss Business."

Pixru scrolled code before Orochi. "This place is the kind of place that Parris would have loved to know about. They have different people from all over the world who have pledged DNA and dollars to make sure they have a backup health dummy for replacement parts and other major health concerns. Kaito Nuboro isn't the CEO of Typhon, Inc. however. Emilio Sanchez is. I've seen his name on some of Parris's stuff, I think Parris knew him personally."

Orochi gritted his teeth. "I wouldn't doubt that."

"The clones are totally being used against contract, however. They reanimate clones whenever they want and use them to steal things, almost like the bodyjumpers but not quite. They have reinstated a clone when a person wound up dead. This clone took over that person's life, and has been doing things for Typhon ever since. It does take a while for a clone to warm up to temp, but they have some tech specifically to shorten the time frame. A lot of it is based on augment technology." Pixru said, summing up her findings.

"Did you have anything on any of the specific families?" Orochi asked.

"I didn't read about them." Pixru said. "There were hundreds."

Orochi nodded. "Do you have access to it now?"

"Yes." Pixru affirmed.

"Look up Michael and Charlotte Hargrove." Orochi said.

He waited while she read through the files. He heard her gasp as she saw the pictures accompanying the files. "Orochi, what on Earth?"

"I know." Orochi said. "I haven't had time to read over the entire file, but I thought you should know."

"Michael... could be alive..." She sounded short of breath.

"Did you ever learn to bodyjump?" Orochi asked.

"Of course not! I never sullied myself with Parris's jump 'ware, the stuff was disgusting." Orochi imagined Pixru's lip-curled sneer.

"Well, bad news. It's in your head, now, and it may be in your best interest to use it to get your consciousness into one of these clones. Pick one and tell me where it is, because I can't think of another solution that doesn't involve you spending a lot of time stuck comatose." Orochi didn't have time to argue with her, and he knew it.

"Your argument is overblown and manipulative. You don't know what I'm capable of in this state. It may benefit me to stay separated from my body." She sniffed.

"What if Michael is at Typhon, waiting for you to wake up?" Orochi asked.

"It would be his clone, he'd have no idea who I was." Her replies lacked tone, but Orochi thought he could imagine what she'd say in person.

"All right, so the standing plan is for you to go to Typhon and intercept their communication, turning everything black so they can't see us or hear us." Orochi ticked off one finger. "You're going to scramble any outgoing signals to make sure they can't call for backup. You're going to keep us appraised of what is going on inside Central Processing. And you're going to get out when the place goes up, so that we can resuscitate you after we get back to our greendome.

"Orochi." Pixru said.

"What?" He asked.

"Something is going on in there. Was there any way for them to be warned?" Pixru asked.

"Check it out, tell me what's going on." Orochi told her.

He waited for long minutes as she went on reconnaissance. Finally she came back. "Hyde."

"Already? Son of a bitch." Orochi growled.

"I think I scrambled most of the message but the fact that he called in a warning, it isn't going to matter how much got through. Someone will understand." Pixru said.

"I know." He looked at the digital clock. "We're going to be there in six minutes."

"That's six minutes for them to prepare for you." Pixru pointed out.

"Try having Hyde call back and give a false message that everything is all right. Give them false coordinates and have as many people leave as you can." Orochi asked.

"You know I don't work for you." Pixru reminded him.

"I'm trying to wake you up, and you didn't listen to my suggestion about how to wake you up fastest. I'm fully aware that you don't work for me."

"Fine, I'll work up solutions to these problems you keep hanging up on." Pixru snapped.

"If you're good I'll bring Michael back to you." Orochi said, signing off quickly to prevent hearing the earful she was no doubt launching.

COALESCE

Mikeru escorted her to the C-pod room, and then right past it.

"Where are we going?" Carnelia asked nervously.

His dark look told her what she didn't want to know.

They walked out and climbed up onto the tank mezzanine. Carnelia didn't fight. Her fight wasn't with Mikeru, even as she wished that he would stop working for the bad guys without complaint. Her problem was with Kaito and his men. Now she had to last until backup arrived.

She could hear the footsteps of three men coming down the hallway. Carnelia stood and faced the stairs, thrilled that her body no longer tremored at the slightest motion. Guards walked in up the stairs. She didn't know the names of the guards, but she recognized Kaito in his sharp black suit and immaculate hair.

"A personal appearance?" Carnelia put her hands on her chest in a flattered gesture. "I feel so fortunate."

Kaito motioned for the two guards to rest. They were close enough to act if Carnelia attacked Kaito. As if she could.

She said nothing further, and Kaito grew edgy. "You're not going to ask me what I'm doing here?"

"Why would I do that?" Carnelia asked.

"I'm your boss, Carnelia. I say 'jump' and you say, 'how high?' That is how it works, and you have not been doing your job since you started here!" Kaito's face flushed and his lips trembled. "You made an agreement!"

"I quit." Carnelia said.

Quick and vicious, Kaito slapped her. "You can't quit! I own that body lest you forget. Typhon owns you. We are not going to let you walk out that door!"

"You're not going to get any use out of me!" Carnelia felt the rage of her incarceration bubble up from her guts.

With a shaking hand, he gripped his gun, and aimed it between her eyes. His hand was shaking.

Carnelia forced herself to stay steady. He'd told her he wasn't allowed to kill her, but he seemed ready to forget that order.

Kaito dropped the gun, holstered it. "There were two ways to do this. The first way, you would live a life of wealth. The second was much less fortunate. I hope you enjoyed your time in the executive suites, because your next room won't be as nice."

She didn't respond.

"Tell me about Orochi." Kaito said, thumb tracing the lines on the butt of his pistol unconsciously.

"He's tall." Carnelia offered.

Kaito crossed the space between them and slapped her again. "You think you are funny because I can't kill you, but you are wrong. I can make replacements. They may take years, but time is on our side. Also, you seem to have forgotten there are four more clone memory sets. I can make you relive those memories on repeat for days or weeks, as long as I want. And I don't have to stop there. That's just your memory. I can do anything I want to this clone body. Your perfect, unmarred skin doesn't have to remain so in order for you to be functional."

Putting her hand to her lip, she pulled her fingers away, tacky with blood. "What do you want, Kaito?"

"Orochi has sent a virus that Atargatis can't seem to fully remove from the system. I want to know what it is and how to get rid of it."

"I'm not a Savvy, that's why I work with him." She couldn't let him win.

It worked. Kaito struck her again. She reeled from the blow. It hurt, but she'd been through worse. Hell, the clone memories were worse.

Kaito's eyes rolled in anger. "Damn it, tell me what you know!"

"My name is Carnelia Cesnos and I am tired of your penny-ante operation!" She faced Kaito, holding herself ready for a strike.

Kaito called in the guards, and Carnelia grimaced. She knew that this was going to hurt. She hoped Atargatis wasn't watching. The guards stepped forward from their quiet observation. One held her by the arms and the other one came in with a punch to the stomach that drove the breath out of her lungs. She cried out, and it was genuine, but she wasn't ready to give up just yet. He punched her five times in rapid succession, each one at a different point on her torso. She felt tears well up in her eyes. She forced her eyes open and saw an open hand coming towards her, a strike that rattled her teeth. She closed her eyes, the tears rolling down her cheeks.

"Stop!" She brought her head back so that everyone could see her tears. "Please, stop!"

Kaito barked an order in Panasian and the two guards backed off. He walked over to her, grabbing her by the chin and forcing her to look at him.

"Tell me." Kaito said, dropping his hand.

"It's lycanthropy." Carnelia said, voice quiet. "A mutating biovirus. That's why she can't grab it. It's meant to change as soon as it's messed with."

"How do you get rid of it?" Kaito demanded, raising a hand.

She flinched away. "System purge. Total shutdown. You have to shut it down, load it up with antivirus, and then turn it on and wait."

"That's all? No secret password locks?" Kaito asked.

"It mutates all the time. Even if there were a password lock, the password would change with each mutation. It's not supposed to ransack your warehouse, Kaito. It's supposed to beat down your system until it's a quivering mound of jelly." Carnelia sniffled for effect.

Kaito brightened. "Then he has no knowledge of Typhon?"

Carnelia gave him a wry look. "Kaito, I've been locked up here for days now. I haven't been in contact with Orochi this whole time. He didn't know why I didn't come back, but I'm not surprised he's looking for me."

"He'll be hard pressed to break down our walls." Kaito said. "We're an impenetrable fortress."

The pain of Carnelia's beating was starting to sink in now that the adrenaline rush was wearing off.

"Time to go back in the cell." Kaito said.

Carnelia sighed. Memories of the basement of the Glass House came rising up in her mind. She hoped Orochi hurried. There was no going back now.

They were standing on the scaffolding of the coffins. Clones lay in rows, breathing through tubes, fed intravenously. They floated in a somewhat hazy substance that Carnelia remembered as being unpleasantly thick. At their feet, an unoccupied coffin lay open and waiting.

Revulsion rose in Carnelia's throat like bile and she screamed despite herself.

He said something to the guards in Panasian. They nodded as one and moved. On either side of her, each of the guards grabbed a handful of her clothing and then pulled in the opposite direction. The thin clothing she wore had no hope against them, and was ripped away, leaving her standing naked before the bay of clones.

"No!" She shot an agonized look to Mikeru. He looked at her, miserable, and then looked away.

One of the guards pushed her, and she fell knee-deep into the nutrient gel. She moved to jump off the other side, but hands grabbed her neck and shoulders, and they forced her down into the gel. Someone slipped a mask on her.

She growled as she went down, struggling. The hands were off of her, and she looked over. Through the haze she could see the lid coming down. She hit the glass but it a futile gesture. The guards waved at her, and as she looked up she saw Kaito spit. The glob slapped the lid, almost impossible to make out except that she knew that it was there.

Calm down Carnelia, calm down, they can't put you under, you can use your mind... She remembered in that moment that they had been able to stop her from talking to Atargatis. She tried to use her 'ware, and it wouldn't respond. *Shit, they have both locked down, how am I going to let anyone know where I am?*

She thought about how she could get Atargatis' attention. She figured the mermaid had a monitor on every clone, although it probably wasn't something she gave much thought to. What would send a signal? Vibrations probably were out, since the gel absorbed most of the energy. She couldn't access any wires except her breathing tube, which she needed...

Carnelia smiled. They had to have some kind of monitor to check on any tube that got kinked or otherwise didn't supply oxygen. Oxygen was necessary to live, but how long would it take the monitor to detect that there wasn't a flow? It would probably be rather quick, thirty seconds or less. So, she could cut off her own oxygen supply for a short time, and get Atargatis' attention.

What to do with it though, if she couldn't talk to her?

It didn't matter. Atargatis would know where she was amid all the clones, which would go a long way to rescuing her when the time came. She was very sad that she hadn't been able to rescue herself. She would have loved the look on Orochi's face as he came striding forth across the Typhon grounds to be the big damn hero, and her standing there already rescued, looking as well as could be expected having the bully boys let loose on her.

Of course, she'd need his help to free Atargatis, so he wouldn't pout long.

Gripping her oxygen tube, she took a deep breath just in case. She clamped down on the tube. She wasn't entirely sure it was working, but the air flow stopped. She held on for as long as she could before unkinking the hose. The tiny trickle of air flow was delicious, despite its plastic aftertaste. She took another deep breath and kinked the hose again.

Atargatis, please. A thought occurred to her. *Do you know Morse code?*

She kinked the hose in an SOS, hoping that Atargatis might understand and that Kaito's crew wouldn't. She had no way of knowing. No one could signal her back. She had to float and wait.

CAVALRY

As they drove through the winding streets of Tokyo, everyone prepared and made final checks. Orochi had his Zerorez loaded and ready, and he was spending a last few moments updating Atargatis with their ETA. Nathan had his gear out and ready. He was going to stay with the vehicle and defend it. While he was in the car he would also continue to attack Typhon from his station.

Emi, Sumisu and Kasshoku were suited up and ready to go, bristling with weapons. Each had a backpack full of explosive charges. Sumisu and Kasshoku would be taking the outside, and Emi would be mining the inside. She pulled Orochi off to the side once they were out of the van. "I can't leave this place active."

"I know." Orochi said. "I'm not going to stop Nathan from doing everything he can to save them."

"Surely you understand the necessity?" Emi asked.

"I understand the system." Orochi said flatly. "Don't ask me to agree with it because that's never going to happen. I see the expediency in what you're doing. My focus is rescuing two girls. I'm hoping that one of the girls is rescuing the rest of the clones and inconveniencing the shit out of you."

"I'm going to set these charges to ten minutes. It's going to take at least ten to set them before we start the countdown. I suggest you do what you came to do and get out of there." Emi said.

"Just another day at the office." Orochi grinned. "I'm going to link with Gatis, and try to sync it to all of our comms. She'll be our eye in the sky."

"You still can't be sure if she's on your team." Emi said. "I don't think it wise to rely on her."

"Not using a resource when we're so pared down is the worst plan ever." Orochi shot back.

"Fine." Emi waved her hand. "I'm going."

They spread out, and Orochi contacted Atargatis. "We're here. I need a way in."

"Hurry quick, they put Carnelia in a clone tank and I don't think she can get out!" Atargatis prodded. She told him which entrance to take. Emi followed.

The door was an entrance for shipping and receiving. There were no trucks for cover, but the setup of the docking bay was a long, slender throat that had a lip that Emi could hide behind. Orochi on the other hand couldn't duck down that far. He did his best to keep a low profile. The door's light switched to green and Orochi grabbed it open, holding it for Emi as they entered the building.

"I'm sticking to the wall." Emi said. "Go do what you need to do."

"Right." Orochi leaned against a wall. "Where'm I going, Gatis?"

"You'll be in the back part of the building. You have to walk through receiving and there's a couple offices.

Walk straight through and you'll be in the clone theater. That's where both Carnelia and I are."

From behind him, Orochi heard the clack of a shotgun being cocked.

"I have been waiting to do this for so long." He heard an unfamiliar voice with a familiar drawl.

He heard the shot and tried to move, but even as he fell he knew he wouldn't miss the blast. His coat absorbed the impact but a bullet moving at three hundred and fifty meters per second still hurt like hell.

"Son of a bitch, forgot about that stupid jacket." Orochi heard as he hit the ground.

With no time to think, Orochi rolled to bring Hyde in his sights. He was wearing a hat, and Orochi aimed below it. He could have more than one.

He shot, but Hyde jumped for cover a fraction of a second faster than Orochi could aim. Orochi was fairly certain he hit, but he wasn't clear where.

"This is stupid, Orochi." Hyde said. "We both know you're here for the girl. Of the two of us, I know where she is."

"What do you suggest?" Orochi asked, scrambling for his own cover.

"A trade. The girl for you. I get her out safe, and you let me kill you." Hyde's drawl was pronounced and liquid.

"Tempting, but not tempting at all." Orochi shot in the direction of Hyde's voice. There was the clang of the bullet hitting metal, and a hissing of pressure being vented.

"Don't care so much about the clone tanks, huh?" Hyde drawled. "They're people too, you know."

"Hyde, if you were such a humanitarian, I might believe your bullshit, but this place is like a fucking closet for you. So shut up already." Orochi cursed the standoff. He had less than twenty minutes to find Carn, set her free, then rescue Atargatis. Hyde needed to hurry up and die so he could get to them.

"Do you know who you're talking to, boy? I'm the man that shot your mamma to death." Hyde's voice floated out from behind the foundation of the glass tanks.

Orochi closed his eyes. "Yeah, you did. And I'm going to kill you for that, one of these days."

"But not today!" Hyde taunted.

"You could jump into anyone of those clones. You could do it now, if you wanted to. They're all waking up." Orochi taunted.

Hyde looked around. "What?"

"That's right, Hyde, a highly competent Savvy has access to all of your dirty little secrets, and now they're gaining a life of their own." Orochi peeked to see if he could get a shot. Hyde had him locked down. This was bad; anyone could come up behind him while he was keeping Hyde occupied. He could feel the clock ticking down.

"Is that supposed to scare me?" Hyde laughed. "They won't even be able to walk."

Orochi snuck another look, and saw nearby Hyde, barely visible, was another one of those pipes like the one that depressurized. *I'll smoke you out.*

He took a moment to aim. "Just like you, able to do anything you want and not pay for it."

"Just like me." Hyde agreed.

276

Orochi squeezed the trigger on his Zerorez, and watched Hyde duck as he heard the gunfire. The steam poured out, hissing loudly as the contents inside blew out, and Hyde yelped and jumped away from the pipe, right into Orochi's sights.

He pulled the trigger again, this time aiming for Hyde's ear.

Watching as the man straightened in shock, and then crumpled to the ground, Orochi jumped out from behind his cover and ran up to the bleeding man. He kicked off the hat, and just to be sure, pumped a three round burst into the top of Hyde's head.

"I'll sleep better tonight." He muttered, then looked around the banks. He linked in to Atargatis.

"Gatis, where's Carnelia?" He asked. "And where are you? I need locations."

"You're underneath me." Atargatis told him through his comms. "Carnelia is in one of the tanks. There are men coming to kill you. And, there are others who are running around the inside and the outside of the building, putting things against walls."

"That's the clean-up crew." Orochi didn't want to explain what they were up to. "We're going to get you out."

"I want to jump!" Atargatis said.

"That would make it harder for me to find you." Orochi pointed out.

"I would splash! And move! None of the other clones are moving, they are sleeping." Atargatis pointed out.

"You have five minutes." Orochi said. "If you can't jump by then you're going to have to abandon your plan and let me get you out of the big tank."

"Okay." Atargatis agreed.

"Where's Carnelia?" Orochi prompted.

"Third row in, fifth from the bottom." Atargatis said. "You're at row two, just go one to the left."

"Thanks, Gatis." Orochi sprinted down the aisle, when movement caught his eye. Carnelia was struggling weakly against the glass. "How do you open it?"

"Her's is locked, I cannot." Atargatis said. "I have tried several times."

"Can you tell her to hold still and scrunch to the right side of the tank?" Orochi asked, pulling out his Zerorez.

"I can try." Her voice sounded uncertain.

He could hear them before he could see them. Two guards who ran towards him from either side of the plank. Both of them had a bead on him.

Orochi aimed his Zerorez and pulled the trigger. He felt bullets hit his back as he saw the other man crumple on the deck. He spun and shot at the man who'd shot him. The man went over backwards from the force of the bullet.

He turned his Zerorez on the glass, and it went click. Hurrying, Orochi slammed another magazine home. He took aim in the far corner, trying to keep as far away from Carn as possible. He shot the tank, and the glass fractured. The bullet took out the top pane and the bottom one, and gel and glass and Carnelia fell onto the top of the next tank. She coughed, then retched up the colorless gel she'd been suspended in.

"It's time to go, dear." Orochi said firmly. He closed the distance on the coffin even as it was disintegrating around her. He scooped her up into his arms.

She wiped her face against his shoulder. He made a face but didn't complain. Her smile was bright if weak. "It's about time."

"We have to get Gatis now. Can you walk? I can't carry both of you." Orochi said apologetically.

"I should." She stepped to the ground and he noticed for the first time that she wasn't wearing anything.

"We need to find you clothes." He said.

"Living is more important, and unless you have more bullet proof clothes, it's not going to help." Carnelia said.

"Well, that's going to go on you at least." Orochi peeled out of his bulletproof trench and held it out. "Watch the bottom, it's long."

"Follow me." Carnelia said, and started running.

Orochi dutifully ran behind his partner. He kept his eyes open for any other guards approaching. He heard people in the distance. The echoes kept him from determining where they were.

"Gatis, we're inbound." Orochi said into his comm.

"Does she know to cut power to this place when she disengages?" Carnelia asked.

"That would kill the clones, wouldn't it?" Orochi asked.

"It's kinder." Carnelia said, not wasting words.

Ouch. Orochi thought. "What about you? You're fine."

"I imported software upon install. They don't have BIOS to start with." Carnelia explained.

Orochi felt a surge of relief. "Gatis, prepare to cut all power on your exit."

"I'm not going to exit, I'm going to jump!" Atargatis said.

"Gatis! Gatis, I told you we couldn't find you..." Orochi began, frustrated.

Atargatis didn't respond.

"What happened?" Carnelia asked, looking worried.

"She said she was going to jump, and now she won't respond." Orochi said.

"Okay, we need to look for one that's thrashing." Carnelia put her hands above her eyes, trying to focus down the long lanes of sleeping clones.

An unfamiliar voice demanded, "How could you do this, Carnelia?" Orochi turned to see a girl dressed in all red approach them. Even her gun was red. "I was going to make a career out of being your attaché."

"Shoot her and let's go." Carnelia said. "She's like Lizbet's evil twin."

"Holy Mother of God that's a terrifying thought." Orochi brought his Zerorez to bear.

"If he shoots me I'll shoot you." Yuuki changed the angle of fire directly to Carn.

"We've got to find Gatis." Carnelia said, dismissing the girl in red.

Feeling the press of time, Orochi squeezed the trigger and caught Yuuki in the midriff. The girl buckled, her expression one more of aggravation than pain. She fell to the mezzanine and coughed once.

Orochi turned to see Carnelia on the ground. He reached down to offer her a hand up. "Are you all right?"

"Yeah, she's a bad shot." Carnelia's eyes met his. They were so beautiful.

He looked over at Yuuki, laying lifeless on the deck. "I got you some clothes!"

Carnelia wrinkled her nose. "I'm not sure I prefer those to being naked."

Orochi grinned. "You can run around naked, it's cool."

Her eyes narrowed. "Keep looking for Gatis and give me a minute."

"We don't have much time, Carn." Orochi said, looking over his shoulder. "We have less than twenty minutes..."

Blood soaked the red skirt down the front, but the scarlet top was reasonably blood free, or just hidden well in the fabric. Carnelia made a face.

"I think I found her." Orochi pointed at a tank where one of the clones seemed to be moving. It was a small clone, from what he could tell.

"Let's go get her." Carnelia ran, Orochi holding back to let her lead. They got to the tank, and it was on the top tier. The haze of the nutrient gel made it difficult to make out the clone inside. Orochi put his Zerorez up to the bottom of the tank. "Prepare for some splash."

He pulled the trigger, and the glass splintered and crashed out, pouring nutrient gel across the tops of the lower clone banks and catching Orochi and Carnelia in the splash.

Carnelia gasped. "Atargatis, no!"

The girl in the tank was young, probably no more than six or seven. She had long, perfect limbs, and blonde hair. "Carnelia!"

"Oh, honey, you shouldn't have jumped into a kid." She said, looking sad. "Oh, honey, no."

"What's wrong, Carnelia?" Seeing her so upset, Atargatis became upset, and tried to cover her small body with her skinny arms. "Why are you sad?"

Carnelia blinked. "I'm sad because we have to leave. Are you ready to go?"

Atargatis nodded.

Orochi picked her up gently. Her arms and legs were weak and thin, and she weighed almost nothing. "This is going to make leaving tricky."

Carnelia held up Yuuki's gun. "I'll shoot anyone who tries to stop us."

"Your wish is my command." Orochi said, turning to lead her out of the land of the living dead.

ESCAPE VELOCITY

Carnelia ran, doing her best to keep up with Orochi's strides. A thin coating of nutrient gel slicked every surface on the way down. Orochi had it the worst, trying to balance Atargatis in his arms. Carnelia dragged Orochi's coat through the puddles of the stuff, and felt the wet slap against her calves as she ran. She could hear the sounds of people approaching, but the echoes kept them from knowing which direction they came from. Orochi held Atargatis close to him to keep her safe. Carnelia wanted to stop and offer her clothes but it would take more time than they had, and she could get Gatis all the clothes she wanted later. She struggled under Orochi's coat but he wasn't in a position to take it back.

Her mind kept going back to the danger Atargatis was in. As they picked their way down to the ground, Carnelia's memories kept coming back. Jumping into children was not allowed. She couldn't think of how many times that rule was drilled into her head. No jumping into children, and if you did, jump out as quickly as you realized it.

It wasn't because Parris was a good Samaritan. He was a crime boss, had never fathered children of his own (that anyone could prove, at any rate) and was not above using children for his work. The reason bodyjumpers had to avoid children was because of the nature of their minds. Children's brains were elastic, still developing major systems. Their memories weren't accessible, either. A bodyjumper that put themselves in that environment was doomed to disperse into the child's personality, like a drop of oil in a bowl of water. The oil would always be there, would always leave a residue, but would not stay cohesive enough to retain its own identity. Eventually a child aged out, but Gatis's new body was firmly in the danger zone.

Carnelia thought that Gatis had two things going for her. One, the clone didn't have a personality of its own, so there would be nothing to disperse into. Two, Atargatis was herself very childlike, and may simply lose memories of a bad and lonely life. It may be the best thing that could happen to her. She hoped.

"Carn!" Orochi brought his Zerorez to bear, holding Gatis in his off arm. Men ran towards them, guns drawn. "Run!"

Gunshots fired, and Carnelia felt the crack of something moving fast and stopping hard in her side. Her breath left her in a rush, and she struggled to take more in.

Orochi caught her gaze and held it, willing her to obey. "RUN!"

Fear shot through her. She ran, knowing she was doing the wrong thing but doing it because Orochi's advice always seemed good at the time. The tank lights flickered off and then on again, catching her eye. She bolted as Orochi held his gun out and took a shot at Kaito's men. She heard another shot and watched Orochi crumple.

She saw two of them break off to chase after her, and she stopped looking back.

Pulling out Yuuki's gun, she looked for a place that could offer her cover. The stacks below the glass coffins weren't pure steel beams, they were manufactured to hold loads but also use less aluminum. Clever unless you wanted to stop bullets.

She tried to think of where she could hide. She ran headlong towards the walls, wondering where they would take Orochi and Gatis, or if Orochi would survive. They were shooting at her, which she didn't think they were allowed to do, but apparently Kaito had changed his mind. She turned and shot back at them.

They dodged, but didn't break off pursuit. She ducked behind some pillars and nearly tripped over a dead man. He wore a duster and cowboy boots, a cowboy hat near where he fell. She frowned in distaste at the mess that his head was in. Not that he didn't deserve it. Carnelia knew Hyde, knew enough about him to know he needed to die. She looked up, at all the clones in the tanks above. She wondered if Orochi had killed him fast enough, or if Hyde was now hiding among a mass of waking clones. She reached down and picked up his hat, which was nicely heavy. She slipped it on. It was too big, but so was Orochi's coat and it had already saved her life.

Kaito's men had caught up with her. They were shouting at her in Nipponese. She turned and shot at the guards, hitting one in the arm. They yelled at her, hiding behind pillars and pointing up to the mezzanine. They stretched their arms over their head, with their hands flat to the floor, indicating something long.

A hand snaked around her mouth, choking off a surprised cry. A strong arm drug her back against someone, and a pistol dug into her back. She looked down to see the hand's skin tone was a twin to her own, deep brown with golden undertones. His fingers were manicured, and his suit was steel gray.

"Mikeru." She hissed.

"They're talking to you." He said. "They say they have a tall friend of yours."

"I got that without the backstabbing." Carnelia growled.

"Kaito wants to talk to you." He said. "I'd be happy to escort you."

"I think I'll take my chances with the guards. They're more honest with their intentions." She tried to jerk free, but he held her fast. He disarmed her quickly and put her gun in his pocket.

"Easy, kitten, save the burns for Kaito. I'm just the messenger." Mikeru said, pushing her forward.

"You know what happens to the messenger." Carnelia tried to dig her elbow into his ribs.

He easily avoided her move. "You were going to go back anyway, why are you so mad at me?"

"I would have rather you were at my back, not stabbing a gun into it." She said, fuming. "I guess you decided to be the one pulling the trigger, huh?"

He didn't respond to her, just marched her up the stairs and into Kaito's office.

Kaito had his gun out, aimed at Orochi. Atargatis was still naked and shivering in Orochi's arms. Blood soaked his shirt, but Atargatis hid where the bullet had made its entry. Orochi's face looked like thunderclouds, promising imminent violence. Whatever tableau they walked in on, Kaito smiled when Carnelia walked in, escorted by her brother.

Striding up to her, he put his face within inches of hers, close enough to kiss her. Quietly, he said, "Well, I hope you are happy with what you've done today. My sysadmin is non-operational, you have ruined an inestimable amount of yen's worth of equipment, and you've killed a rare resource to this industry."

She looked fondly at Orochi. "I didn't kill Hyde."

Kaito's eyes widened as she spoke. He strode up and jerked the hat off of her head, and then he slapped her. "I've had enough of you!"

She looked over at Orochi, who looked concerned. He looked at his wrist like he was looking at a clock, and at once she understood. He had mentioned they didn't have much time.

"Kaito, let them go. It's me you want, and if you let them go, I'll do what you want. No more backtalk, no more conscientious objecting. Just let Orochi and Gatis go." She bit her lip as she realized what she'd done.

"Gatis, eh?" Kaito's eyes squinted. "But that's not her body. How did my sysadmin learn how to bodyjump? Did you teach her? How?"

"I can't explain that now. I need to have them safely away from you before I explain it." Carnelia said.

"I will not lose my second bodyjumper!" Kaito said crossly. "Orochi goes, Atargatis stays."

"You're making a mistake. She won't remember how." Carnelia said. "She's not going to remember how to code, either. You can't jump into kids, it's the first rule of bodyjumping. You lose cohesion and get lost in the body you wear. She's worthless to you now. Let her go."

"But then there's your boyfriend. I should shoot him on principal." Kaito leveled his pistol at Orochi.

"If you do, I'll find a way to rebel. You know what I'm capable of. You have to let both of them go, and I have to know that they're safe." Carnelia said.

"You are not in a position to negotiate." Iron backed Kaito's words.

While he spoke, she felt something hard pressed into the hand held behind her back. It felt like a gun grip. Mikeru only held one arm now, and that considerably less forcefully than before. She wanted to risk a look at Mikeru but that wasn't how these games were played.

Kaito raised his gun, grabbing her attention. He leveled it at Orochi. "I'll set them free."

Mikeru let go of her hand, and Carnelia brought her gun around on Kaito. The gunshots roared inside the little office, and Orochi dropped to the ground, covering Gatis. Kaito tried to swing his gun back at Carnelia at the last moment. His head snapped back as a bullet punched through.

Before Kaito had even hit the ground, Carnelia spun around to face Mikeru. "You asshole! I thought you'd flipped sides!"

"It needed to be convincing!" Mikeru said apologetically. "If it weren't for me..."

Orochi scooped Atargatis off the floor. "Save the sibling shit for later, we have to run!"

They barreled down the stairs, one after the other, and ran for the closest exit. Kaito's men saw them running, and shouted.

There was a loud hiss, so loud everyone but Orochi covered their ears. Carnelia looked up. The clones were moving! Some were grabbing a hold on their lids and pushing them away. Others kicked in the nutrient gel. Their movements were slow, unbearably slow.

"Orochi, what are we going to do?" Carnelia said. "We can't just leave them like this?"

Just then, a section of wall off to their right caved in. Chijo no ashi flooded in to the building, tearing holes through walls as they were too large to take the doors. The brilliant white mechs made booming sounds as they stepped forward on the concrete floor.

"This is the Tokyo Police Department. Please put your weapons on the ground and wait to be processed." The voice boomed in Nipponese and in English.

Orochi eyed the glass coffins, then glanced back at Carnelia. Carnelia raised her eyebrow at him.

"Don't look at me." He said. "You're the one who wanted to go sightseeing."

Carnelia dropped her gun and raised her hands in the air. She'd never been so glad to see the police.

LONG ARM

"I'll take this one, Officer Nguyen." Officer Hayanari put his hand on Orochi's shoulder. "Stand up please."

Without argument, Orochi got up and allowed Daizo to lead him by steering. He felt worried about leaving Gatis and Carnelia, but after talking to Daizo and Takeshi, he thought he could trust the TPD just slightly. The gunshot wound in his side took a lot of the fight out of him, anyway.

"You need medical assistance." Daizo said when he saw Orochi's front.

"It's just a bullet. Nothing fancy." Orochi smiled weakly.

An EMT came over and asked to see the wound. Orochi pulled up his shirt. The EMT pressed a flat metal disk against the wound. Orochi could feel the bullet working its way toward the disk. It didn't hurt at first, which had Orochi worried, but as the shock wore off the pain crept in. He tried to make light of it. "How does that work? Lead isn't magnetic."

The EMT watched as the shrapnel collected on the disk. "Nipponese bullets aren't made of lead."

It was surprisingly comforting, to know that things were working the way they were supposed to. Orochi let the man put a bandage over his wound, and took the two pills the EMT handed him and dry swallowed them.

"No fast motions for two weeks." The EMT cautioned, and then went after his next patient.

Daizo gave Orochi the once over. "You good? Can you walk?"

Orochi nodded, then winced. "Yeah."

Daizo walked Orochi back to the mech. "What do you know about Kasumi?" Daizo asked. "Do you know who she was associated with?"

"I'm afraid I do." Orochi said. "The man she's spending time with is the man who killed my mother."

"Oh." Daizo paused. "I'm sorry to hear that."

"Yes, she's gotten herself in a bad way. He's only a goon, he works for higher-ups that are into slavery, extortion, theft, and all manner of illegal acts." Orochi sighed, his hand resting over his bandage. "She's going to go to jail after this is sorted out."

"I see." Daizo fell quiet.

"What happened to the explosives?" Orochi asked. "I didn't hear anything go off."

"Tokyo PD has good toys for stopping bombs. We were almost too late. Did you plant them?" Daizo asked sharply.

"No. I was just here for the girl." Orochi admitted.

"Hmm." Daizo seemed to understand.

Orochi was grateful for the silence. He focused on not focusing on the pain in his side. They didn't talk much on the ride back to the station. Luckily for Orochi he didn't have to go by Daizo's mech. There were vans lined up to take villains, outlaws and clones back to the station for processing.

In the interrogation room, Orochi was sitting on a hard-backed, plastic molded chair, waiting. His side ached but he was too tired to stand. He wasn't in cuffs, which was a grudging concession but one he appreciated. There was a click as the door opened, and in walked Takeshi Shin. His suit was black and businesslike. It matched his eyes. Takeshi's hair was slightly longer, but Orochi imagined that within two or three days he had his regular haircut scheduled.

"That story you told was frankly unbelievable," Inspector Shin began without preamble.

Orochi nodded.

"It helps that there were two hundred and fifty-three clones. Four, I suppose, if you count the little girl." A trace of sardonic humor touched his thin lips. "Her story makes yours look credible."

Orochi grinned, but didn't say anything.

"We don't know what to make of the situation." Inspector Shin hiked his leg up and half sat on the interrogation table. "We had some Hitochigai files pointing at the possibility of body switchers, but we had assumed clever con artists, not full-blown... technological augments."

"Would it help if I said, 'Told you so?'" Orochi asked.

"No, it wouldn't." Inspector Shin's tone made it clear he wasn't amused. "What would help is if you all blew back to the greendome you came from."

"I can arrange that." Orochi offered.

"Someone has arranged it for you. Your superior officer, Rascati, called, and explained some of the more ticklish details of the situation. I'm certain that it wasn't a full story, but then again, with what we know, I doubt the whole story could be much more believable or understandable." Inspector Shin ran a hand through his hair.

"I wish I could be of more help, Officer." Orochi shrugged. "A full-scale cloning facility has got to be fairly illegal."

"As does colluding to murder a government official." Inspector Shin said.

Orochi shook his head. "I wasn't aware of that."

"Your friend Carnelia told us that the Hitochigai forced her join in a plan to assassinate someone in our government. I wanted to see if this was something you knew anything about."

"I was busy trying to get her out of there, I didn't interact with any of the bad guys directly." Orochi said.

"Except when you watched Kaito Noboro die." Takeshi folded his arms across his chest.

"He had a gun to my head when he got shot. You'll forgive me if I don't feel too badly about that." Orochi shifted in his chair. He wanted to stand, but he didn't want to seem threatening to the cop.

"What was Kasumi Yamamoto's part in all of this?" Inspector Shin asked.

"Not my pay grade." Orochi put his hands up before him. "No one told me."

"Humor me. What did you think they were?" Inspector Shin encouraged.

"She was a mole. I believe she worked for Kaito Noboro, and she seemed to be associated with a criminal that goes by Hyde. Carnelia could tell you more about it, but the reason Carnelia knew anything about her was because Rascati brought it to her attention." Orochi wondered briefly how much he was supposed to tell Inspector Shin. He mentally shrugged and decided he didn't care. After all, Rascati had thrown them under the bus and hadn't apparently dragged them back out again, so at this point they were on their own.

"I don't understand what kind of official you are." Inspector Shin wondered openly. "You're not from any division I'd ever heard of."

"We specialize in Hitochigai cases. There's a group causing trouble, and they apparently have long arms." Orochi explained.

"Perhaps we can share some files." Inspector Shin said casually.

"Rascati would be the one to talk to about sharing files." Orochi said. "I definitely think having more people on board knowing about this technology is the only way to keep it in check."

"What can you tell me about the girl?" Takeshi asked.

"I'm just glad to have her back." Orochi smiled.

"Not Carnelia." Inspector Shin corrected. "The girl clone."

"Gatis. Yes, she's... well, she's special." Orochi said. "Tell me this, do any of the other clones talk?"

"Nothing so far." Inspector Shin said.

"Do any of the other clones know how to walk very well?" Orochi asked. "Or do they just shuffle?"

"They're not very functional." Inspector Shin conceded.

"I think that Gatis is different. If she's a clone, I think she's one that they've activated. Maybe they had her in storage because she didn't behave. Carn suggested that happened to her. I think that Gatis might also be a little... unreliable. How could you be amidst people like that as a child and hope to keep completely balanced?"

Inspector Shin nodded. "That is possible."

"More possible than what she's telling you." Orochi reminded him.

"We are remanding you to the Seattle official Baxley. You are going to take Nathan and Carnelia with you, and leave our greendome."

"Wait, what?" Orochi blinked.

"Gatis will be staying here, with the other clones. They are proscribed, and will be euthanized." Inspector Shin looked at him apologetically.

"What? No! Gatis isn't a clone, she's a girl! With people who care about her and are willing to take her somewhere safe, out of your greendome!" Orochi felt rage begin to rise.

"It is the law, and we are bending them to let you out of Tokyo." Inspector Shin glowered.

"I'm not going to let you take out your national aggression on a helpless little girl. You said that you already can't account for a few of the clones." Orochi pointed out.

"You said there were two hundred and fifty-six. You were mistaken." Inspector Shin said.

"Let me be mistaken." Orochi smiled. "What's one more girl on the books? Especially if she's leaving the greendome?"

"You may exist in some gray hat world where laws don't apply, but as a representative of those who uphold the law, the law doesn't stop existing for you. We have these rules in place to prevent people from doing things that shouldn't be done to the citizenry!"

"These are the citizenry!" Orochi argued. "They didn't ask to be put into decanters and grown in vats! Most of them have been vegetables their whole life. Have you noticed? Some of them are thirty!"

"And don't you think this would be kinder?" Takeshi asked, his eyes meeting Orochi's.

Carnelia's words echoed in his head. "Kinder for them, maybe. But Gatis is autonomous. She is young, she can use her body, and she has her whole life ahead of her. Please, just turn the other way on her. She'll fit in better in Seattle, and she has people willing to care for her."

"You have to give me something. I have given you enough." Inspector Shin said flatly.

Orochi sighed. "Hyde is a bodyjumper. He's the man who turned Kasumi for Typhon. I tried to kill him, point blank. I say tried because he could have jumped into one of those clones, and from one of those clones into one of your men or women on the force."

"Could have?" The Inspector frowned.

"He's done it before. Assuming he's dead is a way to borrow trouble, and then some." Orochi assured him.

"That's information, but that's not the man. I need something concrete." Inspector Shin shifted from one foot to the other, dropping his hands on the table.

"How do you deliver something concrete when he's a ghost?" Orochi asked calmly.

Inspector Shin stood up straight. "You tell a man that a little girl's life is on the line."

EXIT STRATEGY

Their reunion was muted. Inspector Shin arranged transportation for the lot of them to the Chunnel. The docking platform was distinctly unlike the subways. There were almost no people around. There were advertisements on the walls, completely free of graffiti. There were vending machines filled with things to eat and drink. There were families that stood on the painted strip on the concrete surface, huddling together and ignoring everyone else.

When Gatis saw Orochi, she leaped into his arms and gave him a fierce hug. Mikeru and Carnelia joined them, walking side by side. Nathan took a step forward, then paused as he looked at the girl in Orochi's arms. Gatis tilted her head and squinted at him comically. "Hello!"

"Hello." Nathan smiled at her warmly. "Are you Atargatis?"

"Gatis, please." She pressed her cheek against Orochi's chest.

"You got it." He agreed.

"You had people working with you." Carnelia said. "Where are they?"

Orochi sighed. "They're off hunting down Hyde."

"Hyde? I thought you killed him." Carnelia said. She ran her hand over the brim of the Stetson unconsciously.

"Carn, there were over two hundred waking clones for him to take his pick from. I clipped him, but he's been jumping for a long time. If he can jump without a C-pod, which Rascati's story pretty much proves, then he could jump straight up and then pick any clone he wanted. Given Emi's story, the body he was in before he escaped was a clone. He probably wasn't even disoriented." Orochi set Atargatis down. She was dressed, a cobbled together mix of a much-too-big tee-shirt and a bright pink cotton skirt. She was barefoot.

Orochi watched Atargatis wander over to Nathan. Nathan was taller than her, but she was the only person he was taller than. She grinned and hugged him. Nathan stiffened for a moment, then put his arms around her and returned her hug.

"They're letting us go, without making us go get him?" Mikeru asked.

"There's no way anyone can catch Hyde until the tech has been developed to keep him in one body. Emi and her people are going to try to detain Hyde but we're on best behavior until we can be fully certain we've ended that threat." Orochi said. "I promised we'd work on it."

"What else did you promise?" Mikeru asked suspiciously.

"Something to get your ass out of the Tokyo greendome." Orochi glared a warning at Mikeru.

"What is this place?" Carnelia asked, looking around the platform.

"It's the Chunnel." Mikeru said.

Nathan whirled on Orochi. "Why didn't you tell me about this? What is it?"

"It's an underground track below sea level. It's deep and a little scary to travel, and it takes a really long time to get anywhere, which is why we didn't take it before." Orochi said.

"What about McCune? He was all ready to go." Nathan frowned.

"I gave him a retainer. He can stay with his family or go visit his family, either way he got paid for the trip." Orochi replied.

"If my choices are falling to my death or being crushed to death by the sea, I can see why you didn't rush to give me a choice." Nathan conceded.

"The Chunnel has been maintained since before the Crisis. No one wants to let it fall into disrepair since overland travel is so arduous." Mikeru said.

Carnelia laughed. "You sound like a travel brochure."

"You think I didn't dream of leaving that place?" Mikeru asked. "Think again."

Warning lights and chimes advised an incoming train. They watched it roll in, and stood back to let people disembark. There were less than twenty people, Orochi counted.

Orochi gave his friends their tickets. "We have a sleeper car, we can finally get some rest."

They climbed on the hyperloop, and wandered down the cars until they found the one they'd been assigned.

They sat down on their bunks, and everyone looked slightly less stressed.

"Um, who's going to take care of me?" Atargatis asked into the quiet. "I don't have a mommy or a daddy anymore."

Carnelia stood up from the bed she'd been sitting on and threw her arms around Atargatis. "We'll take care of you. I don't know how we'll arrange it, but you can rely on us."

"She has a point, though. You guys are basically owned by the Bureau right now. You're not going to have the kind of free time you need to raise a kid. Ganada might be a good person to ask." Nathan said. "She's always got a few kids hanging on around her house. She's been known to rehome them from time to time."

"I want to live with YOU!" Atargatis said, clinging to Carnelia.

"Aw." Carnelia smiled and kissed the top of her head. "Listen, that will probably be fine, but I have a job that takes me out sometimes, like how long I was in Typhon. We have to make sure that someone cares for you when I'm out."

Atargatis grinned. "Orochi?"

"He'll be with me when we're out on assignment." Carnelia explained.

"Nathan?" She looked at him hopefully.

"Uh.." Nathan blinked in surprise. "I don't know how to take care of kids, I still am one."

"Time to grow up, I guess." Carnelia said, and winked.

Orochi looked among the group. His side was still sore, but less so than it could have been. He had to tip his hat to Panasian medicine. He had his coat back now in any case. He resolved to buy Carn one of her own. He knew that with her abilities that it would probably be unneeded. If he had anything to say about it, he would be getting her retired from the field of bodyjumping. Rascati was due an earful about the way he handled this entire affair, or didn't handle it. He didn't care if Carnelia's ability was an asset. He thought the trouble it caused was well and truly not worth any gain it had ever made.

He jumped as a warm body sat down next to him on his bed. He looked over to see Carnelia, smiling a big beautiful smile. "Hi stranger."

"Hi back." He took his time to look at her. He remembered her lovely skin. He remembered her big, dark eyes, constantly showing what she felt. He wasn't sure what she was feeling now, because he'd never seen it before. It made his heart race to be near her, but what she felt was still a bit of a mystery.

"You came for me." She put her hand on his hand.

Orochi smiled, realization dawning. Maybe she could forgive him for getting her body killed, now that she had it back. "Of course I did. You did pretty well on your own though."

"Thanks." She looked down at their hands, still touching, and flushed slightly. "It turned out okay."

His mind came back to his agreement with Inspector Shin to get them out. He frowned. "Okay."

"You don't think it turned out okay?" Carnelia asked, drawing her hand back.

"Well, I'm happy for you that you got your body back. And Gatis has a new start at life, so that's good." He glanced down at Mikeru, who lay back on his bed and had his eyes closed. "Not so sure about him, but..."

Carnelia smacked him. She looked contrite when he winced. "I'm sorry Orochi, I forgot..."

"It's fine, I'm going to live." Orochi rubbed his bandage, taking shallow breaths.

"You are a bullet magnet." Carnelia joked. "You need to stop that."

"Well, Carn, I'm afraid that would mean ending our relationship. I'm not sure I'm ready for that." Orochi joked.

"Relationship?" She echoed.

"Well, you know, partnership." Orochi attempted lamely.

She looked down. "Right, partnership."

"C'mon Carn, think about how the last few months have been. It's not like I've had a chance to ask you out on a date..." Orochi pressed his lips together. This wasn't how he'd wanted to ask her.

"Are you asking me now?" She pounced on his words.

"Yes." Orochi said. "I am."

In answer, she leaned in, surprising him. Not so much that he didn't put his arms around her and pull her close, his lips meeting hers.

There was applause but Orochi flipped them the universal middle finger of approval.

UNDERGROUND

Carnelia woke up in the underground hyperloop. She saw she wasn't the first one up. Atargatis pulled her by the hand. They trooped together for food and then returned to their car. There were no windows to look out of, no change of scenery to mark their travel. She joined in with teaching Atargatis little coordination games she'd learned as a child. She asked Atargatis math questions. Carnelia was careful to not show her concern when Atargatis stumbled over some of them.

Eventually Nathan distracted her with a game console, and Carnelia went back to her bunk, still feeling exhausted.

Despite that, Carnelia couldn't sleep. She sat up on her bunk, feeling the smooth motion of the ground racing below them. This place felt too much like she was back in the glass coffin, and that was nowhere she ever wanted to be again.

"What's up?" Orochi sat down on the bed. He gestured towards Atargatis. "You've been torn up about her since she jumped."

Carnelia sighed, not wanting to share with him her experience. "It might be nothing. It's just the first rule of jumping is never to jump into a child."

"You mean, because how icky could that get?" Orochi asked.

"Parris was hardly a moral man. The reason why is that kid brain isn't adult brain, and jumpers have lost themselves in the kids they jump into. Their personality matrix isn't strong enough for the elasticity of a child's mind. I was worried for her, but... she's such a kid, and losing those memories would probably be a blessing. And no one was in there to start with, so she didn't have anyone to dilute into."

"Just when I think this stuff couldn't creep me out any farther." Orochi said.

"This from the man whose blood is poison to his favorite toys." Carnelia shot back.

He drywashed his face with one big hand. "My mommy gave that to me."

"I know." She put her hand on his arm. "It's more than that though. I'm worried about Gatis, but I'm worried more about me. I'm a commodity. I hate it. I mean, bodyjumping helped Gatis, but she's the first person I've ever met whose life was made better for it."

"It gave you back your brother." Orochi pointed out. "It gave you back your body."

"Mikeru isn't a body jumper. He's only been alive five years, he's pure clone. You're right though. It did give me back my body. But now I'm ready to stop using the power that goes with it."

"That means we're going to have to stop the man who invented it." Orochi said. "Emilio Sanchez."

Carnelia blinked. "Who?"

"I did some workups on him. He's the guy who financed the first tests out in the Arizona desert. The ones that my mom and dad were subjected to. I found some files." He shrugged. "Seemed a waste not to learn what was in them."

Carnelia nodded. "Well, when I was in Typhon I learned that there were five clones of me commissioned. Four of them were tortured and killed, as part of some kind of experiment."

There was a long, black silence that hung in the air between them after she said that. Orochi looked murderous. She'd never seen him look like this before. "I will kill him if it's the last thing I do. I'll get Pixru to work on this round the clock..."

"Pixru?" Carnelia blurted. "But she's unconscious."

Mikeru looked up from where he'd been watching the console with Atargatis.

"She can access the Web but she can't access her body. So, she talked to me. We need to figure out a way to wake her up." Orochi said. "Then the gang will be back together."

Carnelia saw Mikeru looking up at them. "Then you can meet your... potential girlfriend."

"I'd like that." Mikeru said.

"Huh." Orochi said. "Brave man."

"He's not out of his mind on drugs, so I think he's an improvement." Carnelia admitted.

"Fair enough." Orochi looked over at her. "Listen, Carn..."

She leaned in. "Yes?"

He looked down to see Atargatis looking up, riveted.

"Let me get back to you on that." Orochi said, pulling back from her.

"Ooh, age favoritism." Nathan leaned in and stage whispered to Atargatis. "Just think, you can cash in on that later."

"How?" Atargatis asked, in an equally loud whisper.

"I'll teach you." Nathan promised. "But not in front of the adults."

"Oh, no." Orochi said, and pinched the bridge of his nose.

*

Rascati stood waiting for them on the platform, a gray wolf among sheep that departed the Chunnel's train. His expression was carefully neutral. Carnelia wanted to walk up and slap him. All that she and her friends had withstood happened because he hadn't done a thorough job of checking who she jumped into. Parris was less sloppy, although that was probably due to Pixru.

Pixru!

"Did she wake up?" Carnelia asked.

Rascati's gray eyebrows rose like twin clouds, surprise animating his countenance. "Who?"

Carnelia looked disappointed. "Pixru."

"I didn't think you were that fond of her." Rascati did a double take. "I see you got your... self back. Let's get out of here."

"There's no extradition to Tokyo, I hope." Orochi said behind her.

"There's a conversation that needs to be had." Rascati said enigmatically. "Meanwhile let's get everyone secure before we start spewing company secrets."

"He's old." Atargatis said, staring at Rascati from Orochi's arms.

"I survived this long." Rascati said, and surprised everyone when he winked at her playfully.

Atargatis blinked, then laughed. "He's funny!"

The ride to the facility was quiet, punctuated with Atargatis telling jokes and trying to entertain the somber adults.

Rascati surprised everyone again, by having called ahead and having a room made up for a kid; blankets, toys, puzzles, games, and a hand-held smartboard. He showed her the controls and gave her earbuds. He told her that she'd get pizza for lunch, and asked her to let the adults talk.

"You're really good with kids." Carnelia commented as he closed the door behind him.

"Sometimes your star witness is nine years old, and traumatized. You want the killer that much more, but you have to be that much more careful about how you treat your witness." Rascati explained. "So, I see you found something in your size when you were over there. Care to explain how that happened?"

They walked into the conference room, where Orochi, Mikeru and Nathan already sat. Carnelia took a seat next to Orochi.

"The clone banks were based on Ark's cryosleep technology. They weren't as rigged as your average C-pod, but they were meant for a different task. There wasn't any cryo, but I have a feeling that had we had more time to hunt through their system, there was a freeze and thaw function that we didn't get a chance to see." Orochi said, reaching for another slice of pizza.

Carnelia stood up and stretched. "These chairs are murder."

Nathan and Mikeru nodded their agreement.

"I was contacted by Iha Hiroyasu a few days ago. He was following up with a connection that had recommended me. He works for a politician by the name of Muneo Nakamura. He was ordered by his security chief to find us. He got a tip that something strange was happening with their politician, and he was quite happy to give me the information he had. It wasn't much, but it was something to go on." Rascati said. "Fortunately they have pull with the local police. Kasumi Yamamoto has been indicted, and you have all been forgiven by the Panasian government. They also requested that you never come back."

"It was a nice place to visit." Orochi said, shrugging his shoulders.

"But I never want to go back." Nathan finished for him.

"What about me?" Mikeru asked.

Carnelia sat back down, trying not to slump from exhaustion.

"You are in an interesting position." Rascati said. "Technically you are a *persona non grata,* and the governments have all left clone rights vague because the whole mess brings up more human rights questions than any government body wants to think about. However, your original recently passed, and our division froze his accounts, because we weren't sure how best to deal with them. Of course, it's not a high priority for us, so they've stayed that way, frozen, but still viable. If you'd like to come on and join us, I'm sure we can get those accounts unfrozen within a few days, and you can have a job, a legal identity, and a place to start."

"If you don't want to work for them," Orochi said darkly, "There are other ways to get you viable accounts and an identity."

"Orochi, you promised. Which, you broke by the way, when you hijacked that plane to fly you to Tokyo." Rascati pointed out. "Technically you require a reprimand."

Orochi scowled. "Yeah, you go ahead and reprimand me for fixing a major international incident. Watch me cry in my coffee about that."

Rascati sighed. "You work for us now, and that's keeping you out of jail. I have to remind you of that on a daily basis."

"Your collar's a little snug around my neck." Orochi said.

"Orochi, Rascati's not trying to pick a fight. Let's let him finish, this is about Mikeru, not about you." Carnelia said, hoping it would work.

Orochi looked at Carnelia, somewhat startled. "Fine."

Mikeru looked between the three of them. "What about Pixru?"

"We're monitoring her." Rascati said. "She seems perfectly healthy, we can't determine why she's in a coma."

"I have something I want to try, when we're through barking at each other." Carnelia said.

"Well." Rascati looked at each of them. "I wanted to also offer Nathan a job, as he was so instrumental in helping retrieve our agent."

"Nope, I like being a consultant. It suits me better." Nathan said.

"Okay, that was my last piece of business for today. What were you thinking of trying, Carnelia?"

She frowned, uncertain how to explain herself. "I learned something new in Tokyo, and I want to try it."

Rascati looked at Mikeru's hopeful expression. "Can't hurt."

"Well, take me to her."

*

In the C-pod room, an M-pod and a C-pod stood. Pixru lay still under the glass dome of the M-pod, looking like a princess under a spell. Carnelia was alone, as she'd requested. The boys had kept going after the meeting was declared 'over,' and she was tired of listening to it all. She crawled into the C-pod. It didn't seem wise to give up her secret quite yet. She closed her eyes and sighed, and sought out Pixru's mind.

She could feel Pixru's presence, but her mind was like an empty cup. The cup was there, but nothing filled it. She reached out, not trying to jump into Pixru's body but trying to feel Pixru's consciousness. She felt a bare flicker of something, but she couldn't make a solid connection.

Knowing she would have to get personal, she was loathe to leave her body after working so hard to keep it, but Pixru needed more direct help. She jumped back into Pixru's body, the familiar container that had kept her going for months. She felt the little life growing inside. It deserved a mother, even a woman as frustrating as Pixru. She reached out for Pixru's mind. She remembered when Orochi had disappeared in his body, and tried to remember how she'd found him then.

She realized there was one place that she didn't go as a bodyjumper. The subconscious mind, the place that Orochi called the bento box. She touched the dividing line between the conscious and subconscious, and she could hear a faint voice, swearing.

Pixru!

A faint voice returned. *Carnelia?*

Follow my voice, I can barely hear you from here. Carnelia beckoned.

This place is too loud, I can barely hear you. Pixru said.

Carnelia sighed. And then she pushed through the skin.

Swirls of garbled text in Panasian and in English assaulted Carnelia's senses. She could hear Michael reciting a poem. She saw Orochi, mohawk ablaze, walk through the space, look up, wave, and then suddenly disappear. Then she saw Pixru, long hair flowing down her back, gauzy white gown flowing in an unseen wind.

Take my hand. Carnelia suggested.

Pixru paused. *I'm scared.*

You're not scared of anything. Carnelia reached out. *C'mon, I brought Michael back.*

He's not really Michael. Pixru said dismissively.

You're right. Michael had a drug problem. Carnelia reached out. *You'd be surprised how nice he is now.*

Pixru reached out, and touched Carnelia's hand.

Chimera Systems engaged. A familiar feminine voice caught Carnelia by surprise. She saw a woman appear from behind Pixru. The woman, Diane Lourdes, was unearthly green energy. She pushed Pixru away from the border to her conscious, and Pixru fell down. Chimera disappeared into the hollows of Pixru's mind.

Carnelia helped Pixru up. *There's someone in here with you.*

Pixru looked haunted. *She won't give me any rest!*

I'll help you. We are going to have to push hard to get through to your conscious mind. Keep a hold of my hand, and follow me, no matter what happens.

Lead the way. Pixru gripped onto her hand.

Carnelia pushed her way towards the barrier of the bento box. She kept her eye open for the digital ghost.

How did you learn to do this, anyway? Pixru asked.

I went to Tokyo. Carnelia answered.

Catching the barrier, Carnelia pushed to breach it.

Chimera Systems engaged! The apparition appeared behind Pixru, and grabbed her, pulling her away from the skin of the barrier.

Chimera, stop! Carnelia pulled on Pixru and addressed the apparition at the same time. *You are not protecting Orochi... Jack... with this action! You are keeping a friend away from him!*

It's a program? Pixru sounded affronted.

It's a person. Carnelia didn't want to tell her who. *Chimera, come with me. You can live in my body, until we find you a new home.*

The apparition reached out, taking Carnelia's hand. Stepping backwards towards the skin of the conscious mind, Carnelia walked backwards and drew both women into the light.

COOKIES

The kitchen was clear of most people, and Carnelia hovered over a cup of tea. Orochi smiled when he saw her newly short cropped hair. Seeing her there helped with the guilt of getting her first body killed. It was still a touchy subject, but both of them seemed to feel better about it. He felt like it would be as good of a time as any. He walked towards her table.

Carnelia looked up when she heard his boot steps. "Hi stranger."

He pulled a pink box out from under his arm and straightened the ribbon. "This is for you."

She smiled when he offered her the box. "What's this?"

"You will love me and hate me for this." He said, and grinned.

Inside were twelve golden brown disks, about half the size of a hockey puck. They had little kanji burned into the tops of them. They smelled like vanilla and sugar.

"Taste one." Orochi felt almost giddy, and then he reined it in. He knew what they tasted like. They were sweet, but not cloyingly so. The vanilla aroma permeated the cookie, and it was delicious.

"You can't get these here, can you?" She said thoughtfully between bites.

"Nope."

"I pretty much just hate you." She said, taking another bite, and winking.

"That's okay, as long as you let me have one." Orochi said, snaking his hand in over the box.

She twisted and pouted. "This is my present."

"Hey, I'm the only child here." Orochi said. "Even I know when a present is to share."

She twisted back around, offering him the box. "You did help save my life."

"I wanted to talk to you a little about that." Orochi said, snagging a plastic chair and maxing out its weight capacity. He waggled a cookie at her. "I wanted to talk to you a little more about Emilio Sanchez."

"Can't we be off duty for just a little while?" Carnelia gazed at her cookie before polishing it off.

"Not when I know there's a man out there who tortured and killed four of you." Orochi said, his voice low. "He's on the top of my list."

"Okay, tell me about him." Carnelia agreed reluctantly.

"He lives in the United States, somewhere near where Old Las Vegas used to be." Orochi told her. "I'm not one hundred percent certain the exact location, but it's a place to start, and I can start narrowing things down now that I've got Pixru on my team."

"I'm glad she gets along with Mikeru." She said. "Michael. I have to remember he changed his name on his documentation."

"Only because she's an unrestrained cu..." He stopped talking when Carnelia put a finger to his lips.

"Now, now. Let's be nice. We all had problems with her, but she deserves a second chance."

Orochi almost told her about Pixru not being certain who the father of her baby was. Almost.

Instead, he said, "This guy has spawned all of the body jumping tech variations that have been discovered. He developed the original form of the 'ware in the desert, in an abandoned military base. I'm still trying to grasp what the end goal is, but now that I have some unifying facts I can start making progress."

"You want to go kill him, don't you?" Carnelia said, selecting another cookie.

"Turns out, he was always the guy I wanted to kill." Orochi admitted, fiddling with his own cookie. "I always thought that Parris was responsible for killing my mom. But now I know that Hyde is the one who killed her, and that Emilio gave the word. He popped the cookie into his mouth. "Parris and Kaito both worked for him. You've got stakes."

"I've got stakes." Carnelia agreed. "Will Rascati?"

"Hey, we're part of the Bureau! Our whole division is about finding bodyjumpers and taking them out. It's not about rehoming them, even though that's what we've done on occasion. But that's why we signed on, because they were allies, people who have axes to grind. I'm going to put together a compelling presentation of why this guy is the devil and why we need to stop him."

"In the middle of the NAN." She pointed out.

"Sure, that's going to be a challenge. We have a great guide who can keep us from bumping into the locals."

"Who?" Carnelia asked curiously.

"Ganada." Orochi said.

Carnelia nodded. "She'd be great to have along."

"It seems like what we have to do. This technology does nothing but offer ways to destroy people's lives. I'm in." Carnelia set the box down on the table.

"Okay, now that I got the easy part done, I have a question to ask you."

"Harder than asking me to go kill some people with you?" Carnelia asked, dubious.

"Harder than that." He admitted.

She smiled and leaned forward on the table. "Ask away, O mysterious one."

He leaned in, enjoying the warmth of her smile. "What are you doing Friday night?"

She tossed her head back. "Are you asking me on a date?"

"I might be." He could feel himself start to flush and looked away before she'd see it.

Her hands clapped on his cheeks and she pulled his head around until it was level with hers. "I'll go with you if you promise to take me to your favorite restaurant."

"Beef Noodle?" He asked, choking in surprise.

"That's the one." Carnelia said, and grinned.

ABOUT THE AUTHOR

Tina Shelton lives in Washington State with her son and her husband. Currently attending school, she is an avid student and writes all the time, whether it's an assignment or her own project. She recalls a time when she used to have other hobbies, but figures that time will come again once she's graduated. In the meantime she binge watches Netflix shows and reads.